Carlos C. Solari
John-Patrick Skaar

Perseguir is an e-publishing company jointly owned by the two collaborators in this book of fiction, Carlos C. Solari and John-Patrick Skaar. Carlos operates from the US and JP from Norway. eNikita is the first product of this collaboration across the Atlantic Ocean.

ENIKITA

A NOVEL

BY

CARLOS C SOLARI AND JOHN-PATRICK SKAAR

... for Sabine and Anna

Sarah, Rasmus and Syvert

OUR GRATITUDE

For the many people who gave us a hand reading and commenting. Some names are abbreviated for privacy reasons. John H for the FBI cyber review, Joe P., Ivar Fahsing, Paul Robertson, Art Skuggevik, Steve G, Brandon Price, Uma C., Ches, Jean-Pierre and Gesa. You know who you are. Thank you.

Cover artwork by Alex Shevchenko, @AlexShevchenkoT
Photography by Gunnar Kopperud, @gunnarkopperud
Graphic design by Jelena Scicko, @itissible

This is a work of fiction ...

... but describing real places, everyday events, and computer-hacking methods that are becoming more commonplace.

A **seraph** *(pl.* **seraphs** *or* **seraphim***) is a type of celestial or heav-
enly being in the Abrahamic religions.*

Literally "burning ones," the word *seraph* is normally a synonym
for serpents when used in the Hebrew Bible. A seminal passage
in the Book of Isaiah (Isaiah 6:1-8) used the term to describe
fiery six-winged beings that fly around God's throne singing
"holy, holy, holy."

from Wikipedia

PART ONE

It was Easter 1963. He was writing from an Alabama jail alone with his thoughts… in solitary confinement.

"I am cognizant of the interrelatedness of all communities and states. I cannot sit idly by in Atlanta and not be concerned about what happens in Birmingham. Injustice anywhere is a threat to justice everywhere. We are caught in an inescapable network of mutuality, tied in a single garment of destiny. Whatever affects one directly, affects all indirectly."

Martin Luther King, Jr.

The Internet and Social Media as we know it today were not yet invented in 1963. "We are caught in an inescapable network of mutuality, …" he said, like he knew it was coming.

eNikita is a story about the "network of mutuality", the age where "injustice anywhere threatens justice everywhere," only more so. It is the age where we blend the real and the virtual. We call it e for electronic.

They call her Nikita, but there's nothing virtual or electronic about her. She is real. So real that you can't help but feel her emotions of love and happiness, of extreme fear … and hope.

CHAPTER 1

The Santander Family Home
Torremolinos, Southern Coast of Spain
Saturday, 25ᵗʰ of February

Julia's fingers raced across the keyboard like a virtuoso playing on a grand piano. Her father, Miguel Santander, was in the adjacent room speaking—rather arguing—with someone about work and occasionally typing on a computer.

"No! I'll tell you again, Mauricio. Are you not hearing me? I need you to pay the rent—now!" Cash flow was becoming a problem.

His voice carried across the house when he was mad, the words spoken in the distinct precise intonation of a Madrileño, each letter perfectly enunciated. Julia was lost in her own world. Her cherry red Skullcandy headphones were perched atop her

5

head, her long auburn hair pulled back. The padded cups with the miniature embedded speakers in the earphones were snug to her ears bringing her the music from her computer. It served as background noise, and to keep intruders, her parents, out of her personal space.

If Julia was a virtuoso on the keyboard, her parents were of the hunt-and- peck generation. Spell the words out correctly the first time, the fingers uncertain, the mind needing to perform a slow deliberate sequence each time. Form the thought, tell the fingers to find the letter on the keyboard, punch the key with emphasis, repeat the sequence. It worked like a child putting words together having just learned the alphabet. It came easier to some. Never as easy as for those who had grown up with a computer tablet in the crib.

Miguel Santander took his time typing his password that gave him access to his retirement account. Despite the carnage done to his portfolio over the past couple of years, he knew that he had fared better than most. Diversification had worked, his wealth distributed in a variety of instruments to counter the present-day volatility in the markets. Many of his investments were now worth a fraction of the original purchase price. Still, others had prospered. He had lost millions overall. But it could have been far worse. Now he was counting on the conventional wisdom of the top financiers from Europe and other parts of the world prognosticating that the bottom had been reached. Bloomberg experts were beginning to sound like the market would start to swing back up. The tide was coming back, and all boats would float higher. That's what he thought and hoped for.

He hit the enter key. A small bit of code called keylogger software surreptitiously hidden in his computer's operating system captured the digits and sent out a copy of his password. It traveled in packets of information through a series of network routers around the world. The route was designed to lose the trail of any would-be network-tracer program. The file eventually ended up in a web server hosted by a local Internet Service Provider, or ISP, as they were called. The ISP operated from one of the data centers for British Telecom, the giant telecommunications company. They had many data centers. This one was based in Dublin, Ireland. The ISP was a legitimate company operating as the point of connection to the Internet and other services including data storage for its many clients. They were not responsible for the content carried in the servers inside the bowels of their data center. It said so in the service agreement. The crime, stealing the login credentials, was lost in the ether of complex digital streams and oceans of machine data that no one would look at—no one but one man.

In the second floor of a home on the outskirts of Reykjavík, Iceland, along one of the many inlets of the coastline, sat a computer that served as host to a small software program. The program's sole function was to communicate with the web server in Dublin and download the encrypted file that contained the password to Mister Santander's investments and his personal banking accounts. The ISP in Dublin worked much like a Post Office made of brick and mortar. The software that ran the program was like the letter carrier - pick up the mail and deliver it into the mailbox at the designated address. The digital world mimicked the physical one in most ways. An address of street, city, and country was replaced with a simple number called the "IP Address." Every IP Address allowed the routing system to deliver the electronic data to the right computer device. There was no need for letter carriers. When delivered to the computer in Reykjavik the password file was encrypted so that it looked like a random set of digits. The theft of the credentials was committed like crime has always been done using the legitimate channels and protocols of commerce. It appeared as nothing more than a simple transaction. The encrypted password was an untraceable drop of digits in the vastness of an ocean of data.

Julia had learned this digital world and its language alongside her other memories of childhood. But the digital language was reinforced in the repetition of children playing games on the keyboard. Spanish was her first language, but it was learned intermixed with English in the medium of computers that had always been available to her. There was no translation necessary in her mind. The flow of thoughts to expression on her computer happened as easily as water flows downhill.

At the moment, she was engrossed with chatting – typing in the abbreviated language of teenagers called *txtspk*. As teenagers go, she was an expert. And she was also expert in the mores of online social behavior.

She giggled.

"No, I can't," she typed back.

Her mind was wired for a virtual social world where reality blended with the digital, the two forming who she was and how she thought. Her online friends were as real to Julia as if she were talking to them right there in the room.

She had a couple of conversations going at the same time on the Google chat site.

"Yes, yes, yes, you can!!!" came back the reply.

She giggled again. She was typing to Peter from Birmingham, England. Peter was the boy whom she had met online a month back and who was now visiting with his parents right there where she lived in the coastal resort of Torremolinos.

"He wants to meet??? OMG, will your parents let you?"

She had another session open with Teresa, her childhood girlfriend.

"No, but I will make them."

Julia had met the virtual Peter earlier in the year and now "OMG" she thought, "he is right here!!!"

She could barely contain her excitement. Peter and his parents were in a hotel by the beaches, "right here in Torre!!!" she typed to Teresa, waiting for Peter who was still typing.

Julia knew the hotel.

The boy of her interest was less than a kilometer away. She glanced again to the online pictures on his Facebook account. It showed a handsome boy, blond, thirteen according to the page. He was smoking a cigarette in one picture and holding what looked like a beer in another. He was bad, the cool kind of bad that she liked.

English families like Peter's had been finding their way to the southern coast and vacationing on the beaches of Spain for over sixty years. Northern Europeans loved the beaches on the Mediterranean, a place once called *Mare Nostrum* when the Romans were the power in the region. The tourists came and Spain flourished.

With the Euros' entrance back in 2002 the price of things and services skyrocketed. Tourism took a short-lived dip, but rebounded. The tourists kept coming. A Mediterranean vacation was no longer limited to the affluent. Working-class northerners came to find Malaga and the other coastal towns, like Torremolinos.

The effect was immediate. A young tennis phenom, Rafael Nadal, entered the stage and the nation's soccer teams started winning the cups of soccer glory across the world. It all fueled the passion of the people, symbolized by the success of the national team, La Roja, as it was called. For once it was good to be a Spaniard. New construction started a surge of wealth that sparked economic euphoria, a sense that everything they touched would turn to gold.

It lasted for six years or so. It happened in Spain and across Europe until the seams of the euphoria started to come apart. By the fifth year of negative growth the prices of things and services turned dramatically down. A vacation on the beautiful beaches and the sun of *Mare Nostrum* was now at bargain levels. What was good for visiting tourists was not so good for the owners of property, who faced massive depreciation in their real estate holdings. The burden of high debt accumulated in the banks as collateral was losing value. Spain was slipping, going underwater, and so was the Santander family.

Julia's parents worried more; the conversations at the dinner table became tense. There was no place to escape their own heavy burden of debt that the Santander's held for the place on the beach, the apartment in Madrid, and for the care of their own parents. Julia's father was a banker, well to do, prior to 2008, now worrying if he would have a job the next month. He was unable to answer his wife's question, "How are we going to pay the bills in the future if you are unemployed, Miguel?"

"Our retirement nest egg is still intact," he told her. "We just need to hang tough for a few more years until we can retire. Julia will be on her own with a job, and it will be just the two of us," he told her. The fault lines in his argument were more apparent to her. "What happens when Plan A is gone and we are left going from Plan B to Plan C to end up in …Plan F—'fucked'?" she asked.

It was this retirement account, and his name prominently featured as an expert in mergers and acquisitions, that brought his family to the attention of hackers working for the crime syndicates. These syndicates had also evolved —from breaking thumbs to breaking passwords. The frontline of crime had moved from the streets to underground tech centers in the remote countries where cyber-crime had become an open market of so-called "victimless" theft, as long as the targets were the rich of the West. It had become big business, and the so called *developing countries* were getting even by attracting the disaffected, unemployed, technology wizards being laid off during the recession.

The bank accounts of prominent people became the new targets, what they called *pharming* in the world of cyber-theft.

Names of the *phat* targets were traded amongst the criminals in the cyber underground like an exchange for precious metals. It worked in the same way that online merchants trade the names of their customers to each other. Once a target name entered these databases they remained there in a vicious cycle—sold and resold – an underground market of private information retailers selling credit card and bank account information – all for a market price.

Someone from an address in Dublin, Ireland that called himself Vlad had purchased Miguel Santander's name and credentials from the online black market. Vlad bought it for a very lucrative price. The *phat* target was in the crosshairs; the only thing that remained was to pull the trigger.

Julia found escape from the family's tension in her circle of online friends. She was a Facebook fanatic, Twitter-follower extraordinaire and texting fiend. This too had played into the calculus of why the Santander's got picked as the next target. Julia had badgered her mother to help her get an account, circumventing the required age restrictions. Her blue eyes, dark brown hair and olive complexion were a complete package of innocent but alluring beauty. It was the look of sophistication. She was popular; everyone wanted to be her friend, to "friend" her in the vernacular of Facebook. She reveled in the moment. Julia got noticed online.

Another reply came through before Julia had finished typing with Teresa.

"K, I will be at the entrance to the Pimentel Tower on Calle Las Mercedes at 3 this afternoon. If you show, then I will know for sure that you are interested in me. If not, then I will also know what you think of me. Is it real, or are you just playing with me:-(?"

His name was Peter. And he was already thirteen. Julia was twelve, but you wouldn't know it by her Facebook pictures.

Julia erased her last witty remark and stopped typing. She chewed on her finger, pensive, her ponytail bouncing up and down. Her headphones were playing Justin Bieber. She continued typing on her laptop.

"Julia, I need you," yelled her mother Michaela from down the stairs at the edge of the staircase.

Her mother called again, this time louder. There was no answer, the music in Julia's Skullcandy drowning out her mother's calls. Julia caught the reflection of her mother on the mirror when she entered her room. The mirror was strategically placed for just such occasions. She hadn't heard her mother approaching until it was almost too late.

"I'm coming," she said out loud as she typed back to Peter "K, ciao" and closed the laptop. She raced across the room to join her mother headed downstairs to the kitchen.

In the kitchen helping her prepare the table, she said "Mamá, I'm going to see Teresa after lunch." It was phrased as part statement, part request. Michaela looked at her daughter, letting silence serve notice that requests were acceptable; demands would not get a response. Michaela opened the refrigerator door looking for a salad dressing, finally relenting a bit.

"We'll see. But first we have to talk with your father."

She was already wise to the ways of her soon-to-be teen-ager, but she let her have her way. *Teresa is a good kid from a good family*, she thought The two kids were inseparable. *All the kids are the same these days.*

She smiled. *Today we will not talk about money*, she said to herself.

It was Saturday. La Comida was the noonday meal – an ordeal for the youngster looking at the arrangement of po-tato tortas, chorizos, soups, bread and salad, sangria, olives, olive oil, and butter. This was the only meal that they took together in their busy schedules during the week. It was usu-ally the three of them eating when they could in between the demands of business meetings, schoolwork, and social engagements.

They were seated at the table making small talk about meet-ing friends later in the evening and planning for a much-needed vacation. The setting was of a traditional Spanish home on the Mediterranean Coast, with white marble floors and a lazy fan circulating the air in the dining room. They were seated adja-cent to the veranda that overlooked the other homes with their red- colored roof tiles. The brilliant blue of the Mediterranean was visible just a couple of kilometers to the south. Their build-ing sat on a hillside, with other buildings similarly constructed sitting further below, making for a dazzling array of whites and reds that ended at the blue of the water's edge.

The sunlight lit up every room and even so, there was nary a speck of dust to be found. Michaela Maria Cortes de Santander kept a tidy home. The decorations on the solid white painted walls were modest and meant to offset the brilliance of the sun on the white stucco.

"Julia, are you coming with us tonight?"

Her mother intercepted the question, "No, she's going to the movies with Teresa."

Miguel Santander did not pass on the fact that Julia had not answered his question. He broke the end of the baguette and dipped it in some olive oil, biting off a chunk.

"What movie?"

It was a probative question, more to it than mere curiosity. Julia recognized this—and she was ready.

"We were thinking of seeing *Hugo*."

Her father nodded his head. It was a good answer.

"That's good."

Julia sighed in relief. Apparently her father was acquainted with the movie *Hugo*. The two girls had actually planned to go to the cinema, but not to see *Hugo*. The new *Twilight* movie had just come out and all their friends were intent on going to the opening. That was until Peter had announced, to her surprise, the "secret he'd been keeping for a month."

A half hour into the meal Julia rolled her eyes to her mother so her father Miguel wouldn't see. *How can someone eat all this food?* She was going to be sick to her stomach, she thought. Julia looked at her mother, her eyes pleading to be released from the next course of food.

"Miguel," she spoke to her husband.

Words were not needed to explain the situation. He raised his hand as if to say, "I got it." Miguel Santander was already tired of seeing and hearing all the chafing from his daughter. He was not accustomed to the idea that he was losing control of who could go where and when in his own household. Submission came.

"Julia," he said. "You'll call us, right?"

"Of course, Papá."

Julia jumped out of her seat, hugged her mother and father and raced down the marble stairs before the two could change their minds.

"She will be with Teresa," Michaela said to Miguel who grunted his acknowledgment.

Outside Julia was on her phone texting Teresa. "Hi T. cng Michael. Cvr me???" asking her to cover for her meeting with Peter. Seconds later came the reply. The girls had it all covered. Julia was not headed to the movies, and not to Teresa's house.

The tower was not far. The streets were busy with a mix of vendors and tourists soaking in the sun and the vistas of the beautiful olive-skinned people. Taxis of every brand and Vespa scooters played a dance interweaving with the traffic of private cars. A cacophony of automobile and scooter horns lightly tapped, alerting each other so that collisions were rare. Sailors on liberty from nearby Malaga walked in their white uniforms. They looked splendid in the afternoon sun. The aromas were wonderful, the scene, a kind of convivial chaos.

Julia walked downhill on a slight decline on Calle Las Mercedes. The street narrowed the closer it got to Torre Pimentel. This was the fourteenth century tower from which Torremolinos got its name.

"La veo," I see her, said the driver surveying Julia with a military precision. He spoke on his mobile phone. "*Se cambia al otro lado, tiene traje de blusa blanca, y pantalones cortes de jeans.*" (She is now crossing the street, wearing a white blouse and blue jean shorts.)

"Confirmado," another voice confirmed.

The third man in the trio had followed her from her house so there was no mistaking the target. It was not difficult to spot her. The other two men were in a nondescript white SEAT Inca van. The driver made a quick left turn from his position onto Calle Las Mercedes until it was cruising right alongside the sidewalk and the young girl typing away on her phone.

Julia had her head looking down to her smart phone, texting, barely conscious of her familiar streets. She was following Peter's directions.

"Am in front of the fountain. I c u!" Peter sat back in his chair and smiled. *Job accomplished*, he thought. Now I'm thirsty. He headed for the refrigerator to get another beer. "All in a hard day's work; payday will be sweet."

Peter had a Google Earth view of the street. He was English, but he was not in a hotel on the beach in Torremolinos with his parents. And he was not thirteen years old.

Sitting in his room in Birmingham, England, nowhere near the coast of Spain, his job was to flirt online with specific targets provided by a man he only knew as Vlad. They had never met in person. It was all done online. "The Vlad," as he thought of him, had very precise expectations of his work. "What harm can there be in a little bit of flirting? The girls like it," he thought. He never cared to question to what purpose. He did his job. He got paid. Life was good for the thirty-year-old sitting at home, his mum's home, drinking beer and getting fatter than he already was.

Julia heard the beep and another entry arrived on her phone. "Am in front of the fountain. I c u!" This caused her to pause her walk and look to the left. The bedlam of noise and traffic made it easy for the van to blend in and hide within the crowd.

In happened in the blink of an eye. The van door opened and Julia was gone. All that was left of her presence was a single scream. "That's all I heard." That's what the witnesses all said. The scream was lost in the noise, and the few people who were witnesses, could only say later what was already obvious. Julia had been abducted in plain daylight. The witnesses said that it was "A man, who took her into a white van that then disappeared." It happened in broad daylight right in front of the old tower.

Teresa unwittingly played out her part "covering" for Julia. It was not until a frantic Michaela got the truth from Teresa later that night that it became clear. Julia had never made it to Teresa's house and never went to see the movie *Hugo* that she had told her dad she was going to go see with her friend. By the time the parents got to the bottom of what had happened, the day had turned to late evening. It was dark outside.

Sunshine came the next day in Torremolinos, and the day after, but not for the parents of Julia Santander. In the hours that followed that eventually turned to days and weeks, a force majeure of people from the local authorities to the Cuerpo Nacionál de Policía looked for Julia Michaela Santander. Her photo was plastered on the streets and on news websites, but the kidnappers did their job effectively. They turned her over to another group, a group they knew nothing about, a group called Seraphim. That's the way it was designed. The kidnappers did their job and they got paid to deliver the goods.

The entire operation was run as professionally as any terrorist cell would run it: compartmentalization to keep any one part from knowing the whole of the operation, a strict set of operating procedures, ruthless accountability, money exchanges that made it impossible to trace, and a strict need-to-know set of communications controls.

After several weeks the investigators were nowhere. They knew from the beginning that the old adage was true: the first forty-eight hours were critical. They had lost the *most* critical time, the first eight hours, because of the obfuscation game that the two girls had agreed to play. Julia vanished and the world of Michaela and Miguel Santander fell asunder.

Later in the week, the second blow came. It happened while the parents were in their moment of crisis and frantic anxiety. There had been no word about the whereabouts of their only child.

The Santander's investment accounts were cleaned out. The investment house told Miguel Santander that they had been speaking to him for over two weeks, at least to someone whom they thought was he. They had sent him confirming emails and he had repeatedly approved all the transactions with the right credentials. The shares had been transferred to exchanges and to accounts managed in countries where the trail ended - untraceable. Miguel and Michaela Santander lost their daughter and in the deepest, darkest moment of their lives whatever malevolent being it was that had it in for them had also taken their retirement. To the heap of personal despair was added financial ruin. It happened in the span of a few days.

Dear Diary

5th of March

I want to tell you like Anne Frank did. She told her diary all the little things. I have never written a diary before. I tried it once but it was boring. My family was boring. How I wish that I could have my boring life back. I wish for it with all my heart.

This time I will write to you every day. Almost every day. Until my mamá and my papá find me. I will tell you, only you, the truth, so you can know. I am so afraid!!!

6th of March

I started crying again. I had to stop writing. I am OK now. I am afraid that it is what Mamá warned me about. They warned us in school, too. Why didn't I listen!!!

I must tell someone, but they keep me locked up in this room with a window that won't break. I tried. I hear birds and cows and in the morning I hear roosters. I only heard one car. I don't know where I am.

It was my 13th birthday last week. No one told me happy birthday, NO ONE!!! I am so scared I cannot stop crying. They gave me a rag dog today like I was some stupid little girl. He is brown, no, more like tan. I think he must be like what they call a Cocker Spaniel. I think it was so I would stop crying. I call him Nikita in secret, same as they call me. Last night I slept with Nikita. First time. I started sucking my thumb again. It was all wrinkled in the morning. I had stopped, but now I cannot help myself.

7th of March

I am so scared to tell you this, but I must tell someone. I will tell you. So you can tell Saint Pancras and he can tell Jesus. And Jesus can tell God so he can forgive me. I am so sorry!!!

They made me wear little girl clothes today. They were pink and white. They were too tight and the skirt was so short. Mamá would never, never, never let me wear this. It was a skinny man and an even skinnier woman. They smelled like cigarettes and garlic. I think she was the boss. They made me play like a little girl, as the man, I don't know his name, made a video of me. I was so ashamed. The man said that I was going to have a visitor tomorrow and that I needed to look pretty. I am so sorry!!! I have to stop, they are coming back.

CHAPTER 2

THE BRONX, NEW YORK CITY, USA
SEPTEMBER 1995

"Carolina, wait for me! Caro, wait!" She didn't stop, just kept walking, her head down, shoulders stooped. The backpack was weighing down on her shoulder. Jaime was puzzled. She didn't even look back.

He ran up to her, caught her at the busy intersection. She turned away. Carolina was fifteen – same age as Jaime. The two teenagers were sophomores at Adlai High as it was called there in the neighborhood. The light turned green. Something was definitely wrong. Jaime was alarmed. He had never seen her like this. He grabbed her school bag like he always did, like his grandfather Enrique taught him, to be *"un caballero"*, a gentleman. But she pulled it back and walked even faster across the busy intersection leaving the school grounds of Adlai E.

Stevenson High School. Now he was sure. Something was really wrong.

"Caro, what did I do?" he asked.

"Nothing, leave me alone," she yelled back, finally facing him as she burst into tears. Jaime pulled her to his six-foot frame. She was lost in his embrace, his big arms wrapped around her thin torso with the backpack carrying her laptop computer and her books.

The tide of tears came, her words coming out in short bursts. "I didn't do it!" she said, "now my whole life is ruined." He held her closer still and took her backpack to ease her burden. Caro's tears rolled down his neck. He repeated, "it's okay, it's okay, we can fix it," not knowing what it was exactly that needed fixing.

At least it's not me, Jaime thought. He was relieved about that. Everything else he could deal with, but not having the beautiful Caro mad at him.

Around them the busy life of the Bronx continued. Cars honked their horns and the train rattled by underground. Warm vapors rose from the exhaust grate on the sidewalk bringing up the odors of New York City's subway tunnels. A police siren wailed its strident sound heading in their direction; the Doppler effect increasing its intensity as the waves compressed—a piercing noise designed to get attention. But the two teenagers were only focused on each other, the noisy, odorous world of the city around them in the background. They were young and this urban place with all its manifest sounds, sights and smells was the home they knew.

"Tell me everything he said." He held her at arm's length, bending down so she could see him face-to-face...so she could focus. Between shudders of tears, Carolina told him.

"You know that I had to go to the Principal's office after computer class." She paused again to hold back the thoughts, the shame of having to go see the Principal. Jaime was patient, relaxing the grip a bit, but keeping the same fixed posture trying to keep her talking.

"Mr. Anderson said that I am on suspension. He told me that I broke into the computer network and changed the grades for my friends." Carolina burst into tears once again, at the very idea that she would have done such a thing; the sting of the accusations was more than she could bear.

"I didn't do it, I didn't do it!" she said again, her body heaving with the convulsion of tears, her lungs gasping for air.

Carolina was maybe 110 pounds soaking wet, a Nuyorican beauty with long curly black hair, equally long toned legs and the face of a Latin angel. But not at that moment. Her eyes were puffed and red, spilling a deluge of tears from her diminutive body.

That was until she saw the look on Jaime's face. In an instant the eyes went from puffy red to fiery shrewish anger. She slapped him on the face.

Jaime was stunned. "What the ..." he stammered as Caro went into a machine-gun-style attack.

"Do you think this is funny, am I making a joke, am I a comedian?" The questions came a mile a minute. But she was not interested in answers. Her Latina-girl temper was on full display.

Jaime quickly grasped the situation, got over his indignation at being slapped, and grabbed her again in an embrace that took all the steam out of her. He laughed, this time tenderly, rocking her back and forth telling her "sorry—sorry, I wasn't laughing. I was, you know, relieved, just thought it was, I don't know, something more serious like someone was hurt. I can fix this, Caro. I know you didn't do it. But I can guess who did."

At this thought, Carolina pulled away from Jaime and asked, "Who?"

His first thought was *"Oh no, I have seen that look before. I would not want to be on the receiving end of whatever is going to come from Carolina Maria DelBarco."*

"Who was it?" she asked again, this time more fiercely, if that was possible. Jaime then realized the trap he had just walked into. He knew quite well the temperament of his girlfriend Carolina, who everyone called Caro for short. He knew her *take-no-prisoners* anger could get them both into trouble.

"It's just a guess," he said, trying to backpedal from the trap of his own making.

"No, tell me now, Jaime," this time switching to reason and logic. "I need to know, it's my reputation," now shifting again, her body and facial expressions all in synch, the full arsenal of her very capable persuasive feminine powers on display.

There was a reason why Carolina Maria DelBarco was the top student in the tenth grade. Jaime knew that if he wasn't careful, Caro could easily twist him into a New-York-City pretzel with her logic. He had been there before. Caro usually got what Caro wanted.

He braced himself. In as serious a look as he could give her, he said, "No."

He paused, taking the full measure of a tornado forming there before his very eyes from the 110 pounds of skinny girl still in his grasp. He hurried to explain.

"But I will find out for sure, and then I will tell you, and I will show you and," he paused, drew a breath, and said, "I will get Mr. Anderson the proof so your name can be cleared. But I need to be sure first, Caro," he pleaded with her. The part about clearing her name did the trick.

"Okay, I trust you," she said, which Jaime knew meant that he had better not fail her. He smiled again. "I'll get it done," he said. She kissed him on the cheek and whispered, "Sorry about the slap." She had now given him a kiss—something that she did not give away very easily. That was to seal the deal. His end of the deal would not be satisfied until he came through.

It was a good bargain, he thought. Jaime was mad about the pretty Nuyorican named Caro and there was nothing he would not do for her. He had discussed it with his grandfather Enrique who knew exactly what motivated him.

"*Tienes el amor loco*," he told Jaime, smiling at his grandson like he knew a secret that could only be learned with experience. He said nothing more. Enrique Rodriguez knew there was only so much he could tell his grandson. The real teacher was experience. He blew a ring of smoke from his cigar, got up from his sofa and went to the windowsill to look outside and ponder the question his grandson had asked—"I can't stop thinking about her, *abuelito*. What am I going to do?" But he

SOLARI AND SKAAR

did offer one other bit of advice that Jaime was only starting to understand, *"el amor loco,"* he told him, "ees like it says, it ees jus craazy, makes ju do craazy things, ees like ahn eencurable disease and there ees nothing ju can do about it, but accept it. It ees the eencvitable facts of life. Dat," he said, wagging his stogie in the air, now facing his grandson "ees dee way it ees." Jaime thought he understood.

Back at home that afternoon, Jaime logged into his computer and thought it through some more. He was in love with the girl named Caro and to win her love in return he was going to have to prove himself. Which started with getting to work on the problem of Caro's hacker.

It didn't take long for Jaime to figure it out. He had a theory. It had to be José. There was one other hacker in Mr. Smith's computer class, same as he was, the same class that Caro was in. José, he had figured out, was one of those *malditos* as his grandfather was used to saying, the people in the world who only have malice in their hearts.

Mr. Smith's computer networking class was so elementary that Jaime had a hard time paying attention. And then there was the problem of Caro there in the same room to divert his mind. He stayed interested by helping her in the assignments. She returned the favor in her own way, the little morsels of attention that she doled out. It kept Jaime and all the other boys interested but at bay.

Caro was one of those kids that everyone said, "One day we will all say, 'I used to know her when she was in school, and even then we all knew.'" Caro would be a famous person—someday.

She was so driven; her ambitions were bigger than any room she occupied.

Jaime, on the other hand, treated school like it was something to endure; its only redeeming value was that going to school meant that he could get to see Caro in the hallways or in class.

At the annual parents' conference the year past, one teacher, Mrs. Bates, had put it in straightforward terms to his parents: "Jaime is smart, maybe too smart. But he is, to put it nicely, *coasting* through ninth grade, doing the bare minimum to get through the classes."

Mrs. Rodriguez had looked at her husband, at first bewildered, like she had not heard right. Her face flushed red, the blood pulsing in her, ready to explode. "Coasting" was not anything either of the parents understood, but especially Mrs. Leonor Rodriguez.

"Coasting", what is this word?" asked Mrs. Rodriguez looking from her husband to the teacher and back again. Mrs. Bates was about to explain. Mr. Rodriquez cut her off. "I think we understand, Mrs. Bates." He held his wife's hand firmly and the message was clear, "don't press the point, not right here, wait until we get home."

Jaime never saw it coming. The fact that he was parked in front of the television when his parents got home that evening did not help his cause. A Puerto Rican mother in unbridled anger is something to behold. Jaime heard utterances strung together that he had no idea his mother knew. He got to see a pissed off Latina mother to whom the idea of *coasting* was the antipathy of her life's experience.

"Coasting, *que es eso*, coasting? *Nosotros no somos personas de coasting*," the sound reverberated through the apartment walls. Everyone on every floor knew—Jaime was in deep trouble. The mix of English and Spanish coming from Mrs. Rodriguez sounded just like Ricky Ricardo when he had discovered one of Lucy's *"travesuras."*

Latino parents don't just take away privileges. They get their point across in other ways, and Jaime surely did get the point. Jaime looked for solace in the company of his grandfather, but even there he found that his *Abuelo,* Enrique, was not so stupid as to try and interfere.

"How do they say it?" his grandfather mused, "ahh si, embrace the pain, Jaime," he told him while laughing so hard that he went into another fit of coughing. Jaime was distressed. No one was coming to his rescue—no one in the Rodriguez family was throwing him a rope, not his father or his grandfather. He was going to have to quit the coasting and get focused, that was for sure, on more than just winning the heart of Carolina Maria DelBarco. With time he finally figured it out. The clearest path to Caro's heart was to do well in school—that is what she respected—a serious man.

But he also had another love, the love of computer networks that also kept him focused and proved to give him the intellectual challenge that he needed. Mr. and Mrs. Rodriguez had no notion that computers could be important in making a living. "It isn't like you could be a doctor or a lawyer in computers," Mrs. Rodriguez said to her husband. Little did she know.

At the age of fifteen, Jaime knew more about networks and computers than his teacher, Mr. Al Smith. He had installed his own Ethernet network at home—complete with servers, modems, routers and even a CISCO switch he had bought at a local pawnshop for a song and a dance. He thought back to the conversation—and smiled again—that mischievous smile that he couldn't hold back, the one that had gotten Caro all riled up.

"Hey, how much for the PID, man?"

"The what?"

"The PID, man, you know, the Printer Interface Device?"

The salesman behind the display case gave it his best *I know what I'm doing* face. "This PID's almost new. The tag says 400 bucks. I'll let you have it for $380."

"No way, man, 38 bucks maybe, it's just a PID, you know, to connect several printers. That's what these ports are for, each one for a printer. And besides, this is the 2501, not even top model. I tell you what; I'll give you 40 bucks. Otherwise have a nice day."

"So have a nice day, shithead." Pawners were not ones to back down so easily.

"Okay, I got it, I'm outta here." Jaime headed for the door, holding back his grin.

It was almost closing time and sales had been slow all day for the tattooed salesman. The salesman suspected that the so-called PID was hot property; the guy who sold it to him had no idea what it was, and neither did he. The guy had just wanted some quick cash.

"Hey, wait a minute. Sorry, I didn't mean that," he yelled out. Jaime had the door already open when he turned around.

Calling it a PID was technically not a lie since one could connect a network printer to a switch, but there was no such thing as a PID. But Jaime had bet that the salesman didn't know that. *Just a little bit of misinformation—to get what I needed,* he thought to himself. The so-called PID was an expensive CISCO switch used by Internet Service Providers, the ISPs that made their names selling network access in the 1990s. It was worth thousands, and it added to Jaime's growing arsenal of network devices that kept taking over more of his bedroom and adding a hefty hike to the electric bill.

That night Jaime did his own bit of hacking, including getting into the Adlai E. Stevenson High School network. He got the logs downloaded for the previous week and saw the digital fingerprints left behind by José. From the access logs, he saw that José had gained remote access to Caro's computer. She had her computer set up for full administrative access. *Got to fix that,* he thought, *for later; first things first.* José had then used her computer to gain access to the school network using the default manufacturer's password for the remote access server. The password had never been changed. *Bad mistake,* he thought. All students had remote access privileges to be able to do some of the homework assignments. José had then used a published bug to escalate his access privilege inside the network, found the unencrypted password file in one of the file servers for the database server, and logged in as the database administrator. The trail led definitively back from database server, to network servers, to Caro's computer, and back to José's computer. It was all done in the middle of the night when Caro was getting her beauty sleep. Jaime had to laugh out loud, "Hah, I got you, you jerk." José the hacker knew nothing about erasing his trail.

The following day, Jaime took the courageous step of getting an appointment to meet *the man*. Principal Tobias Anderson was a towering figure of a black man. In an earlier life Tobias Anderson had played Left Guard on the offensive line protecting the famous knees of "Broadway Joe" Namath for the New York Jets football team. The 300-pound imposing figure of Principal Anderson was all it took to scare the living daylights out of students who had an appointment with *the man*, Including pretty little Carolina, and now Jaime Rodriguez.

"Okay, I buy the fact that it was not Miss DelBarco who got into the network unauthorized," with special emphasis placed on the "unauthorized" word. "So how did YOU find the evidence needed to clear Miss DelBarco and find our real perpetrator?" Jaime was taken aback. Principal Anderson had gone straight for the jugular. Now Jaime had a choice.

Jaime did one smart thing in the whole episode of Caro's hack. He had considered that the question of how he got his evidence might come up. The act of breaking into the school network, despite the noble cause, had the potential of getting him into trouble. It seemed to always work out that way when it came to matters of Caro.

But there was no other way. He had to be able to prove it first, and that meant he would have to hack into the network. No one was going to believe him on a theory, nor would they even understand what he was talking about, and there was no way that he was going to get permission to do all of this hacking. He knew that it could mean trouble for him. But he had to do it—for Caro. So he told Principal Tobias Anderson the truth.

It took just a moment for Principal Anderson to think up Jaime's punishment.

Tobias Anderson had to smile—there "were so many upsides to the idea." He stroked his chin, looking every bit displeased with the young Jaime Rodriguez as he had when discovering that Caro, his star pupil, had apparently hacked into the school's network.

"You know your intentions were good, but you still did wrong, right?"

"Yes, sir."

Good answer, Principal Anderson thought to himself. *He's not trying to make excuses.*

"Okay, so your punishment is to work with Mr. Smith, your computer lab teacher."

"Yes, sir."

Jaime had talked to his grandfather about the upcoming meeting. The two were more like pals than anything else; the old man, though two generations removed from his grandson, was the kind of man that loved the plain and simple people, and he loved his grandson like nothing else on earth. Jaime could talk to him about anything. He even discussed Carolina with his grandfather. As to the meeting with the principal, the advice was simple:

"Ju can have only one ahnser, Jaime, and it is made up of only two words: jess sir. Nothing more, no explanations. *Entiendes*?" Do you understand?

"*Si, pero…*", Yes, but…

"*No! No hay peros, solo*, jess sirs," he told his grandson.

Jaime argued it a bit longer, but eventually he accepted the notion that making excuses was only going get him into deeper trouble.

El castigo is algo bueno – porque así se limpia el pecado, he told him. It was not easy for Jaime to understand. He had made an art of avoiding punishment, and his grandfather was telling him that punishment was a good thing; the way the sins were cleansed. And there would be a punishment involved, he told him. "A man is accountable, Jaime; boys make excuses."

His grandfather had never steered him wrong. Enrique Rodriguez explained it further to him in a conversation, not a reproach, just a casual conversation interspersed with stories from his youth back in Puerto Rico and in the Army.

"Your after-school assignment—your punishment—is to secure the school's network so that no one can hack in again, including you. Got that?"

"Yes sir."

"Okay, get out of here, and don't you let me catch you here again."

It was a punishment easy to give. Jaime gulped. What he knew about networks is that they were easy to hack. Protecting them from someone like him, that was not a puzzle he had ever really entertained solving. But for the moment, he had listened and followed his grandfather's advice. In the process he had earned a man's respect.

Jaime had a new challenge, not that he had a choice. In the process of figuring out how to secure the school network,

Jaime Rodriguez became a student of a course that didn't exist. He was creating the process and putting in place the technology for how to secure an inherently insecure network. He had found his life's vocation.

Two years later, he was a senior applying to the universities when he received a letter in the mail from Principal Tobias Anderson. It was a copy. The original had gone to Tobias' alma mater. It was addressed to the Dean of Admissions, MIT, the very same university of his youth where he had been one of the very rare student athletes who had graduated out of MIT and had gone on to play professional football. The letter was titled "Recommendation for Mister Jaime Rodriguez to Attend the Massachusetts Institute of Technology." Principal Anderson and the Dean of Admissions were the best of friends. The letter said it all concisely.

Dear Bob,

Let me tell you about one of my star students. His grades may not be much to clamor about, but there is more to the young man that you should know and which you might not find in the admissions forms. This is a young man who is about doing good, but he needs to learn how to work within the boundaries. He is courageous and smart in a practical way.

Our world is changing. It is being taken over by these young geeks that you keep graduating. We are going to need more of them working for the good guys. I believe we need him. We need him to mature and to gain the knowledge and skills that MIT can teach him. Hope you can find a spot for him in the freshman class.

Tobias

Though Jaime didn't know it at the time, there was another letter similarly written for the school valedictorian—a pretty Nuyorican girl named Carolina Maria DelBarco. They were both headed for one of the premier technology universities in the world.

CHAPTER 3

CYBER SQUAD CONFERENCE ROOM
FBI FIELD OFFICE, 26 FEDERAL PLAZA, TWENTY-THIRD FLOOR
NEW YORK CITY, USA
THURSDAY, 5TH OF APRIL
09:01AM EST, 15:01 CET

Squad Supervisory Special Agent (SSA) Jaime Rodriguez started the meeting with introductions. "Hello Fredrik, good to finally speak again. Thank you for sending the background material."

It was not lost on Detective Superintendent (DSI) Fredrik Hansen that Special Agent Rodriguez had used his first name even though they were not alone.

He followed his lead.

"Yes, good afternoon, Jaime, good to speak with you and your team."

"Folks, on the phone we have Detective Superintendent Fredrik Hansen from the Norwegian Federal Police that goes by the abbreviation KRIPOS joining us from his office in Oslo. We also have Europol Agents from Belgium and France who will be introduced in a moment. We also have our own Legal Attachés from the Legat offices in Denmark and Belgium."

Rodriguez was at one end of the small conference room on the eastern edge of the twenty-third floor that housed the New York FBI Field Office. Outside, a clear sky and early morning sun rose over the labyrinth of towers that make up the New York Skyline. It lit up the conference room. Rodriguez's cyber squad members were arrayed along the old wooden chestnut table that had hosted several generations of G-Men.

It was a new generation of Special Agents that sat around the table, men *and* women. They intermixed—as natural as could be—more likely to speak to each other on a chat session than to speak verbally.

Their faces gave away nothing of what they were thinking. Each was on his or her laptop computer looking up relevant background information about Norway or preparing to take notes. The chat sessions were already up and filling the screen. An informal exchange of small banter was in progress.

Over two years of intensely focused teamwork had taught them to know and trust each other. They knew each other's habits, areas of specialization, and even little quirks. It was all as familiar as a family that had grown up together sharing everything. It did not mean that they were clones. Problem solving meant teamwork; break down a task into its component parts and keep the end-goal in mind. SSA Rodriguez did not pick teammates to fit a specific mold, but he did pick them with certain attributes, and teamwork was one of the key conditions to being part of the Rodriguez Squad.

They were all anxious to get the background for their new assignment. What they knew was that it involved child abductions, an area that was outside their normal assignments. These types of cases went to one of their sister squads, and divisional boundaries were jealously guarded. This was going to be different, and they suspected that more surprises were in store.

Speaking to the voice conferencing phone, SSA Rodriguez introduced his team.

"We have in the room Special Agents Jillian Rose, Randy Pearl, and Mike Gilmer. Two analysts provide support and they are also in the room: Analyst Linda Atkins and Analyst Nick Williams. This team specializes in working cyber cases involving National Security. The international nature and other particular circumstances of this case, that we will discuss shortly, landed us the assignment. Our New York Office Assistant Director, Helen Kozniak, made this case a top priority for the New York Field Office, and the New York U.S. Attorney's Office has authorized our participation. Also on the phone with us are the Legal Attachés for Denmark and Belgium, respectively, Special Agents Norma Miller in Copenhagen, and Roger Levin in Brussels." He paused for a second to give everyone a chance to catch up to all the introductions.

"Fredrik, I also want to let you know that the case is being tracked at Headquarters at the request of our Director and the Attorney General. Please hold for a moment." He pushed the mute button on the Polycom conference telephone, but Atkins read his mind and turned the blinds another notch blocking the sunlight that was now making the room uncomfortably bright. Rodriguez un-muted the line and gave Atkins a nod of thanks.

Gilmer, Pearl, and Rose looked at each other with the slightest of smiles. Atkins, it was said in good humor, could read Rodriguez's mind before Rodriguez had formed the thought.

Rodriguez continued. "For the benefit of my team, DSI Hansen and I met just a few weeks ago in late February, when I was teaching a class at the National Academy in Quantico. He told me about the abduction of a young girl that occurred on the southern coast of Spain that fit the profile of how social engineering is being used for this type of crime. Now there has been another, this time in the DSI's front yard, so to speak, in Norway."

He walked the edge of the room, as was his custom, speaking to the room and then making eye contact when he wanted to make a point.

"There is evidence that these two cases are related, despite their distance on the map." He looked at Atkins and Williams, whose primary task was to do research and help connect the dots.

"Now Europol has learned that the crime in Spain had another facet involving a sophisticated identity theft that wiped out the family's life savings to the tune of several million Euros.

The sophistication of this crime has the financial sector worried." Rodriguez nodded to SA Gilmer, their resident financial crimes expert. "DSI Hansen is head of the Organized Crimes Unit in KRIPOS, which is the federal investigative branch of the Norwegian Police Directorate, our counterpart organization in Norway. You have our attention, sir. Will you take it from here, introduce yourself, and give us additional background?

"Thank you Special Agent Rodriguez." DSI Hansen had now switched to a more formal mode of speaking with his US counterparts.

"First, let me start with introducing our colleagues from the Europol offices in Belgium and Spain who will help us coordinate the investigation in Europe with our various European law enforcement organizations. On the phone is Felipe Navarro from his office in Madrid. Inspector, will you say some words on your background?"

"Yes, of course. As DSI Hansen said, I am Felipe Navarro, based in Madrid. I specialize in the area that is similar to your "Innocent Images Program" in the U.S. I will help coordinate the activities of this investigation as it relates to the young girl from Torremolinos. I am, like our esteemed colleague DSI Hansen, also a graduate of the National Academy, class of 2004."

Rodriquez looked in the direction of Atkins, who was already typing away bringing up his bio on the screen at the end of the conference room.

"Very good. Thank you. Our Europol colleague in Brussels is Patricia Lieuvin. Inspector, can you give us your background?"

Atkins already had the image and background of Ms. Lieuvin on the screen. At the sight of the very attractive investigator shown on the screen, Pearl and Gilmer caught each other's eyes with a smirk on their faces. SA Jillian Rose seated to Gilmer's right did not fail to notice the interplay of her two colleagues. She punched Gilmer on the arm.

SSA Rodriguez's squad was an eclectic assortment of geeks, all young, twenty- and thirty-something professionals hand-picked by their young leader. Getting on Rodriguez's squad was considered the coolest of the jobs one could have in the FBI.

The image of FBI Special Agents in the public's perception was not reality. And this particular team was keen *not* to fit the profile. The tradition to "spot the Fed" at the annual hacker's DefCon Conference in Las Vegas was all about a culture suspicious of being infiltrated. Outing their law enforcement counterparts was part of the game that was played out in the community. It was all for fun at the conference. In their real world, where getting access into the underworld of hacker forums was what made a reputation—these were the credentials that mattered in order to be effective. The game was deadly serious, becoming the newly contested domain of nations. The ethos of the anti-establishment was in some measure the same ethos of Rodriguez's team—to be special, and apart from the norm of conventions, even inside the FBI. It was also a necessary part of the psyche to be effective in their roles. Still, one would not find a set of individuals more committed to the ideal of the FBI's motto of: "Fidelity, Bravery, and Integrity."

The squad was actually twenty-two people, but this was Supervisory Special Agent Rodriguez's inner circle, where playful bantering was the stress reliever. When they were not on a cyber-sleuthing chase, they honed their skills badgering each other. Everything was fair game and they all knew that they had to be able to take as good as they could give. It was not uncommon for a team member to find that his or her computer had been owned or "pwned," in the terminology of hackers, by another member of the team. Getting "pwned," or stopping a fellow team member, meant the difference between losing or earning coolness points. It was sword fighting with training swords. The benefit was that everyone stayed sharp. None of them had yet earned points for getting to their boss' computer. Not that they hadn't tried.

They also knew Rodriguez's mind; how to work within the rules, but also how to be innovative when needing to cross the line. There was no inconsistency if they followed the law. Principal Tobias Anderson had taught the future Supervisory Special Agent a lesson about breaking the rules, but it wasn't to *not* take chances.

Inspector Lieuvin introduced herself. "Yes, my pleasure. I am Belgique as you would guess, but I got both my degree in criminal justice and also my graduate degree in computer science at George Mason University. At our Europol office, I am the lead for cyber crimes. I will serve as liaison to our law enforcement offices here in Belgium."

"Thank you, Inspector." DSI Hansen concluded the introductions. He was keen to make everyone feel included. "Now to the background: As you can see on the first slide, the case involves child abductions." The screen in the conference room had the map of Europe overlaid with dozens of red dots covering the respective countries of the victims.

"What you see on the slide is the location of unsolved child abductions over the course of the past five years. Some percentage of these may be associated with this group, the group that has taken the last victim. We don't know how many. There is a great deal that we don't know. We are also now learning that there appears to be a purpose to the abductions." Hansen paused to create emphasis. "The purpose is pedophilia. As I said, there is much that we don't know, but we are learning more."

DSI Fredrik Hansen proceeded over the course of the next hour, to spell out everything he had acquired in the investigation on the case and the group that, until a month ago, had existed only speculatively. They knew very little. He concluded with a summary:

"What we know was learned from a source that walked into our offices. His name is Becken—more on him in a moment. The group is highly organized and disciplined in a variety of well-known techniques in order to maintain their operational security. Until today, we didn't even have a name for them. Now we do. We call it "Seraphim." That name is derived from information that came to us from Becken, whom I mentioned a moment ago."

Up on the screen in the FBI's conference room Atkins had already populated the Wikipedia description of Seraphim, including the picture of a six-winged burning angel. The agents looked at each other. The connection to the name was not obvious, not at this point.

Rodriguez's team next saw the black and white picture of a man in his early thirties, his hair dark and curly, with a thin, long face and a nose narrow at the ridge. He had the look of a man living too long on the edge—he looked tired. *Still, there is something sympathetic in the eyes*, thought SA Rose. He was attractive. She was intrigued.

"Earlier yesterday, in the early afternoon, to be more precise, we got our first major break from a Norwegian hacker from Oslo. His name is Frank Becken. Becken walked into our offices and told us that he had discovered a website where he saw a young girl on display in a video. To his surprise, according to Becken, what he saw on this website was the very same young girl, Grete Enberg, who is now the leadoff subject in the news. Grete was abducted on Monday morning in a social engineering scheme perpetrated on the grandparents that were watching her. Her parents were away on a vacation. That was three days ago. Becken is a hacker that we have known about, an opportunist that works for hire, but is currently under the control of an organized crime ring here in Norway." He proceeded to the next slide that described the organized crime group.

"As I said, we've known about him for some time, but have not, to this day, been able to gather enough evidence against him to bring him in. The group that controls him here in Norway is called the 'NoSaints.'"

He went back to the slide with Becken's picture. "To his credit, Mr. Becken came to us. He captured critical data when he gained access to a particular website—which is why we have the information we do today."

A series of additional slides went up on the screen to co-incide with the narrative from the DSI. Analyst Atkins kept the slide show in synch. She paused on the pictures and charts long enough for the team to absorb the information that DSI Hansen was describing. What looked like the landing page for the website had the picture of a dark six-winged angel guarding a massive steel door.

"Put simply, the purpose of the website appears to be on-line pedophilia. What we don't know is for whom. And not meaning to be insensitive, but the girls may only have a short shelf life. We know this from a different case that I will speak to in a moment."

Atkins advanced the slides to show what appeared to be an adolescent girl. When the picture of little Grete came up, an involuntary gasp came out from the team seated at the table. DSI Hansen did not fail to pick it up. He paused for a moment before continuing.

"For now, we believe that the young girl, Grete, is alive and safe, but on the move to somewhere within Europe—likely already arrived at whatever location they are using for their operation. We have just gained information, again, thanks to Becken, that leads us to believe it is somewhere in the outskirts of Brussels."

Hansen's voice appeared to change—charged with emotion. He spoke as in a whisper.

"This is no longer just pedophilia. This past February, a different young girl was abducted from a small town in the southern coast of Spain. The remains of Julia Michaela Santander from Spain were just discovered earlier this morning." His voice on the telephone appeared to slow in cadence. "It happened by chance, and what we learned is a major break. The young Santander girl was abducted in the southern coast of Spain and has now been found in Belgium. If the two cases are related then it would mean that the Enberg girl, Grete, is also in Belgium. This is a major break in the case, and why we feel it is so urgent to solicit your help."

There was silence in the rooms and on the phones. On the screen was the picture of Julia Michaela Santander looking like any pony-tailed young girl of twelve or thirteen—a face of innocence and confidence, like the whole world was waiting to discover her talents.

SA Rose broke the tension with a question, "From what you've told us so far, DSI Hansen, it appears that this is a powerful crime ring. Is this where the investigation is taking you?"

"Yes, it is. We believe that the organization behind these kidnappings and subsequent murders has been around for a while, but for how long it is hard to tell. This kind of operation is not easy to conceal and yet it has been, which implies discipline and sophistication. And it may be that this group is behind multiple abductions of young girls. We had believed that the abductions were associated with human traffickers, but now these assumptions are in question. We may have been looking in the wrong place."

Hansen's voice rose. It was the voice of anger. "We still don't have a motive or motives here. It is pedophilia, but for what other purpose is the question, One that we are still trying to understand." He paused. "And to answer your question, Special Agent Rose, yes. That is what we are looking into. Is it an existing organized crime group—or a new one that we have not encountered before—and for what purpose? I will leave that question alone for the moment so we can concentrate on the immediate task. That task—is to find and save the young girl before she becomes the next murder victim like the young girl from Spain."

On the second screen propped against the conference room wall, Analyst Atkins brought up the questions and points of research that she was getting on her chat sessions from each of the team members. The note on the screen about motive was now getting filled with notes. The words *hedonism* and *god-complex* were getting the most votes from the team of Agents and Analysts.

"Why don't you continue, Fredrik? We will develop additional questions as you proceed. We can ask them later."

SSA Rodriguez gazed outside the wall of windows that looked to the east. The sun showed bright against a clear blue sky with only a thin haze of cirrus clouds in the upper atmosphere. On the twenty-third-floor, he could see the bronze-colored appearance of the Brooklyn Bridge spanning the East

River into Long Island. Inside the room, the contrast could not be starker to the brightness of the day.

A dark anger was brewing. He could see it in his team. Nothing could have galvanized this group of young professionals as did those pictures of Julia and Grete presented on the screen for all of them to see. They were now of one mind and one mission. They weren't chasing virtual ghosts in a sea of ones and zeros that they might never see. They were looking at the victims of evil in its worst form.

DSI Hansen picked up where he left off, moving from slide to slide, elaborating on the various bullet points on the screen. "Again, we still don't know the name of this group so we have applied to them the name on the website, "*Seraphim.*"

At this point, and through the remainder of the afternoon, SSA Jaime Rodriguez and his team began to engage with the others on the phone in a free exchange of questions, ideas, assertions, and even some speculation, though being clear to keep the facts separate from the assumptions.

"Again, this is an assumption, but one that is starting to fit the pattern of what we have recently learned. There is no reason for this group to be focused on money as a principal motive, and yet we have the problem that, at least in the case of the Santander family, theft of money was also involved. As I noted earlier, we found Julia Santander, from Spain. It was entirely a stroke of luck. Heavy rains in Belgium created flood conditions, spilling over the banks of creeks and rivers with many buildings in the path of these streams. A local farmer went looking for some of his equipment and he found the body of the young girl on the banks of a creek. The Belgian Police were called. They have secured the area and are planning to search the area upstream when the water levels subside. It is still too dangerous at the moment to be anywhere near these waterways. We now have the first crime scene with evidence that starts to support our thesis that these two events are connected, the abduction in Norway to the one in Spain."

"If I may, DSI Hansen?" Inspector Lieuvin spoke up. "The Belgian Crime Scene Investigation Team just provided their initial assessment for time of death. The examiner says that death occurred not more than a month ago. Cause of death has still not been determined. As you can expect, a large contingent of Belgium's law enforcement resources are being canvassed to assist in the search and pursue leads. Their first task is to get onsite and continue the search for more evidence."

SA Gilmer typed a statement that they all saw on the screen in the conference room. The collection of heads nodded in agreement. *If the bad guys don't know about the discovery, and presuming that they buried the body somewhere in the vicinity of their safe house, then too many uniforms might spook them—they will move the victim and the advantage will be lost.*

DSI Hansen spoke up again. "It did not take long to identify her. The victim was still fresh in the minds of law enforcement thanks to the Europol Alert that went out in February. As I indicated, her name is Julia Michaela Santander from southern Spain." He paused for a few seconds, his voice low and soft. "She had just turned thirteen."

SA Pearl made a fast stab of the back of his hand to stem the would-be moisture in his eyes.

"Your FBI Director and the head of Europol saw this same presentation when they spoke with my boss. If you transition to the next slide, you will see some more that we have been able to determine and why your team, Special Agent Rodriguez, is needed."

Rodriguez held up his right hand, like asking for attention. He nodded to Gilmer.

"One thought before we go there, Fredrik, if I may. I have a question for you, Inspector Lieuvin." He paused a moment to figure out the best way to say it without it coming out as criticism.

"Inspector Lieuvin, am I correct in understanding that the discovery of the girl from Spain has not reached the news?"

"That is correct, we have thus far been able to keep this from reaching the news but, as you well know, there is no telling how long that will still be the case."

"Right. Well, Fredrik, are you thinking what I'm thinking?"

Hansen took his cue. "I believe I am," he responded.

"Inspector Lieuvin, is there some way that you can delay the search and keep the uniformed police out of the area?"

"Very difficult, Detective Superintendent. We did think of that, but... let's just say that I will do my best. From conversations I have had with the Belgian Chief, they will not be keen to slow things down. If this information hits the media... I need not tell you about 2001, right?"

"Thank you, yes, please do what you can. It will give us time to find other leads that might be able to point more precisely to the location of the safe house, if it is in the general area where the body was discovered."

A new message went up on the screen. *2001???* Followed by another. *On it.*

In a moment, the results of a search *2001 pedophilia crime Belgium* came up with the pointed reference from Inspector Lieuvin. SSA Rodriguez muted the call and looked to his two analysts. "Atkins. Get us a quick read on this. Am interested in how this affects the case, could it be the same group morphed into something new, how did it impact law enforcement in Belgium? 9/11 changed us as a country and changed the FBI— find out what happened to them."

Rodriguez looked around at his team. They appeared to be in agreement. The politics of this was getting more compli- cated. He spoke up to shift the conversation back on track.

He unmuted the call. "One more thing, Inspector. Can you give us the precise coordinates for where the body was discovered? We may be able to do some analysis for places to focus the search."

Already moving ahead, Special Agent Gilmer and the Analysts in the conference room were speed-reading the mate- rial presented on the screen and simultaneously working their laptop computers, doing research, bringing up maps of the area—expanding their knowledge of what was being presented. Questions were being captured online interactively with each other using their protected chat sessions—also displayed as a separate window on the projector screen.

"Picking up where we left off, we have also learned that they are adept at using social engineering. It appears that the facts used to lure the victim's grandparents into believing that this was a legitimate request from the girls' school were facts learned from the mother's Facebook account. We looked at her Facebook account and found plenty of details there about her school and her teacher, the same details, used in the conversation with the grandmother. Lastly, your Director and the Director of Europol have both pledged the full resources of your agencies to find this group and help us save our young victim." DSI Hansen paused to catch his breath and to bring his thoughts to a conclusion.

"Ladies, gentlemen, we are racing the clock. Your skills in computer networks are vital. We don't have many leads, and what we need to know is possibly available in the website that Becken discovered." He paused again to let it sink in.

"I believe the place to start is to have you engage directly with Mr. Becken."

Supervisory Special Agent Rodriquez nodded his head as he eyed each member of his team. "I agree," he said. "We have a great number of other questions, but for now I concur that the most immediate benefit will come by way of a conversation with Mr. Becken. How do we make that happen?"

"Mr. Becken is in one of our meeting rooms. It is not safe for him to go home to his apartment. If you would like, I can ask him to join you in an hour, on the phone, which will give everyone a chance to take a break."

"Excellent, agreed. In one hour. It is approaching noon here in New York."

He looked around at his team and saw that they were ready to take a break.

"Thank you all." Addressing the audience on the phone, he said, "As the conversation with Mr. Becken is likely to get very technical, I presume that not everyone will want to join in, but you are all welcome—on the same conference bridge."

With the farewells completed the conference line was closed.

Analyst Nick Williams was waiting for his colleague Linda Atkins to finish up the notes for the meeting. Something was bothering him.

Analyst Atkins looked at him and raised an eyebrow, "What's up, Nick?"

"Something, not sure if I just heard wrong, but . . .," he hesitated.

"But what? Spit it out, Nick."

"We had six parties on that call, us included. When the call ended, I thought I heard six tones as each party hung up the phone. It should have been only the five outside callers into the conference bridge. I could be mistaken . . ."

Atkins interrupted him. "Easy enough to check. Call the bridge administrator and find out. Get the toll data. If it was six, then we need to figure out who the outlier is, figure out why, and pronto. Let me know—get on it, Nick."

Williams was methodical, he saw the tiny details. But he was also not one to take the lead. That he left to his best friend, Analyst Atkins. And he operated at human speed—still fast compared to others, but human fast.

"Will do."

Atkins operated at beyond human speed. Rodriguez always marveled at what she could do. Everyone on the team was fast.

They spoke fast, interacted fast, thought fast, came to data fast, and connected the dots just as fast. Atkins, well, Atkins was "Data Fast." That's what they all said about her. "Data," as in *Star Trek's* "Data." It was not human, not even close. Whatever wiring was in her brain was not normal.

CHAPTER 4

FIRST CLASS SEATING
LUFTHANSA AIRLINES FLIGHT SQ26, AIRBUS 380-800
SINGAPORE AIRPORT
NEAR MIDNIGHT, TUESDAY, 3ʳᴰ OF APRIL

"**Is there anything** else that I can get for you, Mr. Wong?" The flight attendant on the Lufthansa 380 was an elegant, tall, blonde German beauty in her mid-thirties. Aside from her native German, she spoke fluent Mandarin. She knew that Mr. Wong preferred to engage his conversations in English. He only spoke Mandarin with other native speakers. It wasn't arrogance; it was that it literally made him wince to hear his native tongue spoken by foreigners. He was a frequent flier to Europe and always preferred to be assigned the same seat—at the front—seat

1A on Lufthansa's Airbus 380-800, the upper deck of Flight SQ26—the window seat. He gave a thin and brief smile.

"I am quite fine for now. Thank you. I would prefer not to be disturbed for the moment."

"As you wish, sir."

Her nametag said she was Sabine. She understood the message. They had played this little game before. She had to ask—keeping to the required protocol.

Wong would answer politely with a hint of annoyance. It was not a rebuke, just the manner in which Mr. Wong spoke, a man accustomed to power, and service that anticipated his needs, including when he wanted to be left alone.

Mr. Jim Wong was the head of a shipping company based in Singapore, where business and politics went hand in glove. And, as a member of an elite ruling class with personal assets that put him in the mega-billionaire club, the pyramid of power did not go much higher. He seldom flew commercial, but in this case the business trip had to be low key. Flying his private jet would draw attention—exactly what he did not want—not for this trip.

Flight SQ26 was due to land first in Frankfurt in twelve hours and forty minutes, well within the aircraft's maximum capacity of fifteen hours of flight. It was nearly full with a complement of 510 souls.

Before the doors closed he sent a text message to a phone number in Belgium. "On schedule," was all it said.

CHAPTER 5

DSI Fredrik Hansen's Office
KRIPOS Headquarters, Brynsalléen 6, Oslo, Norway
Thursday, 5ᵗʰ of April
19:21 CET, 13:21AM EST

"**M**r. Becken, my name is…"

"Please call me Frank."

"Okay," Jaime paused for a second to regroup his approach. "My name is Jaime Rodriguez. I am a Special Agent with the FBI based out of New York City. I presume that Detective Superintendent Hansen…"

"Yes, yes, I have all the background on you and your team. I don't mean to be disrespectful, Agent Rodriguez, it's just that…," there was a long pause. "This little girl, Grete. She doesn't have a lot of time, Agent Rodriguez. I don't care about titles, or your protocols, I don't care about much these days, but … I care," he stopped for a second, "… I care about this little girl named Grete. From what I have learned so far, I believe that she has hours, a few days at the most."

Supervisory Special Agent Rodriguez looked around the table at his team. Without the need for words, he could tell that what Becken was saying was making a lot of sense to them.

Becken continued, "Again, I am not being disrespectful but, by the time the government, mine or yours, gets around to getting ready to do something, this little girl will be dead - dead as in stone cold, lifeless, lost to this world D-E-A-D dead, … Special Agent Rodriguez." There was a long pause.

"Hello!" The exasperation at the end of the phone line was coming through.

"Yes, Frank. We are all here." Rodriguez was getting irritated. "Will you please ask DSI Hansen to pick up on his private line? I want to speak with him first. We will reconvene as soon as we are done."

DSI Fredrik Hansen picked up the phone on the first ring.

"Are we alone, Fredrik?"

"Yes. Becken is all wound up."

"I figured that much."

"I sent him outside for a smoke."

Jaime was trying mightily to stay calm himself. Still, he could not argue with truth. He could see past Frank's strident talk to the reality of what they were facing. Grete's chances were slim to none.

"The fact is that he's right. And it may be that the best person to find her is someone like Becken, someone who is deeply motivated *not* to follow the rules, but simply to find her, and to find her soon. Is it possible to have Becken be the lead in chasing down this group that has Grete, like we would use a CI—a confidential informant?"

"But a guy like Becken … is a loose cannon on deck." Fredrik was not buying into the idea. "He could as easily turn against us as he would focus his efforts to do one good thing, Jaime."

"Hmm…"

"I don't trust him."

"I used to know someone like him, many years ago." Jaime was starting to see things differently, his voice now lowered, his thoughts back to his past giving him a perspective on the moment.

"And how did that turn out?"

"Well, in this case, it turned out pretty well, I think. That person was me." Jaime let Frank think about that little surprise for a second. He continued. "Someone took a chance on me. I was young and my transgressions were more schoolhouse pranks, but I was headed right where Becken is now. I guess…"

Hansen interrupted him. "Can't do it, Jaime. If it were just *me*, my career, taking a chance on him, that would be one thing. But it's not about me, or my career, it's about the fact that it would reflect badly on the entire department if it were somehow discovered that I violated all the rules. That kind of risk is not mine to take."

"Okay, so what are you planning? It's your case. I need Frank to find out about the group, how they wiped out the Santander's accounts. But that is not going to save the girl. I guess you don't need me to tell you that."

"What I think is that Frank is going to do what Frank is going to do. If he breaks Norwegian law, I will bring him in and charge him if I can. What he does outside of Norway is something else." Jaime didn't respond right away.

"You could…," DSI Hansen hesitated a second, "you could point him in the right direction, I guess. If the loose cannon is going to fire on deck, it would at least be good that it fires in the right direction."

Jaime laughed out loud. "You're a man after my own heart, Fredrik." The two of them had a short-lived chuckle elaborating the metaphor to its ridiculous conclusion.

"Fredrik?"

"Yes, Special Agent Rodriguez?"

Jaime smiled. Jaime remembered his old *Abuelo* Rodriguez, how he taught about the little life lessons in parables.

"Talking about loose cannons on deck, have you ever heard the story of Admiral Farragut from the American Civil War?"

"Where is this going? We don't have time for stories.

"Bear with me …"

"Okay." He said it with obvious exasperation. "Yes, I heard of him."

"Well, the story is that Admiral Farragut was ordered to capture the heavily- mined bay that led into Mobile from the Gulf of Mexico, in Alabama. It´s where the Confederates had their last major ocean port during the civil war. His flotilla of ships started to pull back after watching their lead ship sink after hitting one of the so-called torpedoes, and thinking that their commander would approve the pullback. What they got was the stuff of legends. 'Damn the torpedoes, full speed ahead,' he told them."

"What I'm trying to say…"

"I know what you are trying to say … so now you should listen to me. It's like this, Jaime. I would rather go into my retirement telling stories about how I lost my job but saved Grete, than how I kept my job following the rules, but lost this little girl. I do need your help. And I am not interested in protocols for the sake of protocols—not this time. But I also don't want to take unnecessary risks. Frank is a big risk. We don't know him, not well enough to know whether he's going to be on our side, or go off and do something stupid."

"He did walk into your office. He didn't need to do that—he had no compelling reason, and into your office he walked, offering help."

"Yes, he did, which is why I am saying—point him in the right direction. He may surprise us again."

"Okay, then, damn the torpedoes, full speed ahead?"

"Yes. Just remember, Jaime, that your Admiral Farragut was also blamed for the failure of the Siege at Port Hudson—for being reckless."

Jaime was more than surprised. He laughed out loud. "Okay, okay, message received." The two men shared a laugh.

"I'm going to talk to him. Is he back from his smoke?"

"Yes, he's back waiting outside my office."

"Can I speak to him on this line?"

"Yes."

DSI Hansen found Frank squatted outside his office, his arms wrapped around his legs. Hansen motioned him inside and gave him the phone.

"Hello."

"Mr. Becken, Frank. Again, my name is Supervisory Special Agent Jaime Rodriguez. I have a team of FBI Agents and other specialists here in the conference room who make up the rest of the team. My job in this assignment has two priorities…"

Gilmer, Rose, Pearl, Atkins, and Williams were all thinking the same thing, *uh, oh, wonder where this is going.*

"Priority one for me and my team is to work with the authorities in Europe to help save the young girl named Grete Enberg. My second priority is to help the authorities in Europe take down—as in bring to justice—this group of people so that they will never have the opportunity to harm anyone, ever again, not ever in their miserable lives." Rodriguez was picking up steam. "My priority, as you can see, Mr. Becken, Frank, is the same as your priority. We will do everything within our power, short of missile strikes, to save this little girl named Grete. Am I making myself clear?" There was a unanimous gulp in the conference room. They had seen this before, a "Jaime dressing down" as they called it. Better that it was Becken on the receiving end of this one.

"Missile strikes? Hmm … sounds like an American way to solve a problem. Hey, Mister Special Agent Rodriguez, I …"

Frank caught himself—he was about to have a dick-measuring contest and remembered that he seldom won these. He decided otherwise.

"It's just … I haven't slept, and I want to take a shower, go eat something, but … I can't; not yet. I am worried sick about this little girl. I don't know why."

His emotions came through the phone line. "I don't know why it was me, why I happened to be the one that made this discovery. I feel like, maybe, like I was chosen or something, and that my life will never be the same again— never. I have to find her, Special Agent Rodriguez. I just have to—Before anything bad happens to her. After is no good … you see?"

There was a long pause on the line.

"Frank, my name is Agent Randy Pearl. I have a couple of questions."

"Yes?"

"What was it that triggered your thinking … to look at the other files and not just wait to get the credentials for the financial accounts? The account information was all you were looking for, and yet you ventured further. Why?"

Frank hesitated. He had to think about it for a second, and then decided. "I always look…when I can. People do stupid things with their computers, especially in chat sessions and in email. I also … have always liked the name Nikita. Reminds me of that Elton John song. So I was curious, you know, just poking around, to see what else I could learn about this bureaucrat from the EC." He paused again. "I also didn't like him, smug asshole."

Everyone in the conference room laughed.

"Frank, this is Agent Jillian Rose."

"Hi Jillian."

"Hi Frank. Glad to see you are helping the good guys now …" The statement did not come across as sarcasm, but it wasn't lost on Frank that maybe there was a hint of play in what Agent Rose had said. She continued. "You've run across—to break in, that is—many websites and many computers with different levels of protection, was this computer and the website well protected? Was there a high level of skill involved? And did you get the impression that this was all Tosti?"

"No, not Tosti." He paused. This was an insightful question that needed a moment before he responded.

"There was more. Security tends to be obvious. This wasn't. It was subtle, more than subtle, it was, how do you say it, deflective—like an invitation, almost arrogant."

"Can you give us an example?"

"Yes. That website is probably a honey pot. I would bet on it."

"Then how was it that you were able to see the video and get the chat?"

"That—I think, was all Tosti, all ego and busy … taking shortcuts."

"Okay. Thanks, Frank."

"You're welcome, Jillian."

Rodriguez decided to do the same—to take the high ground. "Frank, this is Jaime. What do you think should be done first?"

It took a second before Frank responded. He had not really thought it through. He knew what he would do, but it would sound stupid to these agents. The problem was time. This, he knew in his heart. He blurted out the first thing that came to mind—that he had been thinking about while waiting there outside Hansen's office.

"I think that I should go to Brussels," he said. He quickly followed it up with an explanation.

"I think that I may be able to act faster and with greater flexibility to find her than the police. The police will act within their procedures. I don't have procedures. I don't have bosses to please, at least not police bosses. I don't have politics to consider. That's what I think we, I, should do first."

"I see. Well, I can't say that I disagree. Grete is not going to be saved from afar. But saving Grete is not your job, Frank. That is Detective Superintendent Hansen's job, and the job of the authorities in Belgium …"

"They won't act fast enough. I've already told you that." The phone went silent for a moment.

"How can I reach you? If we find out more, like where in Belgium they are keeping Grete …"

"I have a mobile phone. You can reach me on my phone." Frank told him the number.

"Okay. Good luck, Frank."

"Thank you, Agent Rodriguez."

"You're welcome. Take care." The call ended.

Jaime was headed out of the conference room when Williams walked in.

He whispered in Atkin's ear.

Atkins spoke up. "Umm, we have a problem." They stopped what they were doing.

She addressed herself to SSA Rodriguez and explained the background.

"Nick, please tell everyone what you found."

"Right, well. There were seven parties on the conference call with Norway that just ended. There should only have been six. There were five that we know about in Europe, us as the sixth. The seventh party joined using a VOIP number. I called that number and it connected to a family in Virginia. It wasn't them that dialed in by mistake. That number was spoofed; the true origin of the call is untraceable."

Special Agent Pearl spoke what they all now knew. "Someone was eavesdropping. And we didn't catch it. So, chances are that the bad guys know what we know."

Agent Gilmer piped in. "What about these other calls? Any chance our other calls could have been compromised, other than the conference call?"

Atkins answered. "No, this was a pure and simple hack of someone's network—gain access to the admin's computer, get access to the calendar, and find the conference call-in bridge number with the access code. Only two parties had this call scheduled, the DSI Hansen´s network and us. We didn't get hacked. It wasn't us."

Rodriquez left the room to call DSI Hansen.

Dear Diary

10th of March

I promised I would tell you all. But I can't. They made me do other things. I cannot tell anyone, not ever, not even you, dear diary. I am sorry!!! I am so ashamed. I want to die, but I can't. Nikita keeps me company all the time now. I have to go.

CHAPTER 6

OSLO, NORWAY
APRIL 1997

The swarthy businessman walked into the first floor shop in the city downtown like he was important. One could guess that he had nary missed a meal in his life.

"God Morgen," he said. But he had to wait a full two seconds before he got any attention from the tattooed, pierced, spiked, emaciated, what-looked-like- a-girl (but he couldn't actually be sure was a girl) attendant at the front desk. He was not pleased.

"Ja?" Yes, she asked. The look of mutual disdain was evident from one to the other.

"I need some web design work," he said to her. He was reading from the company's advertisement on the poster board placed on the back wall. *www.Web2U.no, Your Specialists in Web*

Design, it said. She just looked at him like he had said it in French or something. The name on the desk nameplate said Monika, so he said it again, with a softer tone. "I need some web design work, Monika."

She turned her head around and yelled back, "Frank!" A guy poked his head from behind a cubicle partition. The businessman had the same impression; he couldn't tell whether it was a boy or a girl at first glance. They all looked alike to him—the emaciated face, the Goth dress, and the rest of the outfit of spiked hair, dark-lined eyes, ear and mouth piercings. Except this guy named Frank had a smile and what appeared to be a personality, not like Miss Raccoon, he thought. His second thought was that Frank was awfully young to be a web designer, and maybe not the right person he was looking for.

Frank jumped out of his chair and greeted the businessman with a handshake and a warm smile. Monika rolled her eyes and went back to whatever Goth thing she was doing prior to meeting "Mr. I-never-missed-a- meal-in-my-life businessman."

"How can I help you sir?"

"Yes, well, my name is Tomas Mattsen. I own an import-export business that I would like to put online, as it were." A single drop of perspiration rolled down behind his left cheek. Mr. Mattsen was nervous.

Monika rolled her Goth eyes again. "What an ass," she thought.

"You have come to the right place, Mr. Mattsen," spoke Frank, with the same friendly smile. "You want to establish an online web presence so customers can know how to reach your company on the Internet, and so they can read about the full services that you provide. Is that right, sir?"

"Yes, exactly, except that my customers are actually other businesses."

Frank could almost hear the sigh of relief as Mr. Mattsen relaxed, now that he was on more familiar ground and didn't feel so out of place.

"But I want to discuss all of this in my office so you can see what I want to do, and I can show you around, we can take some pictures of the warehouse and the like for the website. When can I have you visit?"

"I am at your disposal, I just need to tell my boss, and we can head there now, or tomorrow, or later if you wish. I will show you some samples of other websites that we have designed, so you can see our work. You can pick a template to use as a model, and we can get a contract signed. How does that sound, Mr. Mattsen?"

"Tomorrow at nine, sharp. Here is my business card, the address is on the card. I will be expecting you, Frank…," leaving the statement unfinished.

"Becken, sir, B-E-C-K-E-N. nine tomorrow. I'll be there."

It was not much of a warehouse. The office space was old, meant to convey frugality—maybe. Frank was dressed in jeans, a clean shirt, and a jacket, as *business* as he could get from the selection in his closet. Outside of customer visits, he usually dressed in Goth to fit in with a circle of people that he felt were "fun," in that they were eclectic at least. He was eighteen years old, already streetwise to the world. He liked Goth, but he was also aware that business required a different style of attire. So he looked at the warehouse and the office, and the boss of this domain, and he judged it for what it was: fake, unimpressive, and in decline.

Still, while authority did not overly impress him, Frank also knew that the game had to be played. Mr. Mattsen, he had suspected right from the start, was not interested in "putting his business online" as he had said. Something else was afoot. As he waited in the office foyer, he wondered what it would be. The secretary, a plump early-thirty-something woman who wore too much makeup to hide a blemished face, sat behind a desk with a monstrous monitor connected by computer cables haphazardly strewn like spaghetti strings stuck together. The nameplate said that she was Anna Olsen. She offered him some coffee, but he demurred, thinking the coffee probably tasted like the office looked—old and bitter.

It was ten past nine when Tomas Mattsen burst through the door, apologizing for the delay with his hand extended out to Frank, making like the busy man that he wasn't. In reality, Tomas' business was not doing so well. But here, in his office, he was the big shot, and he had to play the part. Even for a Goth head web designer, he thought.

After Mr. Mattsen had left the Web2U Web Designers Shop, Monika had given a name to her description of Mr. Mattsen: *The Man Who Had Never Missed A Meal*. She made it into an acronym -TMWHNMAM—and further reduced it to a phonetic phrase: Tom Whanamum. Frank had to stifle a laugh. He shook his hand and followed Mr. Mattsen into his office, a room of floor to ceiling wood paneling that made him nauseous. It bespoke of 1970s Scandinavian office décor.

He did a quick glance around the room to expand his already growing perception of Mr. Mattsen. What he saw confirmed his earlier assessment. A Compaq computer took up most of the credenza behind the massive wooden desk that faced the front door. The one wall that was not lined in wood paneling was all glass, looking out onto the flat open area where massive trucks and railroad tracks connected with the harbor's ship docks—a lifeline of commerce into Oslo, Norway and beyond. At least there's a view of the harbor and the city in the background, Frank thought. It cheered him up. He did notice as well that a thick layer of dust sat on the keyboard, another sign that this conversation was not likely to be about "putting the business online." The back wall was littered with lots of pictures, the "look-at-me-and-how- important-I-am-shaking-hands-with-other-important-people" pictures. Frank took a seat on the old leather sofa. It was comfortable.

"Did Anna offer you some coffee?" Tom Mattsen asked.

"Yes, she did, but no, thank you sir, I already had a cup," he lied. Frank went through the motions of opening his laptop bag on the coffee table to test his theory that they would not be talking web design.

"Would you like me to show you some of the website templates that I brought on my laptop, Mr. Mattsen?"

"Later Frank. First, I want to talk about a little problem that I have."

Frank smiled. Here it comes, he thought. Tomas Mattsen had taken the other sitting place, a large brown leather seat, also old and comfortable. Behind the sofa where Frank was now seated was the glass wall. Tomas was strategically placed to the view of the harbor outside, while Frank sat on the "visitor's chair" with the view of the "I-am-important" wall of pictures adorned in cheap black IKEA frames.

"There is this other shipping business, a competitor, if you will, that is just doing the most unethical things to take away my business," he started to explain. Tomas Mattsen wriggled to push his massive frame forward on the edge of the seat and continued. He started punctuating his description of his hated enemy—the competition—gesturing with his hands enough to make an Italian Mafioso proud. Frank picked up that this was the rub. Tomas Mattsen, a.k.a. Tom Whanamum, was determined to do something about his "problem."

Ta da, here it is, he thought to himself

"What I need from you, Frank, is to know if you can get information for me. That is the main thing. And, of course, I will also need to, as you described it, get a web presence for my company." He continued on, wanting to finish his description before Frank could react. "But first things first, Frank, do you know how to get information for me from someone else's computer?"

Tomas Whanamum, as Monika had called him, had certainly gone straight to the point, Frank thought. The website was nothing more than a ruse to find a hacker. Frank thought about it for a second, and he decided to do the same— get straight to the point. "For the right price, Mr. Mattsen, I can get you any information you need."

Tomas Mattsen exhaled like he had been holding his breath for minutes. "Yes, yes, indeed, I believe you can, Frank Becken," he said with a garrulous guffaw that rattled the glass wall facing outside. The two had sized each other up and found that they were not so different—in certain ways. Frank was getting tired of the whole Goth thing. It wasn't that he didn't enjoy his Goth friends, just that they lived in absolute poverty. Frank had higher aspirations.

So began the shady career of one Frank Becken, the one where he was now hacking not just for fun, but for paying clients; more precisely, one client, and many targets. Over the course of the following year, Frank was able to gain access to the electronic files of not only "the competition," but also the government shipping inspectors. Frank Becken had been hacking since the days of Phreaking into the Telenor phone systems. His heroes were people like the American called Mitnick, who was wanted by the FBI, and a German named Pengo, who was wanted by the West German Authorities and the old KGB.

With access to these files, Tomas Mattsen was able to know the bid price for shipping contracts from his competitors, and with access to their financial records, he had the information he needed to beat them at the game. It proved tremendously beneficial to the success of his shipping business.

Frank prospered along with his new boss. In the months that followed, Frank said goodbye to his friends at Web2U. Monika may not have looked like she had a brain to the likes of Tomas Mattsen, but the opposite was true. She read a situation for what it really was much faster than a dozen Tom Whanamums ever could, and even faster than Frank.

"This is a mistake," she told him.

But Frank now had a full bank account, and he was concluding that crime did indeed pay, and that there was no way that someone with his smarts could get caught.

Tomas' hatred of his "enemy," as he now openly called them when speaking with Frank, was extreme. He was not just interested in winning more contracts; he wanted complete control of the import-export business in the Oslo harbor. He felt empowered and Frank was the reason.

It was a year later, when the walls came crashing down, literally. Frank arrived at the warehouse one morning to find the blue lights of police cars and the red and white police tape that said something bad had happened. Anna was at the edge of the red and white tape that set the perimeter of the crime scene. Her car was haphazardly parked nearby. She looked like one of those ghoulish creatures in an American zombie movie, the black mascara running down her face from the stream of tears.

He noticed as well that the entire glass wall from Tomas' office had become a debris field of glass shards. He saw the white outline of what had previously been a body sprawled on the ground. It was a big body. It did not take Frank more than a second to connect the dots.

He sidled up to Anna, discreetly mixing in with the small crowd of onlookers. He pulled her aside. "Anna, let's talk." They went to her car and he asked her what happened. She started to cry again, so he gave her some time to calm down. Eventually she was able to get it all out.

Anna told Frank that she had been the first to find Tomas on the ground directly outside his office, in a pool of blood that came from his head, where pieces of his skull were blown away. She had called the police.

Frank clutched at his chin, like he had to hold on to it. She looked at him and she told him what he was already thinking. "You need to run, Frank."

She had not been as dumb as she had looked, he thought. In fact, Anna the secretary knew exactly what Tomas Mattsen had been doing. Frank did not need to be told twice.

He quietly went back to his car and drove to his apartment. Along the way he put together more of the pieces of what had happened. Tomas had gotten greedy. No, that was not right, he thought. *We* had gotten greedy, including himself in the analysis. If they would do this to Tomas Whanamum, what would they do to him, he thought further. The straight answer was: *the same thing.* He hurried home and immediately started packing to get the "hell out of dodge" as they say in the movies. That's when he saw the light blinking red on his answering machine. Not many people knew his home phone number. He wondered, *What's that about?*

He was going to leave it alone, but curiosity got the better of him. A small voice of premonition said, *better find out who called.* Maybe there was a connection between the blinking light and his early morning discovery that Tomas was no more.

He pressed the play button. A male voice spoke:

"Hey dipshit, this is your new boss calling you. Today is your lucky day. Better listen," pause, "if you value your life. Copy this phone number and call it back. Call the police," pause, "you're a dead man. There's only one reason why you are still alive, and it's not because we think you're pretty or something," pause. "You have until nine. Don't call," pause, "again, you're a dead man."

The message ended and Frank ran to the bathroom where he lost his coffee and the corn flakes he had eaten earlier that morning.

PART TWO

In the events of today there is a trail that reaches back in time through a string of other events. Everything is consequential.

Nothing is really new. We just choose to call it so.

CHAPTER 7

Oslo, Norway
Wednesday, 4TH of April
03:40 CET

Frank was in a deep REM sleep dreaming of a girl that had him at full mast—his member poking up from under the down comforter like the stem of a mushroom pushing through a blanket of leaves in a forest floor. His iPhone rang. By the second ring he was awake; his brain had processed the audio sound and he knew who it was. Awareness came with a rush of blood to his head. This was the ringtone, the one that he had assigned to get his attention—in any circumstance—even in the grip of the fantasy that he had been enjoying full bore.

He groped in the dark for the phone—now in a panic—knocking down the lamp on the nightstand before he found it on the floor under a t-shirt. It was still lit, ringing what was probably only one last time. He had to swipe it twice before it opened for him and picked up on the call. Last time he had failed to pick up the phone in time, he had been punished.

His heart raced. He did not want to be punished again. Down below he was at quarter mast and drooping fast. His heart was pounding like a jackhammer working through a bed of concrete.

"Hello," he said. It came out a like a croak, his vocal chords still asleep —muscle consciousness coming slowly.

"Hello," he said it again. His voice recovered. It came out more intelligible.

There was a pause. Frank waited. He could hear the breathing at the other end of the line. A quiet voice spoke. "Making me wait again, dipshit?"

"No sir, I mean, I was asleep," he said, his voice cracking in fear.

"You making excuses again, dipshit?"

"No sir, I mean, yes sir, I'm sorry. It won't happen again."

Frank had learned. He had been schooled at the academy-of-misery, at the hands of the NoSaints for going on thirteen years.

He was a full-grown man, still skinny, but tall, with curly brown hair that he wore long and unkempt. It was the style of the day. Unkempt was cool. But it worked the other way on Frank. He had the look of someone who worried too much, like he had been around the block too many times—and not getting anywhere. The three-day stubble of growth on his chin was interspersed with patches of gray whiskers. He resembled more possum than fox, more prey than predator.

He had aged into a man, but inside he was like a little boy who fears the dark. And he had good reason. Frank feared the NoSaints because in the dark lived the bogeyman, the real one. He was ready to piss in his pants at the mere ring of the phone. He was Pavlov's dog. It was not food that made him quiver— it was punishment: brutal, painful, absurd pain. He had cried like a baby, "Make it stop, make it stop, I won't do it again," he had screamed in sheer agony—so that the memory of it would embed deep into his inner psyche. Frank had been schooled by the minister-of-misery all right—and he had taught him well.

The phone was silent for what seemed like an eternity. It had been a month or more since the last call. Frank knew that it could go either way. He gripped the phone like he was hanging on to it for dear life, pressed it to his cheek, hoping against hope that the voice would speak to him. If not, it meant the punishment was on its way. He almost lost control of his bowels when *The Voice* spoke again, "There's a mark in town," pause, "someone of interest," pause, "details are on the way," click and the line went dead. This is the way *The Voice* always sounded, how the call always ended, sentences structured in packet size, never any elaboration, no thought of questions, then the abrupt end.

In a digital second, the phone chimed. A text message had arrived. Frank reached into his underwear with his left hand to rearrange his parts. With his right hand he opened the text message and saw the picture of the mark, his name, the hotel he was staying in, and the address. The name was Silvio Tosti; Silvio like Berlusconi, the Italian Prime Minister who was always in the news. There was no resemblance.

And there was no question as to what was the task—no need for explanation. Frank knew what the NoSaints handler—*The Voice*—expected from him. He put the phone down, got up from the bed and found the lamp, put it back on the nightstand and turned it on. He looked at the picture on the phone again. The guy looked like someone he would remember; a face comprised of angular features, dark, the eyes closely set, the nose a Roman perfection like it was chiseled from marble by the hand of DaVinci. Not a face easily forgotten.

He had just gone to bed an hour earlier, exhausted from another night spent sleuthing through the 4chan chat rooms, making his connections, keeping his virtual persona in the game, as it were, and doing the dirty work of the NoSaints. He was now on task again. His software developing job as a freelancer was now superseded by the call that had arrived just moments earlier.

He thought about it while he peed into the toilet bowl, emptying his bladder and feeling the relief of getting rid of the Red Bull in his system. *Must be another banker or someone interested in the girls of Oslo, or both*, he thought to himself. He yawned—his mouth opened a mile wide as his brain cut through the cobwebs of sleep.

He felt a chill and his body did an involuntary shudder. He pulled the lever on the toilet and washed his hands, then took a glance at himself in the mirror over the sink. Frank did not like the person that was looking back at him, a cowering little boy who had grown older. He had lost his swagger. He thought about going back to bed. Nothing he could do until the morning, he reasoned. But then he remembered the punishment, and he climbed into the shower.

Under a steady stream of water turned on as hot as he could stand it, he started to form the play. He thought about how he would social engineer himself right into the hotel like he belonged there, and then find out what vices it was that had made Mr. Tosti an attractive mark for the NoSaints. He guessed girls. In the morning he would figure it out. He got out of the shower, dried, dressed and then went to his computer to do some research on Tosti. These days no one could really hide. It did not take him long to find out about the senior government official from Belgium who worked for the European Commission named Silvio Tosti.

This time it was the alarm on the phone that alerted him, a more pleasant ring. It was getting near time to go. Frank went to the kitchen and made coffee. He drank two cups—grabbed a Red Bull for the road. It was game time.

He knew that there was no forgiveness for mistakes; *The Voice* was not interested in excuses. He read the time on the microwave before exiting the small colorless kitchen; it read 05:45. Frank's brain was in full gear now.

Frank made the translation of the time on the clock into action-to-be-taken. First start the car. It would be frozen from the cold of the night. Winter still had a grip on the city. The digital time on the microwave told him that it was time to get going—no telling what time Mr. Tosti got up in the morning and headed for breakfast.

Frank would need to be there when he walked in. He hurried to the bathroom and took another shower. The cold shower started his motor.

His inner drive was starting to get into gear. There was still something left of the younger Frank—the one that had worked for Tom Whanamum—the one that Monika had liked.

He smiled. He thought of Monika. He had started seeing her again out of the blue. She showed up one day at his door a couple of months prior, cool as a cucumber and starting a conversation like they had just met the night before.

"Got a Red Bull for me...Frank?" She had paused before saying his name, like she needed to conserve words, the sentence combining the question about the availability of a Red Bull and a "Hello Frank, nice to meet you; it's been a long time, and I missed you...." She had never been one to chatter. She did her talking on a computer.

"I do. God Morgen, Monika." She didn't reply, just walked in the door, opened the refrigerator and pulled the lid back on a Red Bull, then went over to him and kissed him full in the mouth.

Frank was at a loss for words. She tasted good—Red Bull and all. She tasted real good.

"Getting a rise, are you, Frank?" She let him have the hint of a smile—to let him know that it was just a tease.

Again—he didn't know what to say; just had what is called a "shit-eatin' grin" that was a mile wide.

"You got me, Monika, guilty as sin. And where have you been the last..." he thought about it for a second, "twelve years?"

"Russia."

That's how it began. That's all she said, wouldn't elaborate. He pressed her a bit more, but decided that kissing Monika and taking care of that rise was going to be a whole lot more interesting than getting answers at the moment. She was more than willing.

She had changed for the better; filled out some, in the right places, and she had lost most of the Goth look, but not all of it. She still had that look of the dark and exotic about her, which he had liked from the beginning.

Monika had been the girl in his dreams the night just past. She may not have known it, but over the past months she had rescued him from his growing despair. He feared that it was all over for him, that he was doomed to be at the beck and call of The Voice, always afraid, for the rest of his life, a NoSaints Bitch.

It was a twenty-minute ride in his car out to the central city park where the glitterati of Norway intermixed. He was prepared. On the passenger seat he had his backpack that contained his laptop and his kit of various hacking tools of the trade, each in a small plastic Ziploc bag so he could pick the right tool for the moment. There was no telling what he would need. He navigated the streets. Another early spring foggy morning was in store for the residents of Oslo. Soon the streets would be filled with cars and pedestrians, but not just yet, he thought. Less traffic was a good thing right now. The first to show, he could see a few of them already, were those who walked the streets asking for a Krone to buy a meal, or those setting up their makeshift shops selling street wares: watches, purses, and sunglasses from the best of brands—for a bargain price.

The national theater and other privately-owned theaters bordered Storting's Gate—the parliament street. The streets were called gates—a Norwegian curiosity. On the east end sat the national government building, the Storting. On the opposite end of the park, to the west was the Royal Castle. To the north, on Karl Johan's Gate, was the prestigious Oslo University. The cream of Norway's hotels, and the finest cuisine restaurants were interspersed between the theaters and other office buildings along with the expensive international name brands of retail stores at street level. Hotel Continental was one of the elites of the elite, located strategically across the street from the National Theater.

That Tosti was encamped at The Continental said something. Frank kept thinking about this. His quick research earlier in the morning had revealed Tosti's role as a member of the European Commission—the EC. The website said that he specialized in finance and banking. Financial health of the member states was foremost in the minds of Europeans these days. That, theorized Frank, was most likely the purpose of his visit in Oslo—where the movie stars and government dignitaries stay when visiting Oslo. He drove past the City Hall, where the annual Nobel Peace prize was awarded and started looking for a parking space. *Tosti is important, or at least he thinks himself important enough to stay at The Continental.* He parked a block away and rethought his approach.

The hotel staff was trained to err on the side of decorum, to "never create a scene that will upset our customers." He was counting on that. He knew that they were equally trained on knowing who belonged and who didn't. An attitude of *I belong here* was essential, especially for someone like Frank, who didn't really belong, not with his clothes or his shoes. He had the advantage of years and experience in conveying an image to others—an image of youth and carefree dress.

"I am with the press," he said, "waiting for a colleague," he told the receptionist in his native Norwegian. He was schooled in playing the game. He was good at this. He knew it. The Caroline Breakfast Lounge on the second floor was ready for its well-bedecked, well-coiffed guests.

"Very well, follow me, sir."

"Ahh – can I have that seat, that one over there?" He pointed to the back of the room.

"Of course, as you wish," she said with a smile that generated warmth and professional friendliness.

Another member of the staff quickly brought the coffee. Fine china and all manner of minutiae, the little things, decked the table dressed in the white linen cloth. Everything was arrayed in precise fashion. The table bespoke elegance. Everything was placed just right.

This was the business of the world of hospitality where social structure mattered, a place made for comfort and pampering. Frank took notice, soaking up all the details. It was all a game, he thought. To play the game you have to know the details of how it is played. Social engineering was *his* game, one that he knew worked to his advantage when the playing field involved both the virtual and the physical. *You have to know them both*, he thought. He smiled to himself. *And here, I have the advantage—to know how the two work together.* The aristocrats of money were simpletons in his virtual arena—the easiest of prey.

Working for Tom Whanamum had taught him that. He thought of that song by Garland Jeffries, *Streetwise*. You have to be streetwise—in the city street and in the high-end hotel, but also in the digital world of ones and zeros.

He took his seat at the back of the room, his back to the wall with a full view of the breakfast area to the front and the windows overlooking the main square on his right. The National Theater was visible out the window, just across the street. From this table he would be able to see whoever walked in to sit for breakfast.

He opened his laptop and immediately picked up the wireless signal from the hotel. Other signals began to pop up. When he looked up, he was startled to see that his mark was already getting seated, just two tables away and to his right—in profile. The pictures did not do justice to the sophistication of the mark called Silvio Tosti. Everything about him spoke of symmetry and precision, of attention to all the little details of class that were lost on the general public. Tosti belonged here without need to disguise. His suit and tie were from the finest Italian brands, the cufflinks of gold—opulence, refined opulence.

And then there was his face. Frank thought that it looked like the opposite of him—a moment of panic gripped him. Maybe he was not in his element after all; maybe he was in a league where it would be obvious that he was out of place. He looked down at his coffee cup, the aroma of the dark liquid filling his nostrils. He darted a glance at Tosti—made like he was scanning the room and the abundant breakfast buffet, nonchalant and bored. Breakfast is going to cost me a week's worth of groceries, he thought. They don't pay me enough.

Tosti had the *Financial Times of London* on the table, but he was engrossed in the cover story of the *Norway Post*, provided by the hotel for its English-reading guests. The waitress came by and filled up Frank's cup of the dark rich brew, then went over to Tosti and did the same. Other customers started walking in. The clock on his computer said that it was quarter to eight. He stared at the screen on his open laptop. Tosti looked around the room with a brief glance at Frank, who looked by all appearances to be catching up on his morning email reading. He got up and headed for the toilet.

This was Frank's chance and he knew from experience that he might not get another. The moment seemed to slow, his heartbeat pounding. He glanced around checking to make sure that no one was watching him. In three steps he was alongside Tosti's table, pausing for a few seconds, his right hand holding his iPhone making like he was intent on reading something. His torso hid his left hand. In less than a second he had inserted the small, preloaded USB stick into the left side port on Tosti's open laptop. The stick contained the Trojan code that would automatically install and start to operate—capturing and communicating outbound the information that Frank needed. He removed the stick and went over to the buffet table where he filled his plate—a croissant, fresh salmon, caviar, eggs, bacon. Time to eat and wait.

It's done, he thought. It was so easy. He got a jolt of exhilaration, a hacker's high. Normally he would be making for the door at this point—no need to tempt fate. He saw Tosti return back to his table, absorbed with his own thoughts, no indication that he gave a thought to any of the guests, least of all the poorly-dressed guest a few tables away. The waitress trailed him to remove the empty plates. She poured a second cup of coffee for him.

Frank sat back down to enjoy the expensive breakfast, while keeping an eye on his mark. A small crowd of guests was now busy chatting and picking through the choices for breakfast. It might be days before Tosti visited his financial accounts online. It would happen when it happened, he thought, nothing to do until it did. He started in on his own breakfast, gulping down the eggs and bacon. His mouth was full when he saw his text message application light up to indicate a new inbound sms. Seconds later, his phone lit up as well with the same information.

Frank felt another peak of emotion. It was the exhilaration of the hunter achieving success against his prey. There it was— a web link and its login credentials. He glanced at Tosti from the corner of his eye and saw him reading something on his computer—his breakfast still untouched.

"Can I get you anything else?" He was startled to find the young waitress there with her very pleasant smile.

"No. No, thank you. Ahh, wait—maybe more coffee, and the bill please," he replied.

She left and as quickly returned to fill his cup leaving the bill on the table. Frank launched the link to the website. It came up in a few seconds. It looked like the landing page for a tourist site—to visit Belgian castles. The only odd thing was the image of the angel with the black wings—three wings on each side and a broken chain. His curiosity piqued, Frank loaded the ID *seraph2* and the long password that the Trojan code had captured. The login worked. It opened to a chat interface and a selection of video files. He launched one of the video files and it prompted him for another login. He tried the same credentials but they were rejected. This was obviously not the web page for a travel agency, nor for some financial services or bank account.

Still, "I am in no hurry," Frank thought. He went exploring—still curious about what this website was about. He suspected that it had nothing to do with touring castles in Belgium. He poked around some more and saw that the text exchanges between Tosti, someone named Berta, and another exchange with someone going by the name of Dark Angel were still there.

With every word that Frank read, the blood in his veins pulsed stronger. It was a conversation partly coded in double-speak but it became clear to Frank that the mark called Silvio Tosti, a woman named Berta, someone named Rigo and the so-called Dark Angel were engaged in a conversation about coordinating the escape from Norway *"with their package."* Their package—a girl called Nikita-Norway—was in a van, *"still groggy, but recovering. Crying now, but, that is normal."*

Silvio had responded, *"Ready to meet the client?"*

"Yes'" that was Berta.

Dark Angel had inserted a comment about the *"teaser upload-ed, clients already viewing."* Frank had connected the dots. He almost didn't want to believe it—his life was complicated enough.

It was the other item on the Seraphim web page that caught Frank's eye and settled for him the connection. The file name was a copy of the same name in the list of files that were protected. It was called *Nikita-Norway-Teaser.* He clicked on the file and to his surprise it opened. There was no audio, but what he saw made him look up in Tosti's direction. Silvio Tosti was packing up his own computer. Frank could not draw his gaze away from the man that was somehow directly involved with the abduction of the young girl named Grete. And he knew, from the experience of many years hacking his way into the accounts of the targets of the NoSaints that he needed to stay close to his target, he needed to know more.

Frank Becken had not consciously made a decision, but he had taken a consequential first step that he could not take back. He could have gone home. *The Voice* would have been unhappy about the results—but not all marks returned good results. He had not fully thought out the consequences of what the NoSaints would do to him now. For the first time in his life after his association with Tom Whanamum, Frank felt like the old Frank, like the cocky risk-taker that he was.

CHAPTER 8

HOTEL CONTINENTAL
DOWNTOWN OSLO, NORWAY
WEDNESDAY, 4TH OF APRIL
08:12 CET

Frank paid his own breakfast bill and made for the elevator lobby on the heels of Mr. Tosti. The two got in with only the slightest of glances. Tosti inserted his key card into the slot and selected the fifth floor button on the elevator console and looked at Frank.

"Same for me, thank you."

It seemed like an eternity, but eventually the bell chimed for the fifth floor. The door opened and Tosti made a quick left turn. Frank knew that to follow him to the left could be a mistake. He turned to the right and started walking down the elegant carpeted hallway. He almost sensed it before he heard the footsteps. Tosti had turned around and was now right behind him. Turning left had been a feint—a precaution.

Frank slowed to look at his smart phone and heard a door open behind him. He turned around to see that Tosti was entering room 506. Time to wait. Frank needed to see what else was on Tosti's computer and the most clear path to that end was to gain access to his room and hope that Tosti preferred to carry two computers—one for personal use, the other for work. The personal one was likely left behind in the room. That's what usually happened with businessmen.

There was only one way to find out. He continued down the hallway, connecting to another hallway leading right. He turned, stopped and pulled out the two plastic bags that contained the tools he needed for the next hack. He waited. He had not spotted the closed circuit cameras in the hallways, but he knew they were there. The longer this took, the greater the likelihood that Hotel Security would be coming to visit him.

Patience, he told himself, patience. It was not one of Frank's virtues. With his back to the wall, he edged himself in front of the adjacent guest-room door and felt under the card entry system that controlled access to the rooms. He held his breath, thinking that getting access to the room will be easy or it will be hard. If it's hard then it will take too long. He breathed out.

The lock was the old style that was getting changed out— the type of card entry system with the round-barrel-connector interface. This card entry system was found in hotel rooms everywhere; all the major hotel chains had installed them. The interface was hidden underneath the plate where guests swiped their hotel cards. It had been installed as a safety precaution, to allow hotel staff to gain entry to the room in an emergency, like if the power went out. With time, it had also turned into a security problem for hotels around the world, as criminals figured out that the standard interface, connected to a micro-controller acting as a miniature computer, could run through every iteration of the key code and open the door in a matter of seconds.

Frank had one of these micro-controllers embedded in a run-of-the-mill mobile phone with the external antenna jack replaced by the cable that inserted into the female end of the connector under the card-entry system. He looked at his watch. It was already half past eight and still Mr. Tosti had not exited. No telling how long Tosti would take to exit his room, he thought. What seemed like an eternity later, he checked his watch again. The clock on his phone read 08:45. A door opened. He heard it clearly.

Frank waited a second and then poked his head around the corner. What he saw made him smile—the figure of Silvio Tosti carrying a briefcase made the turn into the elevator lobby.

Frank knew that every second counted. There were two obstacles he needed to overcome—the first was to gain entry into the door. This would be easy, he now knew. The second would be the safe in the room. To open the safe he would need to be in the room within thirty seconds after the safe door had been primed with the code.

It took less than two seconds, and the door to Tosti's room clicked open, the green LED light indicating that the code had been successfully provided. He opened the closet door in the entryway and saw that indeed the safe was closed—presumably with Tosti's *valuables* inside. He couldn't afford to lose any seconds fumbling around.

He placed what looked like a simple miniature screen in front of the keyboard that sensed minute changes in temperature. Frank punched the air with delight. The code was perfectly visible corresponding to the four digits where he had touched the safe's keyboard—the digit reflecting the highest heat rating was the last digit that Tosti had selected, the lowest heat rating was the first digit, and so forth. Frank was able to clearly see the digits in sequence, the code 4 − 2 − 6 − 7. The code Tosti had selected was most likely his birthday—4 February 1967.

Frank spoke out loud for no one in particular—"I got you, you ass." He felt the thrill of victory in his grasp as sure enough the door popped open and seated there in the carpeted bottom was a MacBook Air—the very one, for all appearances, that Tosti had been using in the breakfast lounge. From another plastic bag in his backpack, he pulled out an external hard drive. Seconds later he heard the soft hum of the machine copying files.

CHAPTER 9

REYKJAVIK, ICELAND
WEDNESDAY, 2ND OF APRIL
07:30 GMT (ONE HOUR DIFFERENCE)

Vlad woke to a dim gray light filtering in at the window's edge. He opened the curtains and went straight to the toilet. He looked out the small window in the bathroom to the flat barren landscape along the coast of Reykjavik where he lived on the top flat of a three-story home. It was his home. His bedroom was on the top floor. By quarter past eight he had a cup of coffee in his hand and the computer logs from the night's events. A script, an automated software program, had filtered through the noise of all that data to give him what he needed—the critical information that allowed him to keep an eye on the network activities. What he knew was that Tosti was in Oslo, but the key activity was now happening inside their current base of operations, the house outside of Brussels. Berta would be prepping their new Nikita girl for a rendezvous with one of their new clients.

He almost missed it. Reading through the logs it all looked normal except for the small detail that showed two log-ins—the second one right after Tosti had logged out. That didn't seem right. So he investigated some more and saw the other activity that had been recorded. It was by his own requirement that all Seraphim computers logged everything. He would scan the logs every day and keep a copy for a week. Vlad called Tosti.

CHAPTER 10

MAIN ENTRANCE TO THE STORTING
THE NORWEGIAN PARLIAMENT, KARL JOHANSGATE
22, OSLO, NORWAY
WEDNESDAY, 4TH OF APRIL
09:00 CET

The very dignified, perfectly dressed and smiling Deputy to the Minister for Financial Affairs from the European Commission, Mr. Silvio Tosti, was already working his way through security at the main entrance control point. The entrance was a round atrium designed for conveying authority; the walls and floors made of stone and marble. The customized cabinetry, and where necessary, the modern conveniences that could only be achieved with glass and polished metal and electronics, completed the look and feel of the atrium entrance to the Norwegian Parliament offices. With a smile, a hearty handshake and a brief exchange of kisses on the cheeks, Mrs. Brit Johanson welcomed Tosti. She was his counterpart in the Norwegian government.

"We are so pleased to have you here, Herr Tosti."

"As am I equally pleased to be here. It is so..." Tosti's face went blank as his phone rang with the ringtone that said it was Vlad calling. He fought the urge to show anger. "How dare he," thought Tosti, "he knows my schedule."

"Will you excuse me for just a second, this is family...," his face telling the rest of the story, "family calls occur at the most inopportune of moments..."

"No concerns, Herr Tosti. Would you like a private room?"

Tosti was already at the corner of the atrium where the guests leave their overcoats on a metal rack.

"Yes."

"Did you log in to Seraphim at 08:10, log out at 08:14 and then log back in again at 08:17?"

"No, I don't think so. I was having breakfast at that time. I only logged in once, got the update from Berta, then logged out." Tosti had his mobile phone pressed to his ear hoping that no one could hear the audio in a chamber that seemed to amplify every voice. He looked at his host, and gave her a smile, like saying, "what can you do—family. This will only take a minute longer." She smiled back.

"Someone logged in to the site from a different computer using your login—right after you logged out. We've been hacked, Tosti. Where's your laptop?"

"It's in the room—in the safe. As you require."

"Get back there now, Tosti."

By the time that Tosti was able to explain to his host, Mrs. Johanson about an "unforeseen family emergency" and head back to the hotel, Frank was already headed to his car parked a couple of blocks away.

Frank first went back home to his apartment. He tried to get some sleep but a young girl with blond curls had a hold of his every thought. It came to him slowly; something told him that the world had changed for him. What he had seen he could not un-see. He needed to talk to someone he could trust with his life. There was only one person in the world that fit that description, and that was Monika.

Inside his hotel room, Tosti found nothing out of place. The laptop was still in the safe, but he could see the log entry where the entire contents of his hard-drive, minus the operating system and consumer applications, had been copied to an external drive. Someone had been in his room and inside the most private of his affairs. He was consumed with anger and frustration. Back at the breakfast lounge and then to the front desk he made the polite inquiries looking for a "tall skinny and scruffy man, poorly dressed." As he suspected, there was no trail to follow. The man that had been seated by the window had paid with cash. He was considering what to do next when he heard the familiar ringtone.

"Were you going to tell me?"

Tosti considered the implications of the question. He pushed back.

"Vlad called you." He said it like an accusation.

"That was his job."

"And mine was to get more information before I called you—so I had more to go on than just tell you that someone broke into my room and into my computer."

"Hmm. Fair enough. So what have you learned?"

"That it was a professional. He left no trail behind. I suspect the hotel cameras will not give us more information. He broke into the room and into the safe."

"Vlad says that the Trojan was sophisticated. The hacker got into the main page and tried to get into the video library but failed."

Tosti was silent for a second thinking through the repercussions of the next revelation. "I have to presume that he didn't fail entirely."

There was another pause and then a question, "What do you mean by 'didn't fail entirely?'"

"I had a couple of the video files downloaded to my c-drive." He paused for a second. "For convenience. I wanted to review the file later. It was not encrypted."

The pause on the line lasted longer this time. Tosti waited—angry with himself for the mistake, and for having to play the errant child to Pascal's questioning. Pascal was his friend, sort of; the way a boss can be a friend until he has to turn back into the boss.

"You need to get back to Brussels now. Vlad will be tracking down this hacker. The problem will be eliminated."

"Yes, I agree. I'll be catching the first flight out."

"When you land, call me. There are loose ends. I don't like loose ends, Silvio." The threat was as direct as Pascal would make it. It was left open to interpretation, but not really.

"I'll call you when I land."

When Pascal had finished speaking with Tosti, he called Vlad back up.

"Tosti made a mistake. Figure out what it was."

"He's an arrogant son-of-a-bitch. I told you that. He also downloaded the teaser file that Berta had hosted on the secure page."

Pascal decided to ignore Vlad's comment about Tosti. No sense in hashing out the same conversation one more time.

"Anything else?"

"Not sure yet. I have to review Tosti's logs—see what the files were. If he has any other incriminating data then we had better get to this guy before he does anything with them. We have to assume the worst. And one more thing: What if Tosti made other so-called mistakes?" He posed it as an accusation.

Pascal ignored it for the moment. He was already contemplating exactly that same problem.

"How do we find this guy? Is he operating alone?"

"I'll find him. I have several phone-home applications hidden in various databases. If he triggers one of them it will give me his location. And if I find him, I'll find his computer and gain root access."

"Okay, son. Do what you need to in order to close the holes. I will deal with Tosti."

Pascal had called him "son." It was not often the case that he did so. It made Vlad took note. It thrilled him, like a puppy dog getting a reward. And it made him mad that he felt that way.

𐎒

"Ladies and Gentlemen, we will be arriving in Brussels within fifteen minutes. The local time in Brussels is Wednesday, nine-thirty-two. We will arrive about twenty minutes ahead of schedule. If you would kindly check to make sure that your seat belts are fastened, your seats are brought back up to their vertical position, the trays are secured, and any electronic equipment is turned off. Welcome to Brussels."

Mr. Jim Wong, seated in seat 1A, was looking out the window at the landscape of verdant farm fields and patches of forest approaching the outskirts of Brussels—all appearing so perfectly organized from a height of ten thousand feet. The red-tile roofed homes in townships had well defined boundaries. He could barely contain the growing anticipation he felt the closer he got to his destination. There was very little that stirred him now—he had everything that money could buy. *People are cows*, he thought. But not so the little angels. He assured himself. *I introduce the little angels to the world. Somebody has to do it. What a waste to leave it to the uninitiated.*

CHAPER 11

SOMEWHERE IN EASTERN EUROPE
1970

Roberta arrived into the world at a time when Europe was experiencing its first long taste of peace in three generations. It was an unsettled calm; a "cold war," as Orwell first called it, a war of shadows—the forces of East and West in an endless game of spy, counter-spy. It happened on a rainy night in an old sand-colored Volkswagen Vanagon T1 with its rounded front end.

The van served as transportation and home for part of a troupe of Romanian Gypsies. It was cold inside the van, the kind of cold that seeps into your bones. The heater was barely able to keep the front passengers warm—but not in the back. She came to be with a scream, grabbing her first gulp of the cold air and the world she was about to inhabit.

She and her mother, also named Roberta, were on an old US Army canvas cot bouncing in the back of the van. The wooden framing extended the canvas as tight as a drum so that they felt every pothole and ditch. The two lay prone, mother and child swaddled in the coarse olive drab blankets, also courtesy of the US Army. Berta had made a single long cry and then stopped, like all she needed to do was announce her arrival—no need to make a fuss. An old Gypsy woman helped Roberta and in short order the baby girl was nursing on her mother's breast.

The leader of the troupe looked for a place to set for a while, to give the new mother and her baby some respite from the ordeal of life's beginning. Life was hard—like an endless road trip. The Vanagon was home. And it stayed that way.

What she remembered of her mother was mostly from the men of the troupe, who told their stories when they gathered together for the evening hunched over the campfire, smoking their Gitanes Brunes. The aroma of the dark smokes brought with it a sense of family, the group clustered together for warmth and survival. Her mother, the men told her when she was old enough to understand, was found "on a farm outside of Budapest, sitting by the well." They found her "near death, delirious from hunger, unable to rise." All around her were the remains of "what had been a small but well-maintained farm; the ground churned up from the tank tracks, the family cow bloated and putrefying in the field." Everywhere they looked, they saw the "feathers of the farm chickens that the soldiers had taken into their tanks for making their evening meal." It was 1956. The lesson of Hungary was made clear to the world:

democracy is fine so long as the communists win and govern with direction from Moscow. Nothing had changed.

Roberta was ten at the time that they found her. They picked her up, fed her and when she had recovered, they put her to work in every manner of task, like fetching water from the rivers and springs when they had settled for the night. Her circumstances had improved. She had a new family now.

So Berta, daughter of Roberta, shared her mother's name. Roberta, the mother, had been with the troupe for fourteen years from the day when she was picked up at the farm, and at the age of twenty-four became a mother for the first time. She had avoided pregnancy all the years past, but on one occasion she had miscalculated and little Roberta—Berta—as she was called by the troupe, came to be.

Berta would never know who her father was, because her mother never really knew either. There had been many possibilities and besides, it did not change anything. Roberta's parents had been farmers caught up in a struggle for control among nations, not a political or ideological bone in their bodies. Roberta raised the infant until she was ten and shortly after died of "a bad cough." That's what the other Gypsies told her; that's what she remembered.

Berta picked up the languages of Europe. The troupe she traveled with kept her as a child servant, and one particular kind man kept her as his own personal servant until she came of age. She learned of the world, as she had always known it; powerful men visited, they did what they wanted. And they were interested in her; she could see it in their eyes, they way they were drawn to her like a moth to light. She knew it was because she was young and pretty. If you wanted to stay alive you complied, you stayed pretty. She learned this too, the same lesson that her mother had learned.

When Berta was fifteen, a handsome young man visited the troupe, driving in his new red Fiat 128. The troupe was headed north at the time, traveling through France. He was looking for entertainment and Berta caught his eye.

He paid for Berta; the two spent the night in a local inn. Waking up in the morning, the young man who called himself Silvio packed his things and drove Berta back to the encampment. In a conversation that lasted several hours, Silvio and the troupe leader settled on a price for Berta. It wasn't that she was for sale, but the money would make all the difference to a struggling band of gypsies. "She is not really one of us," was the argument that the troupe leader made in explaining it to the rest of the members. The women of the troupe cried at her departure, and so did the man who had "raised her as one of my own." It occurred at a moment in time when the troupe needed funds and so the trade was made.

Silvio needed someone who had a facility for languages and who was already ingrained in the knowledge that her life was about servitude. With the farewells made, Berta packed her meager belongings and went with Silvio in his red Fiat 128. Life had seemed to take another turn for the good.

It became clear in short order that they needed a story to explain the arrangement, so Silvio told her, "If anyone asks you, Berta, you are my younger sister." The two had a resemblance, so it was not far-fetched. He looked at her and she nodded. She understood. She liked this.

In the months that followed she grew fond of Silvio in the way that the absence of things can be taken as a sign of caring. He did not beat her, did not abuse her, and he appreciated her intelligence. But there was nothing kind in the soul of Silvio Tosti. Berta was soon with child, and the two expanded their story that the father, a veteran of the war, had died, leaving Berta alone—so her brother Silvio had taken them in as an act of goodwill.

It never did occur to Silvio to think of the child as his own, like a son. Silvio was not disposed to be anybody's father; least of all the son of a woman who he only considered purchased property, more like an expensive piece of furniture.

Chaos meant opportunity for those ruthless enough to see the silver lining in the dark clouds. This was Silvio. He saw the chaos of the Cold War as opportunity, but he needed an assistant. Italian was his first language. He was also fluent in French, English, German, Russian and even some Turkish—all the courtesy of an education at an early age that was bought with the money of wealthy parents—their legacy to him until an unfortunate car accident took their lives. Silvio's inheritance had been squandered, he soon learned.

Berta fit the role perfectly. She learned the languages from Silvio, who drilled her to achieve perfection, knowing that kindness is a better teacher than the whip. It was an avuncular relationship, or so she thought. He taught her everything he knew.

It was not kindness, rather practical need.

CHAPTER 12

Brussels, Belgium
November 1987

Silvio Tosti was in the same room with the big shots of Europe. He was one of the young staffers, only twenty and completing his last year of undergraduate university studies. Tosti was considered one of the prodigies being groomed for a future in the leadership of Europe. He sat in one of the comfortable leather chairs around the periphery, on the sidelines, seated behind those that had a place at the conference table. Like the others next to him, Silvio was there to be at the beck and call of the older, mostly men and one woman. "That bitch from England, Margaret Thatcher, with her puffy hairdo," he thought.

His boss, the Finance Minister from Belgium, was at the table; not an equal in rank with the others, but a powerful voice nonetheless. Great visions need great financiers. It was not by chance that these very men at the table now sat there. Most of them had been hand-selected early, like the current staffers—and groomed—so that one day, in the right circumstances, they would be there to take the helm: experienced, able to immediately engage with others of power without being awed, financially well off, ambitious zealots, and protectors of political power. It all had to do with pedigree and acceptance at a young age into the right universities and alignment with the power brokers of the day. Tosti's facility with languages and his regal bearing brought him in contact and to the attention of his mentor the Finance Minister, and one other, his well-connected colleague, Pascal, seated nearby.

Tosti had no problem following all the conversations from all the different languages represented in the room. The conference room was set on the ground floor in one of the government buildings. It faced an inner courtyard that served as a garden. Security guards patrolled the garden, keeping their eyes moving. Forty people were seated in the conference room. It was full and getting stuffy with a thick layer of gray fog building from an hour's worth of continuous smokes lit up in one unbroken chain by the various members of the group.

Everyone talked and tugged on their bottles of Perrier and their preferred brand of cigarettes. The German Chancellor, Helmut Kohl, an HB brand cigarette in his hand, had the floor; talking in his native German while others translated into the various languages. Not everyone spoke English. He continued, "building a single currency with a set of rules to allow free trade between our countries and compete more on an equal footing with the Americans and the rest of the world, as one Europe."

Everyone listened intently; though the big man they called *The Pear* had the most uninspiring voice. The Chancellor spoke in monotone. It was like listening to an old professor give a lecture that he has given a thousand times. His ideas and his words, however, were electric; the ideas of a new Europe, shedding its warring past and cooperating as one, competing as one. It was a dream. A dream that one day, they all hoped, maybe even in their own lifetimes, would become a reality. The thrill of it gave Silvio a shudder up his spine. What a day that would be, he thought, and I will be there, one of the architects, behind the scenes, calling the shots.

"And how will this currency be regulated, Helmut?" spoke Mrs. Thatcher. "What will stop one of the member countries from borrowing more and more money from their treasury, or from wherever? What will happen to the value of the currency then? How will the necessary discipline to operate a single currency be applied, Helmut, when no one here is contemplating giving up sovereign rights, at least not openly. How will that work, Helmut, one currency but everyone with their own banking system?"

She had asked the questions in that arrogant British accent, thought Tosti. Some in the room wanted to ask these very questions, but it was clear that the British Prime Minister was not really interested in the answers. Helmut waited for the translation and just looked at her, they all looked at her with disdain. She had thrown water on their dream—again.

"The bitch did it again," he thought. He could almost taste the hate he had for her.

After the meeting, the staffers met at their usual hangout. Brussels had become the city of convenience when the ministers of the various countries wanted to meet in a non-political setting. It was centrally located in Europe and it had the necessary hubs of transportation.

The beer and wine were flowing freely. Here they could speak without measuring every word, without fear of being overheard and free to be uninhibited by the trappings of power. They were in the separate room that was reserved for them by the proprietor of the bistro. It was conveniently located around the corner from Hotel Silken Berlaymont, a favorite of the power bureaucrats. It was also only a few blocks away from the Gare Bruxelles-Schumann train station and a short walk to Silvio's office, which sat adjacent to his boss' office, the Assistant to the Deputy Prime Minister and Minister of Finance. The room was filled with the smoke of cigarettes. Just like their bosses, they smoked their cigarettes one after the other, a sort of chic habit.

He looked around the room with admiration for his colleagues. "The old men with their titles might be the bigwigs," he thought. "It is here in this smoky backroom where he, Silvio Tosti, the son of a former Italian nobleman from the old aristocracy, and his friends, would make the new Europe."

Pascal caught his eye. The two men smiled at each other across the room. Pascal, the Count Du Relo, also came from old money; but unlike Silvio, Pascal and his family still had it, the kind of money that no one could possibly believe. The privacy laws were meant to hide their wealth. But like Silvio, Pascal was of the new age; he cared nothing about the money because it had never been a concern. He abhorred the old aristocrats and their pompous boring lives. He was the Count Du Relo, an accident of birth, as far as he was concerned. Pascal took it for granted; not to disdain the position, but it was not what defined him. He was interested more in the new order of things, the new Europe. That and the side hobby that only he, Silvio, and a select few knew about.

Pascal pulled out a Mont Blanc pen and what appeared to be a business card. He scribbled on it and passed the note to Silvio across the table. The card had Pascal's name on the front, nothing else. The handwritten note was on the back of the card.

Silvio took a final gulp of his wine and flipped the card over to read the note.

"I am planning New Years in Bangkok. Want to join the fun? And we can discuss a new idea."

Silvio put the note in his pocket and gave him a short nod of his head, with the slightest of smiles. He brushed aside a wisp of hair that had fallen over his eyes. It was perfectly shorn to the times, conveying a mix of elegance and abandon, a perfect match for his classical Roman nose and well-defined cheekbones.

The two men understood each other perfectly. That's what Silvio admired in his friend. He noticed Pascal twisting a silver chain necklace with a pendant. This was something new. He glanced at it askance, not to be overly obvious about it. The pendant was a pair of wings, like those of an angel, but they were black. The more curious thing was the chain that encircled the wings—a chain that was broken in the middle. He had spotted the chain earlier, but now he saw the pendant. He remembered that he wanted to ask Pascal about this and now about Bangkok.

The chatter was dying down. Everyone picked up their coats, gave the customary two kisses, one on each cheek, and went out into the cool of the evening air, some to catch a train and others to their respective hotels.

CHAPTER 13

HSC (HIGH-SPEED CRAFT) *FJORD CAT*
SOMEWHERE BETWEEN NORWAY AND DENMARK
TUESDAY, 3ʳᵈ OF APRIL
09:13 CET

It was ten degrees centigrade on the lower decks of the ferry as it crossed the frigid waters of the Skagerak, the sea between southern Norway and northern Denmark. Ten degrees was not as frigid as it could be for this time of year.

The *HSC Fjord Cat* had undocked from its berth in the port of Kristiansand on the southern coast of Norway at precisely 08:30, picking up speed as it left the harbor. It was on a bearing heading in a straight line due south by southeast to another berth just over two and a quarter hours away. The small town of

Hirtshals on the northern edge of Denmark awaited her arrival, as it did every day at 10:45 in the late morning. From there, highway E39, also known as the Hirtshalsmotorvejen, led south and inland to the heart of the European continent.

The lower decks were where the cars and the RVs were parked. They were bumper to bumper, over 200 of them on this particular trip—busy, but not full.

The ship rocked up, cresting with the waves, and fell gently, its twin jets churning the waters like the contrails of an airliner in a clear blue sky. It was doing a remarkable thirty knots, aided by a strong wind at its stern. Passenger seating, a tax-free shop, bar and business class seating area were on the stern.

Berta and Rigo were at the bar, next to business class seating. Outside, the Skagerak covered the horizon as far as the eye could see—a gradient of hues from the blue-gray of the sea with its tiny whitecaps that merged into a hazy blue at the horizon, turning cerulean blue as the eyes ascended into the heavens.

The two of them sat shoulder-to-shoulder, appearing like tourists who had mistakenly ventured too far north and were now making their escape south to the warmer climate of the mainland. Rigo had a worried look on his face, wondering how Grete was faring in the deck below where they had parked the RV. He was also worried about the security dogs that he had seen when they first drove into the hold. At twenty-three years old, he had the kind of look that made women gape; tall and slender like his mother, hair the color of a rich espresso coffee, wavy and long but well groomed. It was the translucent blue eyes that first caught the attention, which caused the women to inhale and forget to breathe.

And then there was the long aquiline nose perfectly off-set by the subtle cheekbones, the lips thin yet inviting. He was oblivious to his looks. It wasn't that he was unaware of the looks he got; only that it meant nothing to him. Not so Berta.

Berta, seated next to him by the window, looked out to at the sea from behind expensive black Gucci sunglasses. She felt a kinship with the sea; its cold forbidding nature fit her sense of self. She was hard to read, her eyes hidden behind the dark glasses like a movie star; but one could say that she was simply the definition of elegance. Her long slender legs were crossed, one draped over the other, covered in black stretch leather pants that accentuated the impression of wealth and aloofness. Her manner revealed nothing except maybe boredom. Her features were attractive in a classical way of certain Italian women: the eyes almond shaped, the lips full, long dark hair and an olive-smooth complexion. But in this mix, there was a hard edge to her that was uninviting, a soul devoid of emotion. Her forty-one years now encroached in small but clear ways what was still a classical beauty. She had been stunning in her youth.

Berta had resolved the dilemma of who she was and what would become of her and Rigo. She knew that someday there would be a mistake. It could be today or tomorrow, she thought, but she had also long before decided that she would not fret about it.

Berta had trained Rigo to be her accomplice, a choice first made by Silvio, who saw in the mound of her belly not a son to be, but a tool in his toolbox, another resource for his ambition.

Berta looked at Rigo and restrained her desire to smile. "He is so handsome," she thought, like a proud mother. She wondered, "Would he ever know love, unrequited, innocent love?" She knew the answer. It had come to her once in the early days, when she thought that Silvio had been her rescuer. But under the control of Silvio, Berta had made a thousand choices of sin. It was like they said, "death by a thousand cuts." Unwittingly at first, and then with resignation, Berta made one sin after the other accumulating into the worst of all the sins: training her son to be like her—to engage in the business of Silvio Tosti.

Still, in the cold emptiness of her character, Berta knew she had a flaw—like a tiny air bubble hidden inside tempered steel. It was love—a mother's love for her son Rigo. This sentimental flaw, as she saw it, was something that she could never allow herself to show; never to confuse the boy, now a man, that there was anything in their lives but absolute obedience. There was no room for love—not in their lives. Obedience was all there would ever be for her and for him, to the will of master Silvio Tosti and to his master, the man she had never met, but knew was the only person that Silvio truly feared. These thoughts crowded her mind, always there, never a holiday from its truth. Obedience would be her lot, and Rigo's, until it would all be discovered, and then she knew what she was prepared to do. No, there would be no love in Rigo's life.

The rhythm of the engines and the almost perfect rocking forward and back of the great vessel made her more pensive than usual. She thought more on what they were doing and knew that when her time of reckoning came to be, her sins would be uncovered. It would be like peeling a rotting onion; one depraved layer after another, to find that there was nothing inside but an empty center. Berta had been a victim in the early days, but over the course of her lifetime, now over twenty-five years with Silvio, she had engaged in her own willfully complicit sin. She had much to account for. There would be no forgiveness, not for her, not when they discovered the girls; all those pretty, young, innocent girls.

She drank her wine and decided not to go there; better to keep her mind focused on the next steps, like once they disembarked and began the ten-hour journey on the highways leading south to Brussels.

Two decks below them was the reason for Rigo's worried look. It was like any other RV parked towards the bow of the ship, except that this one had a passenger, the-ten-year old girl called Grete that would soon be on the minds of every parent in Norway. She was in the RV, asleep, if it could be called that; a sleep aided by the drug she had been given with cookies and a glass of milk.

That had been Rigo's idea. Berta would have served her water.

The two had picked up the specially fitted Mercedes Benz Sprint RV in Oslo on arrival at Oslo's airport, on the Sunday just past.

Their flight had originated in the early morning the day prior out of Brussels Airport. After clearing through the customs control points at Gardermoen Airport, they found the vehicle as planned, paid for the parking with the Norwegian

Krones they had picked up before departure, and drove straight to Kristiansand stopping only for fuel and the necessities of a toilet. It took them four hours to make the drive, crossing all manner of bridges connecting the folds of the rugged landscape and the many tunnels bored into the mountains. Everything was well thought out with enough flexibility in the plan to resolve for the unaccounted circumstance. The two of them spent the night in the RV off the main road just outside of Kristiansand, eliminating the potential exposure that comes with hotel rooms. It was standard procedure—leaving as few footprints as possible to follow.

In the meantime, the social engineering of Grete's grandparents was set in motion. It originated from a place on the outskirts of Reykjavik, Iceland; the central control for their operations. The grandparents were easily duped by the familiarity and friendliness of the phone call. Vlad, "the engineer", had considered every question that the grandparents might have raised.

It appeared so "perfectly normal," they had told the inspectors who first came to the home. The two grandparents dutifully took Grete to the elementary school on Tuesday morning at the appointed hour, seven in the brisk morning, where a "very nice, elegant lady with blond hair and almond-shaped eyes—she had the eyes of that actress Angelina Jolie," said Grete's grandmother between her tears when she had explained it for the hundredth time to the investigators. The woman had claimed to be Mrs. Lund's colleague and "said she would walk

Grete into the school where Mrs. Lund was waiting for her, getting the classroom ready."

Five minutes later Grete was safely ensconced in the back of the RV as Berta drove and Rigo made all the other necessary arrangements so that the child would stay safe and warm but hidden from prying eyes or security dogs. At precisely 08:30 the great ship released from its berth and headed out of the harbor with the specially fitted Mercedes Benz Sprint RV parked in the cargo hold with little Grete inside, warm and oblivious to her journey, lost in a dream of the last few conscious seconds when fear had wormed its way into her life for the first time.

The RV's modified compartment was where the bed had been. Insulated padding, air vents, and an electric blanket connected to a bank of batteries kept Grete warm enough for the duration of the two-hour-and-fifteen-minute ferry ride from the port of Kristiansand to Denmark. Grete slept soundly. The "sedative would last for four hours; plenty of time to make the crossing in the ferry, disembark in Denmark, and drive south." That was the plan according to Vlad, "The Engineer." Everything had worked out to a T, as he had planned, so that Berta and Rigo now sat quietly contemplating their thoughts, waiting for the ferry to deposit them and the RV in Denmark and far away from where things would unfold as Kristiansand realized what had happened.

Berta knew. This was the most precarious moment in their escape from Norway. There was no place to run if something did go wrong and they were discovered. Mother and son, Berta and Rigo both, succumbed to the only thing left for them to do: sit, wait, and think.

Grete, rather Nikita, will not last long, thought Rigo. She had looked so frightened.

"She didn't even scream when we took her in the van," he told Berta as they walked away from the parked RV and up the stairs into the passenger areas. He spoke to her in the language that Berta had taught him, the Balkan Romani, the language of the Gypsies that had picked up Berta's mother outside the city of Budapest, Hungary. It was their own language, the one that had the benefit of being foreign to anyone but another Gypsy.

She had shrugged, "Not the right time to talk about it, Rigo."

But he could not stop thinking about Grete and how she had looked when she realized that something was wrong. Grete had said only one word and it came out like a whisper, "Mamma…" and then the tears came, like the tears of an angel, he thought.

None of the other girls had ever troubled him, not one, not until now when the cherubic little girl with the blonde curls had said "Mamma" and the tears had rolled down her cheek like she knew something very bad was going to happen to her.

Rigo, a shortened version of Rigoberto, was the "skinny man" and Berta, the shortened version of Roberta was the "even skinnier old woman" that Julia had written about in her diary.

Berta was lost in her own thoughts; charity and kindness were beyond her capability. But she could still remember, still look at her life back to that moment when she too had been innocent.

Berta now sat looking out the window, taking a spoonful from a bowl of fish chowder that she had picked up from the ship's galley. She dipped the elbow end of the bread that they had served into the bowl.

"Did you cover her well?" she asked.

Rigo nodded his head. "But she was still crying before she dozed off."

"They all cry, at first," she added, more a comment of fact. She put the spoon down and looked out the window, the sun was still rising into the clear blue sky. They had escaped from Torremolinos, Spain by train carrying what looked like nothing more than a specially designed oversize suitcase. Its 45 kilograms of cargo was sleeping-away from the strong sedative. Berta and Rigo had easily blended among the travelers of southern and central Europe. No one bothered them. Berta's sophistication and her elegant style put her in a coterie of people that spoke of money and power.

They had arrived in Brussels before the authorities in Spain had galvanized their efforts, and asked for help from its neighboring countries.

"This one is far more difficult," she thought. She and Rigo walked out to the back of the ship. There was a section for smokers. A handful of other souls in need of a smoke were there enjoying the brief moment before the cold drove them back inside. She took a badly needed pull on her Gitanes, inhaling as deeply as she could into her lungs, exhaling out with the wind so that it carried away. Nicotine entered her bloodstream and reached her brain, where it brought a sense of clarity and calm. Gitanes was her brand, the "blondes." It reminded her of who she really was. It was getting harder to get the Gitanes these days, so she smoked it to the edge of the filter before putting it out in the empty coffee cup.

"Tosti sent me a text message," she told Rigo.

Rigo was feeling the cold; he was ready to go back in when he stopped and turned around to listen. She had not said much since they had boarded.

"He says that we have a client who is ready for the visit and the clients, all of them, want a preview video." The wind had caused her eyes to tear as she stared out to the ocean and the ship's twin wakes. It caught Rigo by surprise, a softer look in her face that was transforming, bringing forth a memory that he had somewhere in the recesses of his mother when she was younger.

"Once we get started on the road, we will take a pause and record a short video to put up on the website."

The brief reverie ended. The two of them went back in to get ready for the arrival into Hirtshals and the road through Denmark.

CHAPTER 14

THE ENBERG FAMILY HOME
KRISTIANSAND, NORWAY
TUESDAY, 3ᴿᴰ OF APRIL
14:00 CET

"Hello, may I help you?"

"Ah yes, umm, my name is Mrs. Enberg, I am Grete's grandmother, Grete Enberg, the same name as my granddaughter."

"Yes, Mrs. Enberg," a friendly cheery voice replied, "We have been trying to reach you several times. Thank you for calling us back. We had expected Grete at school this morning but she never arrived. We ..."

Mrs. Enberg cut in, "No, no that is not possible." There was panic in her voice. "My husband and I, we are her grandparents, dropped Grete off at the school early this morning to meet with her teacher, Mrs. Lund, at seven this morning."

The pause at the other end of the phone seemed like an eternity.

"Hello, are you still there?"

"Yes, Mrs. Enberg, but I can assure you that neither Mrs. Lund, nor anyone else at the school has seen Grete at all today, which is why we have been calling."

The office attendant at the school heard a gasp, and then "Herre Gud!" "God in heaven!" with a piercing cry before the line went dead. It was two in the afternoon and the grandparents had arrived in time to wait for Grete's arrival back from school.

The phone rang again in the Enberg home. Grete's grandfather picked it up with a trembling hand. "Hello, this is Mrs. Olsen from Kristiansand Elementary School, I am the Principal here, to whom am I speaking, may I ask?

A somber voice, quaking with emotion, spoke up. "I am Gustav Enberg, Mrs. Olsen, Grete's grandfather. Please," he paused, to catch his breath, "please tell me that you have found our little Grete, Mrs. Olsen, please."

"I just spoke to the police, Mr. Enberg. They are sending someone over to your home right away; they should be there in a few minutes." She paused and then said the words she wished were not true, "but no, we have not seen Grete all day, sir. As my assistant said a moment ago…" but she never finished. The line went dead.

One hour later several cars arrived from the Kristiansand police station. Chief of Police, Politimester Kristoffer Backer made the judgment to initiate Norway's missing child protocol, a process of immediate notifications to all police offices and the media across the south of Norway with notification also made to the network of offices of Interpol and Europol.

CHAPTER 15

MONIKA'S APARTMENT
OSLO, NORWAY
WEDNESDAY, 4TH OF APRIL
SOMETIME EARLY AFTERNOON

Frank's head was spinning. It was becoming clear with each passing moment what he had just done. "There was no getting around it," he thought. The Voice would know soon enough. Frank could not lie, not to him; it was physically impossible for him. The fear of the pain that would be inflicted by The Voice's goons was deeply embedded in his psyche. Frank had not completed the task of getting Tosti's financial account credentials, and worse, he had deviated from his tasking. The punishment would come. He knew one thing for certain. He needed help.

So he knocked on Monika's apartment door. He had texted her in advance.

He heard her steps and the door opened. They looked at each other for a long second.

"Well, are your coming in?" she asked.

Frank nodded his head and said nothing back—he had learned that Monika's questions were more like statements. He walked in the door, took a couple of steps, turned to face her and held her by the arms—at arm's length.

"I am not who you think I am," he said. He had the look of a desperate man who needed to get something off his chest.

"You know that for sure?" It was not a question.

"I work for a group ..."

"Called the NoSaints," she said to finish his sentence.

He nodded, surprised, and yet not surprised by Monika. He was learning not to underestimate her. "They punish me, no, they torture me ..."

She put her hand to his mouth and then kissed him with a tenderness that he had never experienced before, this now from a woman, no longer the young girl he once knew. It evoked a feeling he had never experienced, how to trust another person with complete and utter reliance—to put it all in someone else's hands, in Monika's hands.

"You are Frank Becken," she said to him. "I know who you were and," she paused, "I know who you are, Frank. Inside, you are the same man that I used to know, just disoriented maybe." She took a step in; they were now inches apart, and held him close, her arms around his torso.

"I was in Russia, Frank—I could have stayed there, but I came back. I came back for one reason. I came back for you. You didn't know it, but I was your girl Frank—since then, and the same in Russia. I lost you once to that idiot Tom Whanamum."

He smiled; the memories of those days came flooding back.

"I won't lose you again, Frank, not to any Whanamums and not to the NoSaints. The NoSaints—how do they contact you?"

"I have a minder—someone I only know by his voice, I just call him 'The Voice.'"

"He called me this morning, gave me a new tasking. It was going well until I discovered that the mark—a guy named Silvio Tosti, was not connecting to his bank accounts, but to a different kind of website that he uses with others to coordinate their activities. This guy is involved, Monika. He's behind the abduction of this little girl that they have in the news."

"The cute little blond girl from Kristiansand?"

"Yes, the very one. I," he paused thinking how to say it clearly, "I hacked into his computer, got the evidence that is needed to take this guy down, maybe find this little girl, and if I give it to the police, they ..."

"They will kill you. The NoSaints will kill you." She finished his thoughts one more time.

"If I don't, then this little girl dies, and I could not live with myself, I couldn't just…"

"Well then, you got that right, because I couldn't live with you either, not if you let her die without doing something. That would not be the Frank Becken that I came back for."

He nodded. "I'm going in."

"Good."

"And Frank, one more thing, now that you have decided ... don't look back. Do what you must, not what anyone tells you to do—do what you must to save her. And come back to me."

She kissed him again. Frank left her apartment and found that his head was clear, more than it had been for over twelve years. Monika was left in the apartment, leaning against the door that she had just closed and inadvertently ran a hand across her belly.

Excerpt from the Case File from DSI Hansen

Tuesday, 3 April, 21:00

Put out a Europol alert—watch the borders.

Tuesday, 3 April, 23:33

Talked to the grandparents. Determined why it took so long to notify us. This was their statement verbatim: "We did not notice the blinking red light on the answering machine that was in our son-in-law's study until late in the afternoon when we went to call the school to ask why Grete had not made it home," they said. Both grandparents said the same thing.

Wednesday, 4 April, 04:12

Made the second call at 01:05. The parents' cruise ship was docked in San Juan, Puerto Rico. Talked to the ship's captain, Captain Peter Jensen. Parents were ashore when we first called. It took over two hours to locate them and get them back to the ship. Cpt J passed the telephone first to Mrs. Enberg. Told her the few facts we had so far. She let out a scream, couldn't talk further. Next spoke to her husband—lots of questions and all he could do was repeat what we knew that had already been explained. Afterwards spoke to the captain again. Said he had received lots of family emergency calls in his career, but never like this one. Said that Mrs. Enberg let out screams so piercing that the lights flickered momentarily in old San Juan. His words.

Wednesday, 4 April, 06:00

Left instructions for new shift team to call me if something breaks. Headed home to get a shower and some sleep. Need to be alert.

Wednesday, 4 April, 13:59

We have a break in the case—a hacker named Frank Becken walked in the door. We have a lead and suspect.

Wednesday, 4 April, 16:01

Got the approval to call the FBI for assistance—their cyber team in NY. Met their young chief last month. We need all the help we can get right now.

CHAPTER 16

HIRTSHALS DOCK, NORTHERN DENMARK
TUESDAY, 3RD OF APRIL
10:45 CET

It was late in the morning; precisely three hours and forty-five minutes since Berta had entered through the front door of Kristiansand Elementary School with Grete in hand. She had worn a blond wig and blue-tinted contact lenses that helped to offset her appearance. Rigo had picked open the door lock at the front of the building moments earlier. It was all made to look to the grandparents exactly like what it was supposed to look like.

"The assistant, the pretty lady" as Grete's grandmother described her, "entered the school like she belonged there, taking our granddaughter into the school to meet with her teacher."

Except that the teachers, including Mrs. Lund, were not yet in the school. Berta had entered and had just as quickly gone out the side entrance with Grete in hand where Rigo waited with the RV. Grete realized right away that they were not going to her classroom, but she had not the slightest suspicion—teachers are trusted—always.

"Are we going to play first?" she asked in Norwegian, looking up to the pretty lady that had her firmly in hand. Berta had looked at her, given her a smile and in her best Norwegian said, "Yes, we are."

Four hours and ten minutes later the trio of Berta, Rigo, and Grete still tucked away in the back, were in a queue of vehicles waiting to exit the bowels of the 91-meter-long ferry that had transported them out of Kristiansand, Norway and into the berth at Hirtshals, Denmark. Berta looked around. Everything appeared normal. The bustle of activity had a certain normal urgency—to meet the ship's schedule so that a new manifest of people and vehicles could make the return trip to Kristiansand.

Berta was in the driver's seat. The Mercedes Benz Sprint RV purchased and modified for this occasion was brand new. It had that *new car smell*. Her appearance conveyed a calm exterior. But her thoughts ran through their present predicament—there were no escape routes. She knew that this was the most dangerous moment of their escape. If the authorities in Norway had made the discovery and issued an alert, then the two of them were sitting ducks. She glanced to the side and watched her side mirrors.

Rigo had his own worries. He kept glancing back inside the RV to the back. Sounds of movement came from inside the hidden compartment.

"Keep your eyes ahead, Rigo," Berta spoke the words as calmly as if she were commenting about the sunny weather outside. The sun was up, approaching its zenith for the day, and everything looked ready-made for travelers on vacation. The crew of the ship waved her through to take the ramp and exit the ferry.

"She's starting to wake up," he said. Berta did not reply—there was nothing to do but wait their turn and not draw any undue attention. In seconds they were rolling out of the ship and exiting the small port to what was the start of the E39. The road took them on heading due south. Berta sighed in relief—the immediate danger had passed.

Not more than a couple of kilometers into the trip, they heard an unmistakable moan, and then what was clearly a child starting to whimper.

"Okay," she said. Rigo leaped out of his seat, headed to the back and opened the compartment. Berta drove as quickly as she could to put some distance behind them.

He found Grete curled up, a child waking up from a nap, the wrinkles on the bedding leaving its imprint on her cheeks, her face flush pink from the warmth inside the compartment. She was clutching the comforter in the one hand and wiping her eyes with the other. Her face was wet with tears. He lifted her out of the compartment and put her gently down in one of the cabin seats, all the while speaking soothing sounds.

Grete continued to whimper, too afraid to cry out loud. Rigo spoke to her in what few words of Norwegian he had in his vocabulary—offering and gesturing to ask if Grete wanted some milk and cookies. He showed her a video cover to see if she would like to see the movie *Finding Nemo*. Grete nodded and the whimpers died down. He turned around to open the small refrigerator on the left side of the vehicle.

"I need to go to toilet," she said in English. Rigo reached to the other side and turned the handle to the narrow door that opened into the diminutive toilet that also doubled as a shower. He poured a small glass of milk and opened the Norwegian butter cookies that they had purchased while stopping to refuel on the road to Kristiansand. Grete finished, washed her hands and came out. She took the cookies and milk hesitantly at first, but hunger won the moment of reservation. Rigo indicated to her that she had a milk mustache. She smiled. He gave her a napkin and she wiped her mouth in a motion of such complete innocence that Rigo also smiled. He could not take his eyes away, feeling a sense of tenderness as if he and Berta had nothing but the best intentions for her in the hours to come.

"I'm going to make some lunch, Grete," he said in English. "Would you like a sandwich and a banana?" Grete nodded, she understood. Her fears were dissipating quickly as things seemed to return to normal. She had been on RV trips with her family before and this looked and felt almost the same.

"Are we going on a trip ..." She asked the question in between bites of the sandwich, her mouth half full. Before Rigo could form an answer, she finished the question that her trusting mind had formulated, "... to see my parents?" She didn't like being afraid. There could only be one reason for all the secrecy.

Berta looked back through the rearview mirror.

"Yes, we are. It is a surprise, which is why we couldn't tell your grandparents."

She nodded and smiled—Grete loved surprises. It was as she had expected.

Finishing her milk, she asked a question that had also been on her mind: "Will you take care of me until my mom comes?" Grete glanced at Berta where she sat driving the vehicle. Berta heard the question and shifted her head to see the reflection of Grete in the rearview mirror. Berta wondered, *what's behind the question?* None of the others had asked that question.

Rigo was also surprised, but took a different meaning, that Grete trusted him, but that she was still afraid. It also meant that she had entrusted Rigo—to the task.

Rigo nodded his head and looked down at the DVD he had in his hands. "Ready to watch now?"

"Yes." She smiled, the anticipation of her favorite movie showing on her face.

Rigo inserted the DVD into the player and before long Grete was immersed in the fantasy world of Norwegian-speaking animated fish. There were giggles galore, sighs and tears even, as Grete watched the adventures of the father fish who wouldn't give up looking for his clownfish son.

"Silvio had thought of everything," thought Berta. She occasionally glanced back through the rearview mirror at the young girl watching the movie and wondered at the effect she was having on Rigo. Rigo stayed in the back looking at the map. Normally he would have taken the seat next to her. Berta felt the need to say something.

"You can't take a liking to the girl, Rigo, you know that." She spoke it in Romani. Rigo looked up, but didn't say anything. He moved up to the front passenger seat, staring out the window and checking the back where Grete was eating the banana still watching the film.

A couple of minutes passed before he replied, "I know." And then he turned to Berta. "Will this ever end, Mother?"

Berta had the fleeting thought that he was asking about the length of the road trip. But she knew better. She glanced at him. The road outside was an endless ribbon of paved asphalt in a flat land starting to turn the bright green of early springtime. She had lied to him all his life, and now he was asking for the truth. It wasn't the first time. But she loved him too much to tell it.

"It will one day, but that day is not near." She resolved once again to tell the lie that she had told him ever since he could think for himself. "Our life is in the present, we cannot think on the future, Rigo. We just need to be obedient to Master Tosti and let come what may. He will find a way for us."

He looked at her openly letting his gaze linger a moment. The hum of the diesel engine was the only sound in the vehicle—nothing to distract the mind. She returned the look with a smile. He already knew the truth. Hope made him ask—the hope that maybe she would be honest with him in the manner of peers sharing a common destiny. Disappointment crowded his mind like the haphazard accumulation of cobwebs in an old barn—once again. She might be right, he thought, but he had started to understand that there would be no end to the horror of their task. And he knew why she answered as she did.

Rigo didn't press her. The two went silent on the topic of their future, speaking to each other only in the conversation about routes and plans on arrival. And they also spoke about where and when to take the video. It wasn't all that simple. It all depended on Grete—if she would cooperate.

"What type of video do we make?"

"Nothing contrived, natural, no costume, just her playing a game or eating a meal."

He liked that answer. "Okay, I think she might even like it."

"Yes, maybe it will satisfy Tosti. Not like Spain. I don't want to be on this highway for a moment longer than necessary. Can you do the video as we move?"

"Sure. I'll get started on it. But first, food. I'm starved. There's plenty of stuff stocked in the refrigerator and the overhead cabinets. How about these small pizzas?"

Berta glanced back to the frozen pizza pie that Rigo was showing her. "Yes, that will do."

"I'll start some coffee."

"Good, and close the curtain, I need a smoke. I'll open the window."

After the DVD had finished Rigo started the recording.

"Your English is very good, Grete."

"Thank you," then she stopped and asked him, "When are we going to get there? I can't wait to see their surprise when they see me."

"Soon. We will get there soon. They will be very happy to see you, but you will have to be patient." He was pleased to see that the stuffed dog he had left in the back compartment was having its usual effect. "By the time you wake up we will be there." He changed the topic, "And what are your going to call your stuffed dog?"

"Well, I don't think he's a dog at all. I think he's a prince. I will call him Le Petit Prince."

Berta almost choked on the bite of her pizza that she was chewing. Le Petit Prince had been her own favorite of the childhood stories—a traveler to unknown places—like she had been traveling with the troupe. She watched the recording taking place from her rearview mirror growing more concerned with Rigo. He had never behaved this way. His work had always been done mechanically—something that had to be done; he had never shown any attachment to their subjects nor taken any step other than the minimum necessary. The two of them, Rigo and Grete, were engrossed in conversation, Grete enjoying the idea of being filmed, exaggerating her conversations with the stuffed dog she now addressed as Le Petit Prince.

With a full tank of gas in the Sprint RV they made it as far as Oberhausen, Germany, approaching the border with Holland. They had already traveled over 850 kilometers and the tank was nearing empty. And they needed to stretch their legs. Berta had been driving for just over seven hours straight. They found a gas station off the autobahn, parking at the remote end of the parking lot—near the long haul trucks on their required rest.

While Berta refueled, Rigo uploaded the three-minute video he recorded of a smiling Grete playing with a stuffed Cocker Spaniel puppy doll.

The two changed places. Grete was getting tired so there was less of a need for Rigo to entertain the child.

⋏

Twenty-one-hundred kilometers away, in Reykjavik, Iceland, an alarm pinged on Vlad's computer. Minutes later, Pascal and Tosti each got a text message, "new Niki to c." It didn't take long for the logs to update showing that two accounts had been given access to the Seraphim website, and to the servers that hosted the files of a video that lasted precisely three minutes.

⋏

On the E35/A40 crossing the Rhine River and just short of 40 kilometers to the border with the Netherlands, Berta got her own ping. There was a new text message from an unnamed account. It said simply, "well done. T"

CHAPTER 17

Oslo, Norway
Tuesday, 3ʳᵈ of April
20:03 CET

DSI Hansen was concluding his own conversation in front of the cameras that connected his office to the Ministry of Justice's newly opened information-operations-center. It was also known as the IOC—a place borne in response to the two terror attacks that had occurred in July 2011.

"That is all we have at the moment, Mr. Minister. I now have the task of finding the parents who are on a cruise ship in Puerto Rico. It's their wedding anniversary."

"Very well. I don't envy you that task. Thank you." He was about to get up from his seat. "Ah, ..."

"Yes, Minister."

"I know I don't need to tell you this, but I do need to—off the record." He paused a few seconds to gather his thoughts. "In a crisis like this one there is the justice that has to be pursued, and then there is the political side. Though we both have the same goal, to save the little girl, there are other considerations—especially where it pertains to my role."

He paused again and fixed his eye on the camera as if looking down the barrel of a gun straight into the mind of DSI Hansen. "Your job is to find the girl, find her alive. I will handle any politics that may come up. My assistant will be in touch with you. He will be your direct point of access if you need anything. Keep him up to date. Everything he knows I will know. Do what you must within legal boundaries—but you *must* find her. Everything else will resolve itself if we, … you, are successful in getting Grete back home. Anything you need, you have. I am authorizing you to do what you need to, to use whatever resources you need to find her. Am I being clear, Fredrik?"

DSI Hansen swallowed. "Yes sir, it is clear."

CHAPTER 18

SOMEWHERE NORTH OF BRUSSELS, BELGIUM
TUESDAY, 3ʳᵈ OF APRIL
23:38 CET

Approaching midnight the headlights of the RV telescoped its twin beams through a light sprinkling of rain. The light glittered from the raindrops, lighting the path that was a thin strip of paved road called Paradijs. Minutes later the RV made a left into the short driveway. Rigo stepped out and quickly unlocked the garage doors. He drove in.

The garage was situated to the left of center on what was a forty-meter long brick building that had once served as a barn for farming equipment. The right side of the barn had been converted to a two-floor house. It was the only building for several hundred meters situated between an industrial warehouse complex and a busy waterway—one of the canals that fed into the Scheldt river. Small plots of farmland and unattended growth just over three meters tall created the barrier of brush land to the N17 highway that went east to west.

To the north an hour's drive away was the city of Antwerp. To the south and approximately the same distance was the capital of Belgium—the City of Brussels. The base of this operation was not chosen by mistake. The location and number of ingress and egress points made it ideally suited for getting in and out by various ways. Its isolation served to keep it from the overly curious. It served perfectly for the secrecy that Silvio needed and its other needs. It was also close enough to his principal place of work in the capital.

Berta turned on the lights to the utility room that served as mud-room, wash and storage room. Rigo carried the sleeping Grete while Berta posted the update by text message, "Arrived, all well." Grete's slumber was aided by another of Rigo's concoctions to assure that she stayed asleep as they approached and entered the building. This was the house that served for the next phase of their "service" as they called it.

Silvio got the update in his hotel room. He had been waiting for this before going to bed. He relayed the short message to Pascal and Vlad—who also waited in anticipation.

The inside of the converted barn resembled nothing like the nondescript brick façade of the exterior. It started with its electronic footprint. A host of surveillance sensors fed data to the computer servers in Dublin. A software script performed the simple task of checking for changes in the file directory. An alert was sent to Reykjavik where Vlad operated as the central command center from the second floor of his home. Another bit of software code did simple pattern matching to determine if it all fit the expected profile: something trips the sensor at the entrance to Paradijs Street from the western point of entry, garage door opens and then closes, door to home opened and the electrical power consumption increases. It was also captured by video camera recording the movements as Rigo climbed the stairs and entered the room. A new Nikita had been placed in the holding room.

Rigo placed Grete under the covers with Le Petit Prince in the nook of her arm. The timing of all these actions fit within the profile that was expected—within fifteen minutes from start to finish—all normal.

It wasn't just Vlad's electronics in the house. Silvio also had his hand in the design and outfitting of the supplies. He had spared no expense in creating the kind of luxury appropriate for the Seraphim *guests* that came to visit every few months, coinciding with the new tenants that Berta and Rigo brought into the home. The *guest* room was actually two adjoining rooms each with its own fireplace—one served as bedroom, the other as business and living room. A large bathroom with hot tub, and a separate steam room was accessible from the bedroom. Every room had a full decking of entertainment technology. The living room hosted a three-meter long television screen that rested on a credenza stocked with videos and even a gaming console. A small bar with the most expensive wines and liquors from all parts of the world sat at one corner of the room that connected to a small garden patio with Roman fountains and flowers from the local flora. A local husband and wife team maintained the outside gardens on a set schedule that paused when the house was being occupied. For all anyone knew, this house-farm combination building was nothing more than the expensive occasional home of busy executives.

One cabinet was especially fitted as a humidor stocked with the finest cigars from Cuba and cigarettes of every brand. Each room had its own temperature and humidity controls all with the purpose of creating an environment as close to the home climates of the guests. Silvio had thought of everything.

It was interesting to Rigo that not one *guest* had ever asked what happened to the young girls after they left. It was not something they ever wanted to know, expecting that it would all be taken care of—tidy and without loose ends.

Returning back down the stairs, Rigo found Berta busy with making a goulash soup from stock she kept in the freezer. The two chatted about nothing consequential. Berta had the radio playing. There was a report in the news about a pending rain storm due to arrive in the morning promising torrential rains like the floods they had just a few months back in November 2011.

CHAPTER 19

AIRSPACE SOMEWHERE OVER ASIA
WEDNESDAY, 4ᵀᴴ OF APRIL

Ten thousand seven hundred meters up in the sky, a solitary aircraft flew its assigned flight path like a car on a highway in the sky reserved for the commercial airliners. Airbus 380 Flight SQ26 was a few minutes ahead of schedule. Wong was awake now and famished.

"Your meal will be ready in a few minutes, Mr. Wong." The Lufthansa flight attendant Sabine was busy getting the tray ready for serving. She brought him a combination of salads, an appetizer and entrée readied by the onboard chef who had specific instructions for Mr. Wong's tastes that included a curry noodle fish soup, rice and other small delicacies. Wong's assistant had communicated the details of his needs to the airline in advance. First class meant just that, attention to the small details and individualized service. He took a sip from the glass of Bordeaux Superíeur wine that Sabine had served him.

It was prepared to be a small meal, a transition that would eventually end up eliminating all food. He would enjoy the moment while he could, savoring the exquisite tastes of the foods from his homeland. His battery of pills was in a small plastic container that he kept with him at all times. Soon it would be just pills, no more food. The body was adapting—cleansing itself of the pollutants and cancer carriers as they called it.

Jim Wong looked out the window. What he saw made him wonder, like it always did. Below the small oval window was the vast open darkness that blended with the dark of the night's sky. The heartland of Eastern Europe lay below. The contrast with his own region at this time of night was the wonder of it all. Asia would be lit up like miniature fireflies congregated by the millions in the cities of the Asian continent, from city to city and the same with the archipelago of the island states to the southeast and farther north stretching to Taiwan, South Korea, and Japan.

He smiled to himself thinking; *the time for Asia has arrived. We are no longer the afterthought; the day is coming soon when we will be first in the world economy.* He was also anticipating, with the measured patience that came naturally to him, the initiation of sorts that was to take place within a couple of days. There were business meetings first, and then he planned to meet Count Pascal Du Relo before heading to his entertainment on the weekend. He had no particular preference for the western girls, but if that is what it took to join the club, then so be it, he concluded.

Starting on his meal, he first noted the text message that had arrived communicated over the satellite connection that allowed the passengers to have Internet access. "Anticipating all is well with your journey. Please log in and enjoy your appetizer." He decided to wait until after his meal.

At precisely 05:40 on Wednesday morning, as dawn approached in the eastern horizon, the wheels of the massive jet touched down on the extended runway at Rhein-Main-Flughafen in Frankfurt specially made for the A380. It had been a bumpy approach. Even the massive A380 aircraft was not immune to being pushed around by the cold front from the Atlantic. In less than an hour he was airborne once again. Another two hours after that he was seated in the back seat of a limousine in a driving rain heading west into the city reading the daily newspapers that were placed there for him including the Financial Times of the United Kingdom, the Wall Street Journal, the Hong Kong Economic Times and the German Handelsblatt. By eleven he was settled into his suite at Le Méridien Brussels Hotel, where a plate of tea with a variety of fruits, Belgian chocolates and pastries awaited his pleasure.

Mr. Wong decided that the first order of business was a shower when his new Samsung Galaxy rang. "Yes," he answered.

"Jim, this is Pascal."

"Yes, Pascal, good to hear from you, I have just arrived at the hotel, and am already in my room."

"Very good, am pleased to see that your flight went well—and please excuse the early call, but we have a serious development that occurred while you were in the air." He paused.

"Please proceed."

"You know to what lengths we engage in ensuring the privacy of our affairs, and now I am greatly grieved to report that there is a risk to that privacy."

Wong put the cup of tea down that he had prepared.

"I see. And I presume that you would not be calling me if it weren't serious."

"Indeed. It is serious enough that we need to take certain precautions."

"What precautions are you talking about?"

"First and foremost is your safety. There is a new return ticket getting delivered right now to your hotel lobby. Your departure time is at ten past two later this afternoon, so there is no time for delay. The limousine that picked you up at the airport is already waiting outside. Jim, there is no time to waste."

There was a long pause and then he spoke, the anger in his voice could barely be contained. "I … I am so deeply displeased, Pascal."

Pascal waited a second before responding to cool his own rising temper.

"I can appreciate that, but I can assure you that this is entirely necessary. In business there are always bumps. This is one of them and it is consequential. You need to be on the earliest flight out of country. Am I making myself clear?"

The point was made—Pascal would not be intimidated.

"It is clear. We will talk on this later when I arrive at my destination. And there will more explained on the website?" The last bit of that statement was only part question.

Pascal let it pass. "There will be."

Wong let go a long sigh. "Very well, then."

CHAPTER 20

BRUSSELS AIRPORT, BELGIUM
WEDNESDAY, 4ᵀᴴ OF APRIL
15:30 CET

Silvio disembarked from the Brussels Airline A320 aircraft and made a hasty exit. A host of text messages greeted him as he walked to his Audi A6 in the underground garage. He maneuvered out of the airport to find the highway. The clap of thunder quickly followed a flash of lightning. There were three messages from Vlad, one from his boss, and another from Pascal that said simply, "guest returned to airport, in the air soon."

Vlad's messages were still poking Silvio about the video file he had left unprotected, the "mistake" that had caused them to abandon the guest visit and had put the whole operation in turmoil. Vlad was also still trying to determine whether anything on Tosti's hard drive contained information that could allow someone with the right skills to understand more of the Seraphim operation.

"The limo receipt link is password protected. Are you sure it has no location info?"

Silvio was getting irritated to an extreme. ...*How dare that bastard*, he thought. The rain was coming down so hard he dared not try to visit the website while driving. It would have to wait. He spoke into the phone to relay his text message in reply. "Will check when arrive my apartment."

A ping arrived soon after. "Hurry."

Silvio cursed the *bastard Vlad*, using all of his willpower to keep from letting him get under his skin. He decided to tune in to Radio 1, the national radio station, to see if he could figure out what was happening with the weather.

The Flemish radio announcer was already speaking about the unusual weather. "Finally, there are already reports of flash flooding in the lower lying areas near Antwerp. The Scheldt River canals are spilling their banks. Listeners are advised to stay indoors. This is no time to be out driving. And we have been advised further that Brussels Airport has closed for all but arriving international flights."

Arriving at his apartment Silvio checked his email account and saw the limo receipt link to the company's website that Vlad had noted. He input the long password and opened the PDF file. What he saw made him instantly nauseous. There it was, the address he had specifically told the limo company should never be recorded. And now he had a choice. The first was to tell Vlad, which would further destroy whatever credibility he still had with Pascal. The second was to ignore it, and tell Vlad that there was nothing there. He decided on the latter. This was a needle in a haystack situation that he could clean up at a later point—excise receipt from the limousine company website and no one would know better.

"Right now," he thought, "I need to concentrate on the task at hand; eliminate the evidence that sleeps in the second floor of the house."

There was another more pressing item. His boss, the Director General, had also texted him. "Silvio, disturbing events in Norway. Meet me in the office, 08:30. Confirm ASAP!"

Silvio went to the liquor cabinet and poured himself two fingers of his favorite Cognac. He downed the first glass and poured himself a second two fingers. The warmth of the liquor in his stomach had the needed affect—settling down what had started to be an overwhelming sense of nausea at the compilation of events building up ever since he had seen that "shit reporter at the Continental Hotel in Oslo."

He texted back, "Confirmed." There was nothing else to do. He also texted Vlad. "Nothing there."

Seconds later came back the reply, "Sure?"

Silvio could no longer keep it together, "Fuuuckkk!" he screamed out loud. Vlad had succeeded. The bottle of Cognac was his company for the night.

CHAPTER 21

SERAPHIM BASE OF OPERATIONS
SOMEWHERE IN THE OUTSKIRTS OF BRUSSELS, BELGIUM
WEDNESDAY, 4TH OF APRIL
18:32 CET

On the northern side of the ten acres that constituted the grounds of the address of the house was an old wooden barn still standing but starting to lean from its many years of neglect and the fact that its foundation was starting to crumble. The barn was made to collect the summer hay. It had been unused for at least a decade. An old backhoe gave evidence of its new purpose. It too was leaning, its tires sinking into the soft earth as the water from the creek that breached its banks poured a rivulet of gushing water into the barn, further weakening the structure.

In the center of the barn was a large hole originally dug out with the backhoe. It was also full of water. A large and sturdy-built three-meter long by two- meter wide wooden rectangular cover partly floated in the pool of water inside the barn, banging against the side of the wall. And so did the decomposing body of a young girl that had been wrapped in a large black plastic bag, filling with the rainwater and opening up. The building wall collapsed shortly after, spilling its contents, and the remains of the young girl floated away with the rushing of the water.

A mere two hundred meters away, another young girl, Grete, in the Nikita Room, as they called it, was asking—pleading with Rigo.

"You promised, you said they would be here already. Where are they, Mister Rigo?"

Rigo had no answers. He had brought her another glass of milk, but Grete wouldn't touch it and she wasn't watching any more kiddie videos. The tears streamed down her face, her young body convulsing with the earnestness of her plea that Rigo should keep his promise. He approached her, but she shrank away to the corner of the bed. He reached out his hand to her and she relented. She took his hand firmly, like her mother had taught her—and held it.

Between the shudders of tears, now exhausted, she looked up into his face and asked Rigo, "They are not coming, are they?"

Rigo thought himself immune, beyond the reach of the natural sympathies that humans have for small puppies and little girls. The tears came to him un-beckoned. He fought them but couldn't hold them back.

And he couldn't look away. Rigo tried gently pulling back his hand, but she held it as tight as she could. He shook his head—just once.

"No."

Grete's tears came back, but she still held his hand. In the other she gripped Le Petit Prince.

"My mother always prays with me before going to bed. I haven't prayed ..." Her sobs interrupted her thought. "Will you pray with me, Mister Rigo?"

Rigo couldn't speak. He nodded his assent.

Grete let go of his hand and climbed off the bed, kneeling on the rug beside it with her hands folded, her eyes shut tight, and her elbows propped under her. Rigo first went to the bathroom and returned with a towel that he placed in front of the video lens that looked out into the room from behind a picture of a lighthouse. The lighthouse kept watch over the room. Everything was recorded and saved within Vlad's servers. Grete also got up and got a tissue from the bathroom—wiped her tears and her nose, then resumed her pose, her hands pressed together ready for prayer. He did the same, kneeling next to her, his hands on the bed.

She looked at him. He got the message and pressed his own hands. Grete closed her eyes and began...

"I lay me down, ..."

She looked up at him.

"You have to say it with me."

"I don't know it."

"Then say it after me. And you have to close your eyes."

"Okay."

"I lay me down,…"

"I lay me down,…"

She continued the prayer, parsed a phrase at a time while Rigo repeated it. He thought they were finished.

"And help Mister Rigo keep me safe."

"Is that in the prayer?"

"No. I added that part."

"I see."

Grete gave him a hug around his neck and climbed in the bed under the covers.

Rigo took the towel off the picture of the lighthouse and left the room.

CHAPTER 22

OFFICE OF THE DIRECTOR GENERAL (DG)
EUROPEAN COMMISSIONER FOR ECONOMIC AND
FINANCIAL AFFAIRS (ECFIN)
EUROPEAN COMMISSION, BRUSSELS, BELGIUM
THURSDAY, 5TH OF APRIL
08:44 CET

"I was at a dinner party last night, Silvio ..." The Director
General got up from his chair and walked around his desk
to the long storage unit that served as a table for all the to-
kens of a thirty-year career working himself up the ranks of
the European Commission. The table spread along the length

of the windows looking out to the lush green park across the street. There was a small refrigerator discreetly hidden in one of the doors. He opened it and took out two of the green bottles of Perrier—walked to the round table at the corner of the room and offered one to Silvio, breaking the seal on his own. The DG poured half its contents into a glass and took a sip, finishing the sentence.

"... when I got a most unexpected and unwelcome phone call from Oslo, from their Minister of Justice, of all people. He called me first, Silvio. He would have called the Commissioner himself, but he is not predisposed to, how should I say it, my boss, the man from Poland. So he told me. It was a call made in friendship, one might say. Or maybe more like a friendly political shot across the bow."

Silvio listened as impassively as he could, his training telling him that to speak now would be a mistake. He broke the seal on his own bottle of the expensive water and did like his boss, pouring half its contents into the glass and took a sip, never taking his eyes off the Director General.

The DG looked at Silvio and leaned forward. "I told the Minister that there must be some mistake, that there is no possible way that a deputy from my office whom I have known for over fourteen years would be engaged in such a thing. And to miss such an important meeting in Oslo ..." The DG left the statement unfinished. "You have forty-eight hours, Silvio, to clean up this mess, whatever it is. In forty-eight hours there will be a Europol Alert issued in your name, at which time it will also be in the press, and there will be nothing that I will be able to do to help you." He was now bristling with anger, "And you will have damaged me, Silvio. Fix this, whatever it is—now—before the forty-eight hours, now, actually only forty hours remaining. Am I being clear, Silvio?"

"Yes, you are, Director General, perfectly clear." Silvio's face was chalk white but his demeanor was a mask of control balancing naked fear and seething anger. He felt nauseous once again—for the second time in so many days.

The DG turned his back without saying a word and went back to his desk. Silvio was effectively dismissed. He was about to say something and thought better, turned and exited out the office door, taking a right turn to find the toilet.

In the office, the DG was on his personal smart phone texting with Pascal, the Count Du Relo, using encryption software that protected its contents.

"Gave him forty hours. Tell me again, Pascal, can S fix? If not, then you must—we cannot let explode."

"It is getting fixed. S is a question," came the reply seconds later.

"Do what you must!"

⚔

The Count Pascal Du Relo was in Paris, staying at the Mandarin Oriental Hotel by the Eiffel Tower, getting ready for a meeting with a potential business contact from the Ukraine. He was in his suite finishing his café au lait and croissant. It was close to nine-thirty in a morning that had started with a rigorous workout. Along with the meager breakfast, he opened the sandwich-sized plastic bag of pills of various sizes and kinds—vitamins and supplements carefully combined in his own laboratory to maintain his vigor. He hardly ate normal food any longer; café and croissant were his indulgences. The Count was in his early fifties. No one would have guessed it. He had the look that placed him at least ten years younger. And he felt young—but not at the moment. Breakfast was started late, having just finished his morning workout in the hotel exercise room finished off with a long hot shower. Exiting the bathroom Pascal heard the ping that meant a new text message had arrived. It was from the DG.

Pascal had a plan. It had worked itself out while he slept the night past, his mind unfettered by the conscious control of logic, to find the unconventional links. He would set two plans in motion—the first would save Silvio and create the firebreak to sever the link leading back to him and Seraphim. The other plan, Plan B, would be working in parallel—just in case—and Silvio would be *the* firebreak. He looked at his watch. The business meeting was planned as a working lunch, right there at the hotel. He had plenty of time— *time to catch up on the news*, he thought.

He opened the newspaper, but a new text message announced its arrival—from Vlad.

"S lied. Situation worse. Call secure."

He called him.

"They know the location of the safe house."

"How did you figure this out?"

"Probably not good for you to know, *father*." There was a hint of irony in the statement.

Pascal raised an eyebrow. "Father" was not in Vlad's vocabulary—not since the two had first met. His mother, Pascal's tryst in Iceland, had sent him the message that he had a son. Pascal had introduced himself to the young precocious lad that looked like a direct descendant of a Viking warrior. "I am Pascal, you can call me Uncle Pascal if you wish," were the precise words he had used.

"I made the discovery late last night. There was nothing that we could do overnight, so I let it wait to discuss this morning. It was not much to conclude that KRIPOS, the Norwegian investigative team would be involved, including their Detective Superintendent, someone named Hansen. I found a presentation for a conference call that is supposed to occur later today. The rest is … technical."

Completing the call, it was clear to Pascal that Silvio Tosti, his longtime friend of over twenty years since the days at university, was now the ultimate liability. Pascal was shocked and deeply disturbed. It could mean the ruin of the entire operation. Plan B was now the only plan available to them. And it had a new dimension; the hacker now had a name, Frank Becken. That was a gift.

CHAPTER 23

KRIPOS Headquarters
Oslo, Norway
Thursday, 5ᵀᴴ of April
22:02 CET

Finishing up the conversation with SSA Rodriguez, DSI Hansen felt like at least there was a now a chance, a whisper of a chance to save the young girl. The hacker Frank Becken was somewhere headed to Brussels with strict instructions to "check in and wait there until morning." He had also purchased a ticket for him—to depart in the late morning. He now needed to call the assistant to the Justice Minister to provide him the update. And he needed to brief his own boss, but she would have to wait for the update to the Minister.

"The most important thing," he told the Minister's assistant "is that we now have evidence that puts the deputy to the Director General, Mr. Tosti, in our path as a lead suspect, and hopefully on a trail that can be followed leading to Grete. We are also ...," he reported, "keeping the search inside of Norway going, especially in the area around Kristiansand. A copy of the hard drive that Frank had copied from Mr. Tosti has been provided to the FBI forensics team in New York. They are currently conducting an examination to see if there are additional leads and evidence."

He yawned a Cheetah-like yawn, baring teeth, hoping no one was watching him. To say he was bone tired didn't do it justice. He needed a cigarette, a glass of wine, and sleep—in that order. Outside he found Brit Jahn, his boss, also smoking a cigarette before heading home. Hansen was grateful for having Brit, she was everything one could want from a boss—always told the truth, understated expectations instead of exaggerating them, took the blame for the team when things didn't go as planned, and demanded of everyone no more than she was also willing to give. He hoped he was equal to her with his team.

"So, Fredrik, are we getting anywhere?" Fredrik took a long draught on the cigarette. He exhaled and sighed.

"We have a chance, Brit." He called her Brit when they were alone, the formalities dispensed. He explained the rest. The two were on their third cigarettes and already shivering from the cold by the time DSI Hansen had finished. He was wide-awake now. The evening prior he had only slept an hour before he had the first call of the evening. It was now well past midnight. "Time to catch some sleep," he said to her, "I need to be clear-headed for tomorrow." He said goodnight and headed for his car. He had barely started the engine when he got a text message from Frank, "Will be on flight to Brussels in the morning. Not waiting."

PART THREE

Convergence is the coming together of things that were separate. Something happens when they do—converge. The world of information technology and biology, what happens when *they* converge?

CHAPTER 24

OSLO, NORWAY
THURSDAY, 5TH OF APRIL
22:11 CET

Leaving KRIPOS Headquarters, Frank booked the earliest flight to depart in the morning. He thought about going home first, but decided that was a chance he did not need to take, so he headed instead to find an ATM machine, what they called a minibank in Scandinavia, and from there he headed to Gardermoen—the Radisson Blue Hotel there by the airport. Settled into the room, he was tempted to leave the planning to the morning. The bed was inviting him. All he wanted to do was to climb into the clean linen sheets and to forget his troubles for a while. It would be a mistake and he knew it. He needed a plan, something better than to get close to the action. But before he could develop a plan, he needed more information. So he took a shower and got back on his laptop computer and his phone.

It began with calling Jaime.

"Where are you now?"

"At the airport—in a hotel, waiting to catch a flight in the morning to Brussels."

"What time do you arrive?"

Frank hesitated a moment, thinking through how much to reveal.

"Arriving Brussels at ten."

"And then what?"

"That's why I called."

"I see. I have some more information. Just got it. Was going to call you. I'll text you the details after we finish the call. I think it's the address…"

"You mean for where they took her?"

"…Yes. Not a hundred percent certain, but it makes sense. We did a Google Earth look and it fits the profile—the kind of place one would choose."

"How far is it?"

"Not far, just short of an hour's drive from Brussels. Looks like a converted barn."

"What makes you think this is the place?"

"We found a link that came from Tosti's computer to a limo service that picks up at the airport, takes its passengers to the same hotel, and from the hotel to the address. Tosti's been the one who's been ordering the service. Same company each time, same driver, same routine, one such service just yesterday.

Tosti had a link to the limo company in an email that he had saved on his hard drive. We called the limo company and social engineered our way to get the password."

"Can you send me an image of the receipt?"

"Yes, will be on its way shortly."

"What hotel?"

"Le Méridien, City of Brussels."

"Anything more?"

"Yes. It could be unrelated. But…"

"What is it?"

"Remember the call we had last night in Hansen's office?"

"Yes."

"Prior to the call with you, we had another call with the authorities in Europe including Hansen. There were six parties supposed to be on the line and there were seven on the call.

"So they know I'm here?" Frank's stomach did a somersault.

"Not certain, but we have to presume so …"

"How the fuck …?"

"I called Hansen. His computer had a Trojan. Someone else had access to his computer, his email, and calendar. The bridge information for the call was on his calendar." Jaime let that thought sink in a moment.

"You're not the only one who knows social engineering, Frank."

"I'm fucked!"

Jaime saw that Frank had gone to the same conclusion.

"Hold on, Frank. Agreed … we have to assume that whoever that seventh person was, untraceable by the way, heard the whole conversation, the most important part of that being that you were headed in to Brussels. At the time of that call we did not have the precise address. From what we had discussed, they would know that we are close."

"That means they will feel like they still have some time to escape."

"Yes." SSA Rodriguez had to admire how quickly Frank deduced the same key conclusions.

"But also that they will be more cautious. And they'll have time to set a trap."

"Did you send the image of the limo receipt?"

"Yes, it's on its way."

"I think we can turn this into an advantage."

"You mean the limo?"

"Yes."

"That's what I would be doing."

"Okay, anything else?"

Rodriguez heard the question dripping with sarcasm.

"Yes, I guess there is ..."

"Don't tell me there's more?"

"No, it's not like that, just ..." Rodriguez let the sentence hang for a couple of seconds.

"When I was fifteen, I hacked into my high school computer network ..."

"You! You the FBI Agent?" Frank was incredulous.

"Yes—me Frank, me the FBI agent was a bit of a hoodlum when I was young."

"You know why I hacked in, Frank?"

"No, but I'm sure you're going to tell me, Jaime."

"It was for a girl, Frank. For a girl that I loved more than anything! Not for me. To save a girl from some asshole who wanted to destroy her reputation. I would have done anything for her. She's my wife now."

There was silence on the phone.

"Thanks for telling me about the eavesdropping on the conference call. I know that you didn't have to tell me. But you did. Thanks. At least now I know what I am getting myself into." Frank paused.

"You're walking into a heap of trouble."

"Yes, well. It is what it is."

"Okay. You have my number. Call if you need anything. If I get any more news I'll call you."

CHAPTER 25

SERAPHIM BASE OF OPERATIONS
SOMEWHERE IN THE OUTSKIRTS OF BRUSSELS
FRIDAY, 6TH OF APRIL
10:08 CET

Berta was in the den on the first floor. She was finishing stocking up the guest room from the supplies that they kept in the cellar. Rigo was upstairs with Grete. The girl had eaten a breakfast and was in better spirits this morning—thanks to Rigo.

Berta went to the staircase.

"Rigo."

"I'll be down in a minute."

"I'll be down in a minute."

Her phone rang. She seldom received calls unless it was from Tosti, but this number showed as "unknown."

"Hello?"

"Berta?"

"Who is this?"

"This is Pascal, Berta." She walked into the kitchen and sat down at the nearest chair.

"Yes, Monsieur Relo."

"It's the first time we have actually spoken directly, Berta, I understand."

"Yes, sir."

"It is important that you pay close attention. This is an important call, and I need to make sure that you understand everything that I say, and …," he paused, "that you do *exactly* as I tell you. Do you understand?"

"Yes sir, I do."

"Very well. Your master, Silvio Tosti, will be arriving this afternoon. He should be calling you soon. There will not be a guest arriving as had been previously planned. It will actually be Silvio and he will be there on a specific task. You are to assist him in his task, but under no circumstances, is he to know that you spoke with me. That is the first task. Again, I ask you, is this instruction clear?"

"Master Tosti will arrive, I will assist him with his task and I am not to mention this conversation."

"Good. His task is to ensure that the girl, Nikita, the Norwegian girl, is eliminated. You will help him with the first part of that task and when that task is finished, …," he paused, "you will eliminate him; you will eliminate Master Tosti, Berta … tonight."

The phone was silent for a moment. Pascal was letting it sink in.

"Am I clear on that instruction, Berta?"

"Yes sir, I am to assist Master Tosti to eliminate the girl, Nikita, and then I am to eliminate him—tonight. I understand."

"Good. I am sure that I don't need to tell you how to do this. Rigo can help you. There is to be no delay. Once your task is completed, you and Rigo will burn the house down with the bodies of Mr. Tosti and the girl inside, and then you and Rigo are to escape in the RV to a place that will be disclosed to you shortly. You will receive new instructions when you get there." He paused again.

She was stunned, her hands trembling.

"You have been together a long time, you and Master Tosti, right?"

"Yes sir."

"He has failed us, Berta, both you and me. His actions in Norway have compromised us. I can't say more, but there is only one thing that can be done. We have to eliminate Mr. Tosti. You cannot fail in this, Berta. The life of your son depends on it. Am I clear?"

Her hand flew to her mouth to stifle a gasp. Her eyes watered, she tried to pull them back, but they came uncontrollably.

"Yes, sir, you are clear. It will be done as you instructed."

"And one last thing. When this is over, we will not be conducting this kind of operation any longer. You and your son will be employed in something new—no more Nikitas. But that day will not happen if you fail in your task. I need to make that absolutely clear—the life of your son depends on you."

"I understand."

"Good. You have everything you need—yes?"

"We do."

"Discreetly Berta, this must be done so that Master Tosti does not suspect. He trusts you. That is your advantage. The authorities will tie the operation to Mr. Tosti, who is already the prime suspect, and that will be the end of it. You will get a new start."

"Yes, sir, I understand."

"Send me a secure text when it is done."

"I will."

The line went dead. Berta set the phone down, her hands still shaking.

A hand touched her shoulder from the back. It was Rigo. The two of them looked at each other.

"Did you hear?"

"What you said."

He had a look of anguish on his face. She got up and held him, her face wet on his neck.

"He is all I have known, almost all my life," she said, wiping away her tears.

Rigo pulled her away, a look of disgust on his face.

Then he brought her forcibly to his lips. She shrieked, "Rigo, no!"

He released his grip.

"And why not?" he screamed at her. She could see the torment in his face. "Your Master Tosti, he is why I have never kissed a girl, never got to know what it feels like. I am the monster that you and Tosti made me, the one who is left to wonder at the feeling, with only my mother left to experiment with, to show me. But it's not the same thing, is it? You can't teach me about kissing a real girl, one my age. It is not the same experience, is it Mother?"

Berta stayed there transfixed, unable to say a word, the lie she had swallowed and fed to Rigo all the years lay there between them now, naked and unvarnished.

Rigo softened his look.

"Don't worry Mother, I did not mean anything by it. The kiss ..." he hesitated, "I dream of a kiss, but not with you, and not with little girls, with someone my age. I can no longer have that, you see. Because I won't do ... to someone I love ... what you did to me. The kiss was just to show you what you have created."

He turned around and started up the stairs, stopped and came back to the kitchen. "But just so you know, you will kill that bastard Tosti. I will help you. Time to make a choice." He left those words hanging in the air as they prepared for Tosti's arrival.

CHAPTER 26

LE MERIDIEN HOTEL
CITY OF BRUSSELS, BELGIUM
FRIDAY, 6TH OF APRIL
11:15 CET

Frank was seated at a corner table inside Le Méridien's restaurant, the same hotel where Jim Wong had been the day prior. This was part of his plan. He was drinking his third cup of coffee, contrasting the brilliant clear sky outside the restaurant with the outlook for what was still to come. A waiter came by.

"Will there be anything else, Monsieur?" He looked like all the other waiters at the fancy hotels, perfectly outfitted in black pants and a white shirt, perfect manners.

"Yes, can I order a breakfast? I know it's late ..."

"Very well, Monsieur, that is not a problem. What would you like?"

Frank ordered the eggs sunny side up, croissants, salmon, potatoes, a fried tomato and bacon.

"I will bring you more coffee, yes?"

"Yes, thank you." Frank got up and headed to the bathroom. Breakfast was his favorite meal—when he had time to indulge in a meal that wasn't just a Red Bull. In the bathroom he had a moment to see himself in the mirror, to reflect again on the man that looked back at him. It satisfied. That is all he felt; apprehension, fear even, but for too many years he had not liked what the reflection in the mirror told him. He went back to the restaurant, sat down and waited. At this moment, what he had was time, time to refuel the demands of his body for nutrition, time to think through the plan that had developed the night before and on the flight, when he spoke first with the FBI agent, SSA Jaime Rodriguez and afterwards with Monika.

Frank had bought some time by providing The Voice an update: "code loaded, waiting for access." The Voice had responded with his own text message, one letter, the capital V, which meant it was acknowledged, nothing more. It often took a week or more for a mark to access their websites, so this was not unusual.

The limousine would be arriving in an hour as he had requested. The company dispatcher had been very accommodating on the phone—and did not ask too many questions. They were paid well to ask few questions. Frank smiled at the breakfast being served by the young waiter.

"Bon Appetit, Monsieur."

"Merci," Frank dug in.

His hunger sated, he started to feel better, to see his surroundings, all the well-dressed people going about their business, and to breathe in the air outside. The doors had been opened. Yesterday's deluge had gone, and in its place was the cleansing air that follows the heavy rains. It was promising to be an uncertain day, but the moment could be appreciated for its calming effect.

The overnight stay at the hotel in Oslo had served its purpose—had given him time to rest his mind and to think. The flight had now taken him closer to where he needed to be. In his sleep, a semblance of a plan had started to form. On the flight it had taken more shape—just enough to start to rebuild his confidence. He would figure out the rest as he went along. That's how it always worked, anyway. Social engineering needed an adaptable mind, not one needing to work out all the details in advance.

SSA Rodriguez's team had broken the encryption and gained access to the contents of the hard drive. They had found the address to the house by following the connection to the limousine company. That was about all the information he had. He needed more but it would have to do for now.

The caffeine was working, but was also fueling an anxiety about whether it was too late to do anything for Grete, about what he was walking into, and about the NoSaints. On that last point he had decided to leave it all in Monika's hands. She had told him that he needed to concentrate on one thing and one thing alone. He recalled the conversation.

"I'll talk to The Voice. You just focus on the girl."

"I don't want to involve you. You don't know these people, Monika."

"Actually, I do, and besides, I am already involved. Getting involved is not up to you, Frank. That's my decision."

A ping came across his phone to break his reverie of their conversation the night prior. It contained a number for him to call. He dialed it while beckoning the waiter for the bill.

The phone was picked up on the first ring.

"Rodriguez."

"Jaime?"

"Frank?"

"Yes, it's me. You got something else?"

"We do. Hansen will be arriving there in the afternoon linking up with the Belgian Federal Police. Once he does that, ..." he paused for a second, "no telling how this will play out. My guess is the Belgiques won't delay acting. That's the good news and the bad news."

"You mean that they may tip off the kidnappers?"

"Yes. It's not that they won't be competent; just that everything we know about this group tells me that they have tripwires in place. All it will take is for the Belgian police to trip one of the sensors, one alert and its over—they will take whatever actions are necessary to get rid of the evidence and cover their tracks. You know that don't you?"

"I do. A hacker can only be bested by another hacker, the others will just be fumbling."

"That's what I'm saying." There was a long pause on the line as both men thought through the implications of what they just discussed.

"Do you have a plan?"

"I do."

"Another thing, once you get into the house, whatever you can find that will give us more evidence will be helpful. There is more to this group than what we know right now."

"Will do."

"Let us know if there is anything else we can do from here. We're going to start looking at other aspects of this group."

"Thanks, Jaime. Hey, I do have one question."

"Sure."

"Does this mean that I'm a deputy FBI Agent?"

Frank heard some laughter in the background.

"We call it G-Man. You will be an honorary G-man if you pull this off, Frank, that's for sure. Good luck. Keep us posted."

"Okay, wish me luck."

"Good luck, Frank."

"There is one more thing, Jaime ..."

"Yes, Frank?"

"Please take me off the speaker."

"Okay, it's just you and me."

"There is a woman in Oslo, like your Caro. Her name is Monika. If I don't make it back, tell her, please tell her ... tell her that my last words and thoughts were of her, that I love her. She will be embarrassed, but I don't want to leave this world without her knowing. Will you do that for me, Jaime?"

Jaime was about to say the expected, that Frank would be able to tell her these things himself, but he remembered what Frank had asked when they first spoke.

"I will Frank. I will tell her exactly. And I hope I don't have to—that you get to tell her yourself. Deal?"

"Deal."

Frank went outside to wait for the limousine. It was already there. He got in and the driver took off without hesitation and without any conversation.

CHAPTER 27

SILVIO TOSTI'S APARTMENT
BRUSSELS, BELGIUM
FRIDAY, 6TH OF APRIL
12:24 CET

In his apartment suite in the City of Brussels, not more than a few miles away from the hotel that Frank had used for the limo pickup, Silvio Tosti was gathering his own set of things to take with him and thinking through his next action. He was drinking his third cup of coffee while packing trying to clear the pounding in his head. Tosti had come to his own set of conclusions. He had called Pascal several times the night before needing to get reassurance, to know that Pascal was still on his side. Pascal was the only real friend he had in the world. He had called him on his private mobile number until he lost count.

It happened the same way each time, on the seventh ring a digital voice came on, "Leave a message …" is all it said, and the line had gone dead. Pascal always picked up on this phone. That he didn't pick up told Silvio volumes.

Silvio felt something he had not experienced since the day when he sat with the family attorney in Bologna, Italy, as a young man. He felt alone—completely. His hands trembled. The brandy multiplied the effect of abandonment that he felt—and rage.

The attorney in Bologna had told him. The life of luxury he had lived as the son of the super-wealthy Italian engine-manufacturing magnate was over. His parents had left him nothing. They were both dead, caught up in the millstone of the war—the family fortune had been lost in the political upheaval that had seen Il Duce, the fascist, Mussolini, come into power in Italy. It did little good that he was the only heir. All that remained, according to the family attorney, was a small bank account that had been preserved in his name. It had enough funds to give him a start; to start to build a career. The playboy life was over.

The eighteen-year-old Silvio Tosti had gone outside the attorney's office, had started his red Maserati and drove it straight to a dealership. And he drove out in a red Fiat 128, plus the difference in cash. He had decided then and there. There would not be any tears. He would never trust anyone again, and he would rebuild his fortune.

The moment of reverie passed. He realized that he had made a mistake. He had trusted Pascal. But there was one other in his life.

In the morning Tosti called Berta's mobile number. As the phone rang, he had a swell of emotion about her that he never knew existed, that maybe had always been there, just suppressed within his ambition to succeed.

"Master Tosti?" The way she said it swung the pendulum of emotions in his head to a different feeling —ecstasy.

"Yes, Berta, it is Silvio."

It had been a long time since he had addressed himself to her with his first name. It had been back when they first met and the two had spent all those glorious days and nights in bed, exploring things she had never known were possible, not with a young, uninhibited man. Her sexual experiences had always been with older men who expended their fire in a few minutes of sweaty exertion and then it was over, not a caress, not a thank you, just a coin or two for her troubles.

"Our guest was supposed to arrive but plans have changed. He will not be joining us. I will be arriving late this afternoon. We have much to talk about and much to do."

He paused for a second and then continued, "It's been too long, Berta, you and I, talking—really taking the time to talk and gather the situation. That's what we need to do now. I expect to arrive there around five. Can you have dinner ready for just the two of us—an early dinner? Ask Rigo to give us some time."

"Yes, of course." She hesitated a moment. "Not the pills?"

"No, not the pills. No more pills for me!" he said with some satisfaction. "In fact, I would like my favorite, foie gras. Can you prepare foie gras and ... also a bottle of champagne, the Besserat de Bellefon?"

"I will have it ready for you. Would you like to use the guest room, Master Tosti?" Berta had reverted back to the familiar role being obedient, he noted. "It would take time to change that," he thought.

Silvio's heart lifted, "Yes, that would be quite welcome, actually. Until this evening then?"

"Yes, Master Tosti."

"No—no more master. I am Silvio to you."

"Yes ... Mas," She caught herself. "Yes ...Silvio."

"Ciao, Berta"

"Ciao ... Silvio." He ended the call.

"I still have a friend," he thought, "and even a lover? She has always been there, neglected, but always there, still there."

Tosti finished packing his papers with a renewed energy. He packed a suitcase and opened the safe in the closet to gather his money in the different denominations that he kept there— just for the occasion that was now before him. Looking around the room Tosti realized that he felt elated. It was not the feeling he had expected leaving behind the titles and the promise of even greater power with Pascal. He also took his other passport, the Italian one that he kept current under an alias. "It's time to initiate his plan B," he thought.

He looked around at the luxury suite in the upscale apartment complex and realized that there was nothing left inside that he really needed—that was not already in his valise and in his suitcase. He still had his secret bank accounts, and there was enough money in those accounts that he could start over. The money would be able to replace anything that he left behind.

First, he needed to see Berta and take care of the loose ends that would chase him like a vicious dog around the world if he had not prepared for this very day. He had always suspected that someday this contingency would be necessary. Now that it was here, he was prepared. It all depended on the small external hard drive that he kept—the one that was worth a thousand times its weight in gold—the one that gave him leverage. The bastard Vlad had not been so smart after all. Tosti smiled to himself and walked out of the apartment headed for his car, the Audi A6 that he now preferred to the Fiat of his youth.

CHAPTER 28

GENERAL DIRECTORATE JUDICIAL POLICE
CITY OF BRUSSELS, BELGIUM
FRIDAY, 6TH OF APRIL
13:01 CET

DSI Hansen was in the office of his counterpart, Louis Betón, the Deputy to the Director General of the Judicial Police in Belgium. The two of them were getting a cup of espresso from the cantina.

They knew each other, had shared leads in pursuing past cases and suffered through few successes and far too many failures. With time they had also learned to trust each other.

"I have an address," he said.

"So why are we not going there right now?"

"We are. I just got the address. It is not far from where the body of the young Spanish girl was found."

"Fredrik."

"Yes, Louis."

"You know what happened here in Belgium in 2001—right? The girls ..."

"I do," Hansen interrupted, "like what happened in Norway in 2011 with Anders Breivik."

"Precisely. It cannot be that we know something and have not acted. I get the feeling, my friend, that you have not told me everything."

The big burly man's temper was starting to flare. The members of the force called him "Gerard," as in Gerard Depardieu, because he was the spitting image of the French Actor.

"I will tell you everything—in the car. Now we have to go in. We need to have a big presence Louis, to block every possible exit."

"I have twenty cars ready to go. They have the assignment. We are handling this entirely as a federal case. The local force will be invited to help handle the street blockades. Here, put this on."

The two men put on their coats with the word *Policie* emblazoned across the back and front while they walked the stairs down to the garage. They mounted the DG's white and blue police car.

Pulling out of the garage, the Deputy Director General spoke into his handset and a parade of cars made their way out of Brussels into the countryside.

DSI Hansen's phone rang.

"Hansen?"

"Yes, this is he."

"Frank should be getting there soon. Are you headed in?"

"Yes we are. I'm in the car with my counterpart, Louis Betón of the Belgian Federal Police. There is a convoy of cars headed that way."

"Hurry, Frank won't wait."

"Understood. And so you understand ..." as he looked at his friend the Deputy DG, who was glaring back at him, "... once we get there, the police will be heading straight in. There is nothing that will stop them. They won't care about a politician."

"Yes, I understand, it's out of our hands now."

"Let's hope that he has success."

The car holding the two senior law enforcement bosses was weaving through the Brussels late afternoon traffic. Deputy DG Betón was trying to concentrate while glaring at his long-time friend.

"You ready to tell me what's up, how you come into my country and hold back on me about a crime? And who is *he*? You are testing our friendship, Fredrik."

DSI Hansen told him everything. The Deputy DG pushed the pedal to the floor, barking orders on the radio to hurry.

CHAPTER 29

OSLO AIRPORT
NORTH OF OSLO, NORWAY
FRIDAY, 6TH OF APRIL
13:25 CET

On a United Airlines Boeing 777, two harried passengers were hurried off the airplane and into a waiting KRIPOS police car. The tall, elegant woman in her late forties and her distinguished husband got into the back seat and spoke by telephone with the grandparents. Mrs. Enberg burst into tears again, as she had repeatedly since they had learned the horrible news aboard the cruise liner. Arriving back home, there was some news from the grandparents, but not the news they had hoped for.

"No news is good news, darling. Hold strong, for her, for Grete. Be brave for her, dear."

Mrs. Enberg wiped away her tears and tried to put on a brave face. The Police Inspector in the front passenger seat turned around to face them.

She had the most earnest face she could put on, trying as best she could to convey the caution of her update.

"You must not read anything into this more than what I am going to tell you, Mr. and Mrs. Enberg. They know where she is ..."

A gasp escaped Mrs. Enberg's lips. She was unable to bear the next words that came from the mouth of the inspector. Her husband held her about her shoulders. "Tell us Inspector, the simple truth, just tell us."

"Grete is in a place outside of Brussels, in Belgium. We don't know if she is alive. We have no news on her condition, only that the police are in route, to include our own Detective Superintendent, DSI Hansen."

She reached out to Mrs. Enberg, woman to woman, and held her close. She whispered in her ear, "It is easy to say this, I know, but, if you can, ...be brave Mrs. Enberg. If anyone can find her and bring her back safely, it is our beloved Inspector."

Excerpt from the Case File from DSI Hansen

Friday, 6 April

Arrived Brussels late morning, met with Deputy Director General of the Belgian Federal Police—D-DG Louis Betón. FBI in NYC with SSA Rodriguez updated. They are working the forensics of the copy of the hard drive. They found the address of the house where we believe they were taking the girls, including the child Grete Enberg. Mr. Silvio Tosti of the Director General of ECFIN continues to be our prime person of interest. He had accomplices. A woman who did the abduction and at least one other sus-pect—undetermined yet. Investigating video and other data from border control. D-DG Betón was ready with a force to get to the target location. Briefed him. Force departed. Found out from SSA Rodriguez that Becken had arrived Brussels and had proceeded to the target location.

CHAPTER 30

On the Way to Paradijs Street
55 Km North of Brussels, Belgium
Friday, 6ᵀᴴ of April
12:22 CET

The black Mercedes limousine was the same vehicle that had picked up Jim Wong. It was just the right symmetry of power and luxury with a wide range of conveniences; a harbor from the worries of the day or a private office on wheels, with all the necessary communications accouterments.

An internal glass partition between the front and back seats provided additional privacy. Frank was alone in the back with his thoughts as they travelled through the quaint Belgian countryside approaching their destination. He pushed back the urge to think through the plan in greater detail. In any case, the information he had was all there was. Experience told him that the best preparation he could have was his own well-developed ability to improvise. Frank had survived this far on his wits; knowing when to go with the flow was as important as knowing when to be audacious. Right now he needed to go with the flow, come what may.

He thought some on Monika, but decided that now was not the time. Instead, he decided to think about the little girl named Grete. Grete is what made him sure. Whenever he thought about her, he was certain. This is what he was meant to do. It might only be one time, and he was likely to fail, but he had to try. It was the only certainty he had in his life. Frank was going to chase this down until whatever end fate gave him.

The driver had made this run many a time without incident. Guests of Mr. Silvio Tosti traveling in the limousine never spoke to him, conversation was not expected and certainly not welcome. In less than an hour after picking up his guest, the driver made a right turn onto Paradijs Street. It was the last five hundred meters of the ride.

⋏

In Reykjavik, an alarm pinged on Vlad's computer and kept pinging away. It was programmed to continue nonstop until Vlad turned it off. It had one purpose.

There were two discreetly placed laser tripwires on the side of Paradijs Street, one for each end of the road that ran east to west. Anyone walking, riding a bike or driving a car down this road would unknowingly interrupt the laser signal and the alarm would start to ping away unceasingly. Whoever it might be that was on this road was either headed to the safe house or was very lost.

Vlad walked from his kitchen with the wide-open view of the bay. It was another gray dreary day. He headed back to his command post. That's how he thought of it. He sat in the ergonomically designed hi-tech chair and turned the alarm off. Six displays staged in two rows, three to a row allowed him to monitor various functions all at the same time. The upper center display provided a continuous stream of CCTV video from the camera placed on the roof of the converted barn. It showed a black limousine. He wondered why Tosti had decided to ride the limo. He usually took his own car.

⚓

"I should bill this to the same account, sir?"

Frank answered, "Yes." He looped his backpack over one shoulder getting ready to exit.

"There's a button on the back of my seat, sir. It should be lit red. Please push it to speak. The light will turn green." Frank did as suggested.

He repeated the answer. "Yes, same procedure."

"Very good, sir. Will you require a return pick up?"

"No, not for the moment. We will call you if needed."

"Very good, sir."

⚓

Vlad adjusted the joystick to keep the camera centered on the limousine. He leaned back in the chair and saw the dark vehicle pull into the driveway of the house. A lean, tall man wearing a gray hoodie got out, his face masked by the hood of the jacket. This was not Tosti. Tosti would never wear a hoodie. He dialed Tosti's number.

⚔

Inside the house, Rigo and Berta were still packing the suitcases, each in their first floor rooms on the backside of the building. They heard a loud knock on the front door. Berta came out into the hallway, finding Rigo already there.

They looked at each other. "I didn't expect him so soon," she said. "If it's not Tosti, then who could it be?"

"Don't know."

"Silvio is still half an hour away, unless ..." Berta left the statement unfinished.

"I'll find out." Rigo headed down the hallway to the front entrance."

"Wait!" Rigo turned around. Berta was holding a gun in her hand. She held it by the barrel, with her arm extended like she was making an offer. He looked up to his mother with a curious look on his face.

"I didn't ..." She interrupted him, "Don't read anything into this, Rigo." She handed him the Glock 17 weapon with the full clip and a silencer attached.

"Master Tosti told me to get it from the safe." She gave it to him.

"Just in case," she said. "Hide it. And be careful. If it's Master Tosti, then let me know right away so I can meet him."

Rigo nodded. There was a second knock on the door, louder this time.

Rigo stepped through the hallway and into the atrium that served as the reception area when guests came to visit. He went to open the door when he heard Berta's phone ring.

He half opened the door, placing his left foot behind it to act as a backstop. His left hand was also behind the door, holding the Glock. Rigo didn't know what to make of the man standing there, wearing a hoodie. For the briefest of moments the two of them looked at each other with the curious notion of seeing themselves—like a reflection.

"Yes?"

"My name is Frank."

"And how can I help you? Are you lost?"

Frank knew that he couldn't waver, not now. "I'm here for Grete and to make a trade."

"I see. You are lost. I know of no ...Grete, did you say?"

Frank could see that either Jaime had been completely wrong about the address or whoever it was that was inside this house was a good poker player. He pressed on.

Frank had practiced the speech in his head. "The police are coming." It came out whiny.

Rigo stared at him. "What are you talking about?"

Frank found his voice. "If you let me have her ... you can escape now and I will turn her over to them." He continued. "I am not a policeman. But the police *are* coming. When they get here it will be too late. I only want to get Grete back to her parents."

Frank expected to see anger or fear from the young man standing in front of him. A smile, he didn't expect. The perfect poker player.

Rigo opened the door fully and pulled out the gun. He pointed it at Frank, motioning for him to come inside.

Frank sighed. This had been his whole plan. He stepped through the transom.

He put his hands up and walked into the foyer, following Rigo into what served as an anteroom. He saw a kitchen to the left and a living room to the right.

Berta came in from behind a wall. She sized up the situation.

"He knows about Grete," Rigo said.

"Hmm. And I just got a call from Master Tosti. His name is Frank. Master Tosti knows him. Says he's the reason we're leaving."

"What now?"

"He said to take him to the garage. He wants us to tie him up and wait until he gets here, which is in about twenty minutes. After we get him secure, we'll continue to pack."

"Okay. This guy says the police are coming."

"Master Tosti said nothing about that. But he wants to leave as soon as he gets here—'don't want to be here any longer than necessary,' were his words."

"Okay. I'll take care of it. You keep on packing, Mother. I'll tie him up and rejoin you."

Frank was breaking out in a cold sweat. Experience had taught him to keep the initiative. He broke in on the conversation. "You should listen to what I'm telling you. You have to get out now…"

Rigo swirled around with an upper cut that landed on Frank's solar plexus. Frank keeled over onto his knees, gasping for air. The punch caught him by surprise, expelling the air in his lungs.

Berta bent down to look closer at the man called Frank that had been the cause of why they were now packing. "He doesn't look like much," she said.

She got back up. "Tie him well, Rigo. We can't let him escape. Silvio wants to deal with this himself."

Rigo grabbed Frank by the back of his hoodie and pushed him past the kitchen and into the hallway that served as mudroom and utility room for the washer and dryer. He stopped.

"Sit down on the floor. With your back against the dryer."

Frank was only too eager to obey. He was just getting his breathing back to normal. The NoSaints had trained him well. All it took was a bit of physical pain and Frank complied. Whatever bravado he had puffed himself up with in the limo was gone. He looked around the room, his head still spinning.

This had been the sum total of his entire plan. There was nothing to improvise with or on. Frank took stock of his situation. That bastard Tosti will arrive and he will shoot me, they will escape with Grete, the police will arrive to find another dead victim and nothing else. I will not see Monika again, not ever. He started to hyperventilate.

He didn't know why, but all of a sudden, he had only one thought left in his brain. "Monika," he said out loud.

"What?"

"Nothing." Frank looked entirely despondent.

"Now take off your jacket, drop your backpack and empty your pockets. Turn the pockets inside out."

Frank continued to do as he was told. He recovered his composure—thought he would give the plan another try. It couldn't hurt.

Out of his pockets came his wallet with his identification card and the money he had been able to get out of the cash machine prior to boarding the flight. There was also his mobile phone.

Rigo searched through the backpack and found a newspaper from Norway. Grete's picture was on the front page. There was also a phone charger, a bottle of water and a can of Red Bull. He took Frank's phone and put it in the backpack.

"They don't know about you ... whatever your name is. They, the police, only know about this guy Tosti ..."

He looked him in the eye. Frank's breathing slowed. It looked like Rigo was hearing him. Rigo nodded.

And then he shot him, in the gut. And he fired again—and again.

The silencer muted the sound of the three shots, but Berta heard it as the round exited muscle tissue and entered the thin metal skin of the washing machine. She heard it and came running into the mudroom.

"What happened?" she yelled. Frank was on the floor laid out flat. There was blood all over his t-shirt. This wasn't like in the movies.

CHAPTER 31

SILVIO TOSTI'S AUDI A6
187 KM/H ON HIGHWAY A12 HEADING NORTH, BELGIUM
FRIDAY, 6ᵀᴴ OF APRIL
13:09 CET

Tosti ended the call with Berta and accelerated the Audi. He now had less time than what he had thought. His mind was racing as fast as his car. He wondered how the hell that bastard Frank from the hotel in Oslo found out about the house and its address? He did not want to think about the receipt at the limo website. "No way he could have found that receipt, that needle in a haystack, broken the password and found the address," he thought. Tosti was trying to convince himself.

"Fuck!" he yelled out loud. A drop of perspiration leaked down the side of his face. He pushed the button on his steering wheel that controlled the air-conditioning in the car.

It triggered a memory of Bangkok over twenty-four years back when he and Pascal had roamed carefree, two young men with their futures bright, their escapades bonding a friendship. "It's our time, Silvio. Fuck the old aristocrats!" Tosti had been driving the old British Land Rover in the lush Thailand countryside through a mud road dodging the rain filled potholes. The two of them were drenched in sweat, no air conditioning, and loving every minute of life. He let his mind wander; he smiled.

"Yeah, fuck the old aristocrats!" Tosti had replied. Looking to his left, he remembered the intense look on Pascal's face. Tosti had asked him, "Why do we need to fuck the old aristocrats?" Pascal's face had gone from deadly serious to schoolboy laughter at the image. Tosti would always remember. They had gone there as colleagues, Pascal insisting on paying for everything.

It was in Bangkok in the evenings where they had gone exploring the underside of the densely populated city to find that their Belgian francs were able to buy anything—including the services of young girls. He remembered the conversation like it was yesterday: "They just *look* young, Silvio, they're actually already of age. Don't be prissy. And besides, I have big plans for us." They had gone back to Bangkok many times. And the friendship had become a bond—like brothers.

Tosti fought back the growing emotion of betrayal he now felt and the anger brewing inside of him.

The GPS said that he was ten minutes from his destination. His mind came back to the task at hand. He was planning on the fly. One after another plan that he considered in his head had its fatal flaw. He thought about keeping the girl as a hostage, but realized that escape would be greatly more complicated. Traveling the roads of Europe with a young girl, while trying to stay undetected would not be easy.

He came to a conclusion, *stick to the original plan, just make it happen faster.* Tosti started to calm himself down, thinking more logically.

He shifted next to think about Frank. "If Frank is already there, then the police could not be far behind." He wracked his brain to find a silver lining in the whole mess. Maybe there's a way to divert the investigation; pin all of this on Frank, he thought. I would need Vlad's help to create the electronic fingerprints. That wasn't going to happen. He hit the steering wheel with the palm of his hand. The droplets of perspiration kept slivering down his face.

His phone rang. It was Berta.

"Berta?"

"Yes, it's me."

"Is everything in place?"

"Yes, but that's not why I am calling ..." She hesitated.

"What is it Berta?"

"Rigo shot the man. He's dead. He had tried to escape, there was a fight and Rigo shot him."

"What! Wait a minute ... actually ... that's okay—that's actually not bad news. Means that he won't be any trouble when I get there. Tell Rigo good work. I should be there in less than ten minutes. Do you have the benzene can ready?"

"Yes."

"Hold on a minute." Tosti was thinking clearly now. Having Frank there in the house was a god-send. It would cause some confusion in the case—with the media—that the police would not be able to explain away—not without implicating themselves in a botched effort. If the girl died in the same place as Frank, and if the press learned of this, then the whole thing would be about the incompetent police. He could pin the whole thing on Frank the hacker and the police."

"And the girl?"

"Still the same, Rigo has her calmed down."

"Well, it won't matter anymore whether she's calmed down or not. We're leaving as soon as I get there and we take care of things. See you soon, my love."

Tosti was starting to see a way out of the tangle that had been the feeling of betrayal, and the collapse of all the plans they had been working on. His heart soared, now for a good reason.

A wave of emotion also rose in Berta's heart. Love, that's a word that Master Tosti—Silvio—had never used before, not with her. For the first time in more than twenty years she started to feel, to have a sense of a future, to think that there was more than servitude to the relationship. Berta's step lightened. She was walking on air. She made up her mind. She would tell Silvio about Pascal's call, about the betrayal. Berta was casting her lot with Silvio come what may.

"Ciao Silvio."

"Ciao Berta."

CHAPTER 32

THE HOUSE
FRIDAY, 6TH OF APRIL
13:14 CET

Berta was in the kitchen. She finished loading the food into the cooler that they would take with them. They would not be eating at restaurants, not until they got to their destination and took on their new identities.

"I'm going to get Grete ready." Rigo started to head to the stairs when Berta grabbed him by the arm.

"She's not going to be making the trip with us, Rigo." She looked into his eyes, pleading for him to understand. She held him closer. "We're going to be starting a new life as a family, together, but we can't take the girl with us. She is just like all the others. You understand, don't you?"

He looked at her, as impassively as he could. "Sure," he said, then broke away heading to the stairs.

Berta smiled back at him and let him go. Rigo took the short flight of stairs in a few bounds and lightly tapped on the door. He put his ear to the door but heard nothing. He turned the key and let himself in. Grete was in the bed asleep, curled up with her rag dog tucked under her arms.

He walked to the bathroom and pulled out Grete's clothes from a towel closet, the ones she had been wearing when they found her in Kristiansand. He came out and sat down on the edge of the bed with his back blocking the view of the video camera.

"Grete, Grete, wake up." He gently shook her by the shoulder. She roused from her sleep. Rigo could see the streaks of teardrops that had dried on her cheek. He touched them gently.

She sat up, wiping the sleep from her eyes with the back of her hand.

"I dreamed of my mother." Her eyes watered and the edges of her mouth turned up. She started to cry again.

"Shshsh, no, no, don't cry, Grete." He brought her to his chest, wrapping his arms around her and rocking her back and forth. "There's no more need to cry, not anymore."

He used the sleeve of his shirt to dry her tears. "You will see your mother soon. I promise, Grete." He said it all in a whisper, so only she could hear.

He let go of her and the tears stopped. A small sob escaped her lips. Her Le Petit Prince was still tucked away under her arm.

"You are very brave."

She looked at him. "What do you mean?"

"What I mean is that you don't need to cry because you *will* see your mother, not just in your dreams, Grete. That is my promise."

"But you broke your first promise, Mister Rigo." Her eyes swelled again.

"Yes, I did," he told her. "And so I made another promise to myself after that one. I promised myself that I would never lie to you again. The difference is that now you are my friend. I cannot lie to my friend." His own eyes started to swell.

"Are we friends, Mister Rigo?"

"Yes, we are. You are my friend. Can I tell you a little secret?"

Grete let go a small smile. She loved secrets.

"I have never had a friend. You are my first and only friend."

She scrunched her lips trying to understand. She thought all grownups had friends, lots of them.

He wasn't talking to a child any longer. There was earnestness in his question like she was the only person in the world that mattered now. "Will you be my friend, Grete?"

"Okay. I will be your friend."

Rigo smiled.

"Good. But now you need to go to the bathroom and put some clothes on. I laid them out there for you. When you come out, I will not be here. I will be downstairs getting everything ready for you. There is a man downstairs. He will take you to your mother. His name is ... Rodrigo—like my name, only longer. I am going to ask you to wait for him. Make sure that you have your shoes on and also your coat. I asked him to come here. Do you understand?"

She looked puzzled. Her eyes welled up again. "I thought *you* were going to take me to her, Mister Rigo."

"No, that is not what I promised. I promised God that I would take care of you. I did not promise that I would be the one taking you to your mother. Remember?" He smiled at her.

"But I will keep my promise. You will see your mother. Won't that make you happy?"

"Yes." She lunged at him with her rag dog clutched in one hand and wrapped her arms around his neck. Rigo didn't know what to do. He patted her back.

"It's okay now. We have to keep this a secret between us. There's a man looking from a camera and we can't let him know." He pulled her arms off from him, gently. The two were facing each other, only inches away. She dried her eyes with the knuckles of her hands.

"I understand." She kissed him on the cheek. Rigo had to fight off his own tears.

Grete jumped off the bed and went to the bathroom. Rigo watched her go in and exited the room.

Outside the door to the room, he put his head against its wooden frame and wiped away the tears that could not be held back. He heard the garage door opening.

Tosti had arrived.

He went down the stairs catching sight of the back of Berta as she headed through the mudroom into the garage. Frank was still lying there where he had last left him, his t-shirt drenched wet with blood. Rigo followed Berta out through the door to the garage.

The converted barn that was now a house at one end and a garage on the other was large enough to hold three vehicles. In the first bay was the Mercedes Sprint RV and now the Audi A6 sat alongside it in the second bay.

Silvio Tosti got out of the car. Berta was there, waiting for him, her hands clasped in front of her.

He exited the car, went to her and then kissed her briefly on the lips. Berta put her hands to her face. She could smell the stench of the alcohol from his breath mixed with sweat. He whispered something in her ear. Rigo saw her blush. And then he saw that Tosti also had a gun—the same kind as he had in the small of his back, under his jacket.

"Where is he?" Tosti addressed the question to Rigo. Rigo pointed behind him—with his head. Tosti walked around the RV and up the steps from the garage into the mudroom. There he saw the figure of Frank lying on his left side on the floor, his legs stretched out to his front, his back against the dryer.

"Where did you shoot him?"

Rigo was standing behind Tosti. Berta was at the head of the stairs inside the mudroom.

"In the gut. Three times."

"Good. I wanted the pleasure for myself, but dead is dead."

He kicked Frank in the thigh for good measure. Tosti was waiving the Glock like he was holding a knife. Frank groaned and Tosti got startled looking back at Rigo. "I thought you said he was dead?" Rigo just stared back.

Tosti got a grin on his face. Then he brought the gun up with both hands in a straight line. He aimed the gun at Frank to satisfy an urge to pull the trigger on the man who, dead or not, had precipitated the whole series of events that forced them to abandon the house. The sound of gunfire at close quarters reverberated like a lightning bolt striking nearby. Berta jumped and instinctively brought her hands to her ears.

Tosti dropped the Glock. It fell with a clatter on the tile floor. He stumbled forward, his torso folded in half. Berta shrieked. She tried holding him up. His full weight leaned into the washing machine, pushing it backwards a few centimeters while making a screeching sound as the legs of the machine scraped along the ceramic tile. It kept him from falling further.

Tosti tried to straighten himself by gripping the top of the white washing machine. His hands slick wet with his own blood made a shocking contrast of blood red on the porcelain-white machine. Half bent over, he turned around to see Rigo's own Glock still smoking from the barrel. His face was ashen white. Tosti couldn't hold himself upright anymore. He stumbled to the floor, lying on his side next to Frank. Berta had stopped shrieking. She found a towel and gave it to Tosti. He looked at it and back at Berta like he was uncertain what it was for.

"No, no! What have you done?" Berta looked at Rigo as her eyes filled with tears and confusion. "He's your father! What have you done?" she shrieked.

"He shot me. Fuckin' Rigo shot me, that's what he's done!" Tosti choked out the words as he looked for his gun on the floor that he had dropped. Rigo kicked Tosti's Glock out of the way. He could see a spittle of blood foaming around Tosti's mouth as he groaned from the pain.

"What the fuck?" Tosti looked up to Rigo, the pain like nothing he had ever experienced. He threw up, a yellow-green watery gruel mixed with the dark red blood spraying against the opposite wall of the hallway in the mudroom and on the tile. Tosti tried again—screaming, and managed to get half way up.

He went back to his knees and fell to the floor, squirming and screaming from the pain. Berta sat down on her side with her hands in a frenzy, needing to do something. But there was nothing to do. She looked up to where Rigo stood transfixed to the spot, his two hands gripping the Glock like he was still ready to shoot. His face was a mask of loathing for the only man that he had ever really known.

He spoke slowly. "You may think this is pain, Master Tosti, *father.*" Rigo's face was a conflict of emotions. His hatred of the man that *was* his father was plain to see. "Pain is a relative thing." he said. "This is nothing. You don't know what's coming."

Berta stood up; her hands and blouse were covered in Tosti's blood. She faced Rigo, who had his back against the wall. She wiped her tears with the back of her hand. "What have you done?" she asked him again. Rigo didn't answer. She slapped him.

Rigo's face showed the red handprint of Tosti's blood where Berta had slapped him. He cleaned himself with his sleeve and punched her in the gut—the same as he had punched Frank.

She folded, gasping for air. Rigo pushed her down next to Tosti, who was still looking for a position that would lessen the pain. He put his weight on his left side, away from where the bullet had entered his torso. Tosti was moaning from the unbearable pain, holding his back with one hand, the other on the floor trying to lighten the weight on his hip. The bullet had lodged in his back.

Berta slowly recovered her breathing, but Rigo already had her legs strapped together with plastic tie-downs. He took her hands and placed them together. She resisted but Rigo was too strong. He wrapped the plastic strap around her wrists and pulled it tight through the ribbed square hole. She just looked at him, her mind lightheaded and nauseous.

The body of Frank Becken was on the gray-tiled floor to the right of Tosti, who could barely keep himself seated.

Frank lay there motionless; looking very much the dead possum. He took in the whole scene, starting to get the sense that there was still hope for him, and maybe even Grete.

Rigo bent down in front of Frank's body. "Get up," he told him. Berta's mouth dropped, as Frank obliged, straightening up with a groan. He found a dishcloth that was there in the washroom to stem the flow of blood still seeping from the bullet wound.

"Was this necessary?" Frank asked, putting pressure on the wound with his hand, not really meaning to get a response.

"Would you have preferred that Tosti here," he motioned with his head down to where Tosti was still struggling on the floor, "put a bullet in your head?"

Frank didn't answer.

"First tie down Tosti with these." He gave Frank another pair of plastic tie-downs. "Clean yourself up. There's some tape in the bathroom around the corner from the hall that you can use to hold a bandage in place. There's also a clean shirt in there. Put that on and come back. I'll tell you what's next. Frank did as he was told.

Berta was starting to recover. She looked over at Tosti and ran a hand of tender caress over his face. He was delirious with the pain, groaning, his body wet with perspiration, his face like the washing machine behind him, a contrast of red on white pale skin. Berta looked back to Rigo, who was staring at her. The two looked at each other for a long moment. This had happened so quickly that Rigo had not had time to think what he was doing. But now he was certain. It made perfect sense to him, with perfect clarity where this was all going.

"We cannot, no, I ... I cannot escape ... who I am, Mother." His gaze softened. "And you too. As for Tosti ...," he looked over to Tosti, "... he deserves all the suffering that I am giving him and the one that is still to come. He will not leave here alive."

Berta looked at him. It was the look of resignation. "I understand," she said.

"Do you? Do you really?" She didn't answer.

Tosti glared back at Rigo, fighting the pain. "You are my bastard son. But I never wanted you." He laughed; a spittle of saliva and sweat intermixed sprayed the air as he laughed.

"Berta, talk to him." The laughter died off, the pain returning. "We can still get out of here ... make a new beginning. Tell him, Berta!"

She turned her head in his direction with a look of calm settling over her face. Berta looked at him and back to Rigo.

"He doesn't want a new beginning, Silvio." Rigo also sat down on the floor; his back to the wall, his knees propped up facing the two of them.

Berta spoke. "What is it that you want, Rigo?"

"You will see, Mother." He got back up.

"By the way, is the benzene can still in the garage?" She nodded.

Frank walked back into the room. He was wearing one of Rigo's shirts, a slim fitting brown long sleeve polo shirt. It fit him perfectly. He looked better.

"What are you doing?" It was Tosti asking. Rigo ignored him for a moment, and then he looked at him.

"You said that you wanted to burn the place down, right? Well, I'm going to do just that. Frank here is going to help me set the fire."

He looked back at Frank. "There's a can of benzene in the garage, by the entrance to the door. I want you to start in the living room past the kitchen and douse the place from there to the garage with the benzene. If you do as I ask, I will give you the keys to the room where Grete is kept. You can ..."

"What are you doing, Rigo?" It was Berta asking, her voice rising, sounding more like a plea.

"I told you Mother, you will see in a moment."

Tosti fell over, his head leaning on Berta's shoulder. He was barely conscious.

Rigo kicked him. "Wake up, Tosti. You're part of the show!" Tosti groaned, his eyes struggling to open.

"As I was saying, Frank. Do as I ask, and I will let you take Grete out of here to safety. Go—now!"

Frank stepped out gingerly into the garage pressing the dressing tightly against his abdomen and came back through the mudroom with the benzene fuel in its red container. He stepped into the kitchen and exited from there to the front entrance foyer and to the living room entrance. It did not take long before they could smell the gasoline vapors.

Tosti tried to get up, but Rigo kicked him back into place. Berta just sat there watching her son the whole time.

"There's a place outside of Budapest, Rigo. It's a farm. That's where we came from, where my mother was born. I bought the place some years ago for Master Tosti, for Silvio ..."

"Berta, no!" Tosti was screaming, now fully awake.

She looked at him, but continued. "There's a safety deposit box in a bank in Budapest. The identification information and key are in my purse. You are on it, on the account, Rigo. I was going to tell you later." Berta's eyes swelled with the thought of what had been her dream.

"Take it Rigo, take it. It's yours now. Go there. Start a new life for yourself." She looked at Tosti, who was now staring at her in disbelief.

She looked back at Rigo. "The farm is also in your name. It was supposed to be our getaway place." Rigo kept staring at her, understanding more of the pieces of the puzzle that was his life. He finally spoke to her.

"You don't understand, do you?" His lips trembled, the eyes filled with tears that leaked into the small cavity by the bridge of his nose and trickled down the contours of his cheeks.

"How do I escape the girls, Mother? All those pretty young girls, I see them in my sleep every night. How do I escape them?" He was yelling now. The tears came as a flood, mixing with the flow of mucous from his nose in a rivulet of pain.

"There is no getting away from who we are. I cannot escape who I am … not any longer." He bent down again, folding down with his back against the wall and his knees in front. Rigo reached over and kissed his mother on the cheek, leaving it moist with his tears. "There is no place to hide, there is no getaway from the dreams of the girls who come back to haunt me every night."

He wiped his eyes and got back up, looking at Frank.

"Wait here." Rigo first went to the living room and stopped in the kitchen. He came back into the mudroom, closing the door behind him. Rigo had Berta's purse in his hands. Inside he found the envelope where he also found the papers that Berta had just described. It included an identity card from Hungary and a key to a lockbox, the lockbox from the bank in Budapest.

They all jumped when the smoke alarm went off—a strident blaring noise meant to penetrate through any conversation and any depth of sleep, stifling anything but the urge to turn it off. Tosti understood now.

"You bastard!" Tosti screamed a string of obscenities at Rigo, laughing at his own words like a deranged animal. He kept trying to get up but fell back each time, the effort giving way to the intense pain that cut into him like a knife's edge piercing through skin and muscle to find the nerve endings in the bones.

Frank grabbed Rigo by the shoulder.

"The key, Rigo, where's the key?" he asked him. The first wisps of smoke had already worked itself into the mudroom.

"I have a package for you ... Rodrigo. It's in your backpack. Your money's in there too."

"What about my wallet?"

"I'll be keeping that. It's necessary."

He gave Frank the backpack and then looked at Berta, speaking the surprise he had been keeping. "I'm not leaving."

"No, Rigo," she screamed, "that was for you, for a new beginning!"

Frank was puzzled. Rigo had called him Rodrigo.

Rigo held out the key to Grete's room.

"Hurry. She's upstairs. Take her." Frank grabbed for the key, but Rigo held it tight.

"Take her out of here, Rodrigo, take her back to her mother."

"I will. I swear it. She's why I came here."

Rigo pulled Frank in to him and grabbed him in a bear hug. "Thank you ... brother." He then whispered in his ear, "Start a new life, Frank ... a life as me. It's all in the backpack. Live the life I wanted to live ... please."

He let go of him, and Frank ran out of the room holding his arm across his face, dodging the flames that had already started in the kitchen. The smoke was getting thicker in the mudroom and it was getting unbearably warmer. The smoke alarm kept up its wailing, tormenting the mind with its peal for attention. Frank entered the kitchen and ran up the stairs.

Rigo sat back down with his back against the wall; his knees perched in front of him facing Tosti and Berta. All three of them were now coughing. The room was filling up with smoke.

CHAPTER 33

THE HOUSE
FRIDAY, 6TH OF APRIL

Outside, a bevy of police vehicles had just arrived. A scene of chaos greeted the police. They could see the flames enveloping the farm converted into a home as they leaped out of the windows, licking the sides of the brick front. Smoke was everywhere getting whipped into odd-shaped patterns by the dry, cool winds that had arrived to replace the rains of the night before. The federal policemen wearing their windbreakers with POLICE emblazoned across the front and back fanned out to surround the building. Inspector Betón approached the house, but the heat from the flames was already too great. He spoke into his radio that he wanted everyone pulling back. A voice came across the radio channel that the Brandweer, the fire department was alerted and would be on their way.

✦

Frank reached the room and fumbled with the key, finally inserting it into the keyhole, turning it and opening the door. It was already stifling warm inside but so far free of the smoke that was everywhere down the stairs. He looked around but was surprised. He had expected to find Grete in the room.

"Grete! Grete!" he yelled. He ran to the closet and pulled it open, desperately flinging its contents to the ground to see if she was hiding in the back. He ran to the bathroom, opened the shower stall door, but it too was empty. He was frantic.

The smoke was now also in the room filling every space. He went back into the room and yelled out again, "Grete, my name is ... Rodrigo." He said it in Norwegian.

There was a whimper. He heard it clearly. He looked under the bed and there against the wall was the young ten-year-old blonde little girl that he had been looking for. She started to crawl out and he reached in to help her. As soon as she was out from under the bed, she turned and tried to wriggle out of Frank's hold.

She kept saying "Le Petit Prince!" Frank held her tight.

He ran out the door but saw that the steps headed downstairs were now impassable. The whole first floor was in flames. He went to the window in the second floor foyer, looked out and saw that it led to the roof with a sharp drop-off a meter or more. Frank held Grete tight. She kept screaming "Le Petit Prince!" and was now fighting him to let her go. He opened the latch on the window with one hand as the flames leaped up into the second floor, sucking in the new supply of oxygen.

He looked around to see if there was any other option, but this was the only choice. Out the window he went, feet first, still holding on to Grete as tight as he could. For a moment he had to release his grip on her to hold on to the windowsill. Otherwise he was going to slip and go head first over the edge. At that moment, Grete flung herself free and went running back into the foyer and into the room where they had just left.

"Grete!" he yelled.

He started back in, but the flames were now leaping up to the foyer, the noxious brown smoke filling the room as wallpaper and curtains in the hallway caught fire. Frank saw Grete running back out with a rag dog clenched in her arm but lost sight of her for a moment. He then saw her trying to get around the flames. There was no way for him to get back inside the room and there was no way for Grete to get to the window without walking through a wall of flames and smoke. Frank was screaming and crying "Grete! Grete!" He hung on to the edge of the windowsill from the outside framing, screaming her name and wanting to not let go. The heat from the flames was now making it unbearable to hold on.

In a last desperate try he screamed "Grete! Grete!"

As if on command, at the very moment when he was about to let go and slide off the roof, a figure emerged out of the window wrapped in a large white towel dripping water and steaming from the flames that had enveloped it. Frank grabbed Grete, towel and all, letting go his grip on the windowsill. The two of them slid down the meter-long distance of tiled roof, over the rain gutter and over the edge, going airborne for what seemed like an eternity.

The bundle of flailing arms and legs that was Frank and Grete still wrapped in the steaming towel turned in the air, landing on the hedge that served as the perimeter of the small patio-garden. The hedge broke their fall. One of the branches ripped open the bandage that he had just placed on his wound. Frank clambered off the hedge, still holding Grete as he took the towel off her. She was shaking.

"Are you hurt?" he asked her in Norwegian.

"No." She saw his blood-drenched shirt. "Are you?"

Grete had the rag dog, Le Petit Prince, still clutched in her hands. They were immersed in a thick fog of noxious smoke, crackling sounds from the burning house, pulsing blue lights and wailing sirens in the background. She threw her arms around his neck and held them there.

"You can let go now, Grete. We have to move out of the way from the fire." They backed away a few meters. She released her grip on him and the two of them paused to see each other in the relative safety of the garden. Frank was on one knee, with one hand cupped to the side of her face holding the young girl that he had never met before.

"Hi Grete, I've been looking for you, my name is ..."

"Rodrigo, yes, I know. Mister Rigo said you would take me to see my mother." She started to cry. "Will you do that, Mister Rodrigo?"

"Yes, yes! I will—sort of ... it will actually be the nice policemen who are waiting for you."

"Mister Rigo said *you* were going to do it! You were going to take me to my mother!"

"Shsh, Grete. It's okay. The police are right over there on the other side of this little garden. They are all waiting for you. All you have to do is walk through that walkway and you will see them. Ask them for policeman Fredrik Hansen. He is Norwegian just like us." He took a small pause catching his breath, "Will you do that? Will you trust me to walk over there and go see the policeman so he can take you to your mother?"

Grete nodded. She was shivering now.

The wind was blowing the smoke in the other direction, away from them towards the other side of the house. They could hear the sirens and engines of the emergency vehicles arriving to put out the fire. The house continued to hiss and crackle reaching its final death throes.

Grete could see the walkway in the garden, but not to where it led—there was too much smoke.

She was about to let go and head through the walkway, when she stopped. "Mister Rigo ...?" It was spoken as a question. Her small face was asking the question with as much earnest as she could muster.

Frank held her by the arms. "He told me to tell you that he kept his promise."

She nodded. Then she gave the rag dog to Frank. "This is for you, Mister Rodrigo. The secret is in his heart."

Frank took the shabby tan stuffed dog and Grete took off on a run through the pathway as Frank had instructed her.

⋏

Inside the mudroom the two doors were already blackened and buckling from the flames on the other side. The heat was unbearable. They could barely see each other. Tosti was delirious with pain and couldn't stop coughing.

"He will burn alive, same as the two of us." Rigo hacked away in a convulsive fit of coughing for a moment. "It is hell that waits for us, not Budapest."

"How long, Rigo? How long have you known?"

"For a long time now. I've known for awhile. I did not know it would end like this. But I knew ... I knew it would not be ... a happy ending."

The coughing resumed. When it stopped, he saw his mother holding the other Glock that he had kicked to the side. Berta looked at the weapon, resting her hand on her lap.

"If hell is where we're going, then it will be soon enough, Rigo." Her face told a story of resignation and a lifetime of regret. "I never meant this for you. I never meant it for me." The tears poured out from her, the tears that she had kept pent up all her life.

Rigo kept his eyes focused on her, his own tears and the snot dripping from his nose mixing. He looked at her, both of them now facing the final moment and afraid of what lay in store on the other side of life.

Berta pointed the gun at Rigo's head, held it firm to steady her aim. The door from the kitchen was now in flames. He was speaking something to himself, like an incantation. She fired one shot. It caught Rigo at the top of the bridge of his nose and cratered his face between the eyes. The bullet deflected upward as it hit bone, losing most of the energy so that it entered and bounced inside of Rigo's cranium. He was gone, mouthing Grete's bedtime prayer.

Berta turned to her side, where Tosti was already unconscious. She decided to give him one last mercy. She placed the Glock to his temple and also fired into his head. The bullet entered and exited with maximum force, spraying the mudroom with Tosti's blood, pieces of cranial bone and brain matter.

Her hands were shaking violently. With both hands held steady she placed the barrel of the gun in her mouth and did not hesitate.

⚓

Outside, to the astonishment of the police on the western side of the building, a solitary figure came out of the smoke. Grete came running out of the smoke and into the arms of an incredulous police woman who wrapped her up in her arms like it was her own child emerging from the flames. A voice came on the police radio frequency, "The girl is here! She's unharmed! We have her!"

She was no more than just over a meter and a quarter tall, with blonde curls, wearing a red jacket over a white blouse with a pattern of two cats playing with a ball of yarn. She had a pair of blue jeans on and a pair of white sneakers on her feet.

Grete started talking to them in Norwegian, then realized her mistake and started back in English.

"I must speak to policeman Hansen," she said.

Excerpt from the Case File from DSI Hansen

Friday, 6 April

Arrived target location outside of Brussels. The complex was on fire. The young girl Grete Enberg is safe and unharmed. Inside the house we found three corpses consumed in the flames, tentatively identified as Deputy to the DG of ECFIN Silvio Tosti, a woman named Roberta Tosti (sister) and Frank Becken. No sign of the other accomplice that was involved with the escape from Norway. Determined through video at ferry border crossings that the other accomplice was a young male, twenties or early thirties. Briefed bosses and the parents of the young girl. Success. Must say it was the happiest day of my professional life. There remain many unanswered questions. Forensics may still yield some answers. Who else was involved? Was there another motivation beyond the obvious pedophilia? Who were the clients? Questions for Europol and D-DG Betón. Returning to Oslo tomorrow. Saddened by Becken's death. We would not have succeeded without him.

Friday, 25 April

FBI found another piece of evidence, an address to a crematorium in a nearby town where the house burned down. Passed lead to D-DG Betón. It may be where the other girls ended up—cremated with no records. The Spanish victim may have been in temp place until they took her to the crematorium—why she ended up in the stream. D-DG Betón indicated that the ME provided an update on the forensics. Told me that there are no medical or dental records for the woman and the man. They are confirming

Tosti died of a gunshot to the head, same as the other two. All three were consumed in the fire. Tosti had also been shot in the torso. Two Glock 17 weapons were found, one gun lying next to the woman. She had been tied down on the floor. Likely was the shooter. The younger man was her biological son, from DNA. He was also shot in the head. Died from the gun wound before he burned. The woman's gun had four bullets expended if the clip was full. It was obviously not Becken who died in the house. These records are being sealed at the request of the FBI to hide Becken's identity. We owe him this much. There is more to this case that is now in other jurisdictions.

CHAPTER 34

OUTSIDE THE HOUSE
FRIDAY, 6TH OF APRIL
LATE AFTERNOON

Frank looked around for how to make his own exit from the swirls of smoke that poured out the windows and from the rooftop. The winds were mild, but pushing the smoke easterly precisely in his path. It was getting hard to see. He started walking to the south side of the farmhouse heading in the opposite direction that Grete had taken. All he needed to do was walk directly away from the fire that was the farmhouse, but the smoke was dictating his path. Avoiding the densest smoke that changed direction with the erratic winds, he unknowingly started angling back towards the house. From one moment to the next he was in a real and present danger.

He was also distracted. Rigo's words resonated in his head. The idea had begun to sink in. The smoke was all around him but his spirit soared with the possibility of what could be. Rigo had just given him ... "freedom," he thought. He could hardly contemplate the notion of freedom. "A new chance, a start-over to my miserable existence as the hacker bitch of the NoSaints." It felt like being in a dream, the one he had every morning while lying in bed, thinking about what had happened to him and more recently about the emergence of Monika back in his life. In all those dreams the dark anchor of reality was his constant companion—a resignation that life was over for him. "He had never intended to be a criminal," he thought, just to help even the score, to make it a "level playing field for the little guy, a romantic type of Robin Hood." That was all it had ever been about even when he had been working for Tom Whanamum and his shipping company.

And then the NoSaints had left him that message on the phone and his life had taken a different turn when all he had left was dreams of freedom. It had been just a dream until Rigo had whispered in his ear about a life as Rodrigo with the new identity credentials parked there in his backpack on his shoulder.

"But first get away from the crime scene," he thought, "... and stay hidden if the possibility of freedom is going to have a chance to work."

The wail of emergency sirens, and blue, red, and yellow lights was a problem. If he walked into the hands of the police then "the new identity would be discovered for the falsehood that it was," he thought. The problem was clear in his head, "they would see the fire, the girl and the three dead bodies as murder and arson, possibly even try to pin the abduction on him." His chance to become Rodrigo would be over before it could take form. But the lights were also the answer to his immediate need: a doctor and a hospital, in that order.

He continued forward staying low to the ground cutting a path away from the searing heat. To his rear he could hear the hissing and popping of a house in the grip of an all-consuming fire, dying a painful death and taking its secrets with it in the dark gray-brown smoke that lifted to the sky and dispersed with the capriciousness of the wind. A section of the roof caved in, sending new tendrils of flame that sucked in the fuel of oxygen from the sky.

He plowed on a few more steps walking through the same swirls of noxious brown smoke that Grete had just escaped. Frank had the bottom of his t-shirt pulled up to his face. It helped in small measure by filtering the smoke. But it wasn't enough. He knew. The wound continued to bleed, warm and pulsing at the point where the bullet had entered his side. He was starting to feel nauseous; the combination of smoke, loss of blood and exertion to escape through the second floor window was taking its toll.

The backpack felt heavy. And then he remembered the Red Bull that he had saved for himself. He rolled the backpack off his shoulder, pulled out the precious can, popped the aluminum lid back and downed half the yellowish liquid in a long gulp, pouring what remained over the bottom section of his t-shirt that he had been using as an impromptu air filter. Frank dropped the can, repositioned his now Red Bull soaked t-shirt over his face, picked up his backpack and continued heading in the direction of the lights.

The smoke stung his eyes, tearing profusely as he tried to block it with the back of his hand. Frank realized he was in deep trouble. His lungs were searing, his whole body consumed in trying to cough out the foreign object that was the smoke-filled air. His mind had switched from the exhilaration of freedom in his grasp to shear panic.

The dark heavy anchor of reality was back. His vision was reduced to blurry shades of gray, nothing distinguishable for what it was until it was right in front of him. He stumbled forward like a drunkard. His right shin caught the edge of a chair that sent him flying head first into the edge of an outdoor patio table, catching it just above the right eye and opening a gash that quickly swelled with blood. He screamed and cursed out loud, sucking in more of the vile smoke that filled his lungs until the world spun into darkness.

And then the explosion came.

In a microsecond of time, the farmhouse went from a dying, hissing and popping smoke-filled structure to a spray of brick and wooden shards traveling outward at terrific speeds from the force of the exploding gas tank inside the garage.

CHAPTER 35

REYKJAVIK, ICELAND
FRIDAY, 6TH OF APRIL

Vlad got an alert on his smartphone. It contained a simple message that part of the network was offline. He walked back to his desk and checked the logs. He saw that first the primary and then the secondary backup router in the safe house had gone offline. "House Brussels" had gone dark. He called Tosti but got his voicemail prompt.

Vlad launched the text messaging application and sent Pascal a message, "Something very wrong in B. We are blind. Tosti not answering." Seconds later his phone rang.

He saw that it was Pascal.

He didn't bother with hellos. "Am pulling up the video logs. Hold on a second ... okay, got it ... hm, I see Tosti entering.

I'm going to speed it up. I thought burning the house was supposed to happen later tonight or tomorrow?"

"It was. What about the guy who arrived earlier?"

"There's no sign of him after he entered. Wait, I see Rigo walking into the Nikita Room and talking to the girl. He's got his back to the camera. Nothing appears out of the ordinary ... just looks like what he's been doing all along. There it is. I can now see the fire. From the garage level camera for about a minute of video and then it's all smoke until it stops. Same with the camera upstairs. The girl looks frightened like she knows something is wrong. She hides under the bed and then the video feed dies."

"So it could be that they did as planned and then got out— just sooner than we anticipated?"

"Tosti would have called. Or he would have answered. I've tried several times. Nothing."

"Right. Me too. Either he's not answering or something else happened there. I'm heading that way now. See what else you can find out. Do you still have access to the Inspector's computer in Norway?"

"No. It's been taken offline. But there is one more thing."

"Yes?"

"I've got GPS tracking on all the phone and laptop computers. They all stopped reporting about the same time that the routers went offline."

"What do you mean ... oh, shit!"

"That's right. Tosti would never have left the computers and his phone behind. Either they figured out how to disable the GPS or the devices were left there with the house. No way they found and tampered with the GPS. Which means that ..."

"That Tosti, Berta and Rigo never left the house, same with their laptops and phones. I'm headed there now. Keep a watch to see if this makes the news. Keep me updated."

CHAPTER 36

OUTSIDE THE HOUSE
FRIDAY, 6ᵀᴴ OF APRIL

The last thing Frank remembered was the yellow lights getting brighter and being dragged through the back yard by a fireman in full fire battle gear. There was a ringing in his head that drowned out every other noise.

The explosion saved his life. It took away the fuel that was the house and the smoke started to dissipate with the winds. A fireman from the local community found him moments later and placed the clear plastic mask over his face. It was tethered with a thin tube to an oxygen tank that allowed Frank to start clearing his lungs. He was prone, laid out flat on a grassy field, the sunny clear day above a sharp contrast to the hell storm of smoke he had been in just moments prior.

"This is one lucky bastard," the fireman told his companions around him. They were now moving Frank on a wheeled gurney as quickly as they could into the back of the bright red ambulance. "Another few seconds and we wouldn't be bothering with oxygen. Get him to the hospital quick."

They shut the back doors and started the engine. Inside the back of the vehicle the paramedic found Frank's wallet. He got on the radio channel with the hospital and registered the vital signs of one Rodrigo Kajetan, "he's got severe smoke inhalation, what appears to be a gunshot through the lower torso that exited cleanly, looks to have avoided any organs. He is bleeding from one ear, his forehead, and other smaller cuts and abrasions. Blood pressure is 180 over 100. He is unconscious, lost a lot of blood, vitals are…erratic. I have him on an IV … wait …"

"What are you doing?" The paramedic put the oxygen mask back over Frank's face fighting off Frank's attempts to remove the mask.

"Min hund." Frank spoke the words in Norwegian, realized his mistake, and said it again in French, "mon chien."

The paramedic chalked it up to nonsense talk when his partner found the rag dog lying by the side of the gurney and put it in Frank's hands. Frank passed out again, the dog dropping to the floor once again. The paramedic picked up the rag dog and put it into the backpack that was also there on the floor.

"I'm back. As I was saying, I have an IV going, he regained consciousness for a moment …"

Hansen opened the back door of the Belgian police car where Grete was seated. Outside, the afternoon was turning into a mild evening, the sky still cloudless and the smoke of what used to be a farmhouse dissipating in the winds. A maelstrom of specialized technicians in their respective uniforms were gathering evidence while camera crews with their satellite vans hovered in the periphery looking for someone, anyone, who would talk to them. They were waiting for Inspector Betón to provide a report.

Grete scooted over to make room for Hansen. He poured some water on a towel that he had been given by one of the paramedic's. She was in good health according to the quick check. They had been quite impressed by the little blonde girl talking to them in English.

"Here, wipe your face Grete." She took the wet towel and cleaned her face. He took the towel back.

"April I?" he asked. She nodded. Hansen cleaned the rest of her face, the parts she had missed.

"I've got a granddaughter about your age," he said as he finished. She looked at him with no expression. "You're safe now, Grete."

Her eyes started to swell. "Would you like to talk to your mother?"

The expression in her face changed in an instant, a smile found its way that she couldn't hold back. She nodded again. DSI Hansen pulled out his phone from his side pocket, input "+47", the Norwegian country code and offered it to her. She took it from him and dialed her mother's mobile phone number. It rang twice and the familiar voice of Grete's mother came across the phone speaker. "Hei?"

Grete tried to speak but she was overwhelmed with the moment. When she did speak, it came out as a shrill scream, *Mor! Det er meg!*—Mom, it's me.

"Grete!"

DSI Hansen could not help his own tears and the big smile that fixed across his face, the mixed emotions of joy and relief to hear mother and daughter reunited, even if just over the phone. The two of them were speaking over each other until Grete's mother took control and they talked, the two of them more like best friends laughing, her mother asking if she was all right, Grete answering that she was fine.

"Grete?" Hansen interrupted. The paramedics would be getting anxious about now. They had been adamant about keeping her for only a few minutes before he had to bring her back to the ambulance so they could get her to the hospital to be fully checked out.

"Can I talk to your mother?"

Grete handed the phone back. "Mrs. Enberg?"

"Yes, yes, I do need to end the call now. She is well, no apparent signs of harm, but the authorities here in Belgium will want to have her checked out by a doctor and there are many more things we need to do ... yes, you are welcome, Mrs. Enberg. You have a very brave young girl. As soon as I can I will call you back so you can speak later. The doctors may ask her to spend a night in the hospital and I also know that the Belgian authorities have to follow their procedures ... that is no problem, I can have someone pick you and your husband up at the airport. Thank you, Mrs. Enberg."

He hung up the phone and took Grete by the hand out of the car and back to the paramedic, where Betón was also waiting. The paramedics took her in the back of the ambulance and Hansen got in with her.

"Fredrik, don't forget. We have lots to talk about."

"I know. I will meet you at the hospital."

"Okay. Soon as we can get the investigation going here, I will head there myself. The crime scene team is on its way. Anything I should be looking for inside this house or what's left of it?"

"Yes, the guy Frank ..."

"Wait ..." A strident voice looking for Inspector Betón on the radio interrupted the conversation.

"Sorry Fredrik, let me see what this is about." He returned a few minutes later. Hanson noticed a curious look on his face.

"What's the matter? You okay?"

"Yes, yes, that was my boss ... that's all ... you were saying?"

"Yes, the guy Frank that I told you about ... we don't know where he is right now. I'm concerned. And computers, phones, printers. Anything like that. If you find any, don't let anyone turn them on or anything."

"Okay, will do. But just so you know, this is Belgian evidence. I will share what I can, when I can."

"Yes, I know. Thank you Louis. I am most grateful. The girl is safe. Everything else is secondary." The two men shook hands. Hansen got into the ambulance with Grete and the paramedic closed the back door of the ambulance van. The driver took off.

DSI Hansen got on the phone to call his boss Brit and then afterwards he called Jaime, updating them on the good news. Frank's whereabouts were still unknown. The two men feared the worst, but until they knew further there was still hope.

Hansen was watching Grete as the ambulance rode through the Belgian countryside. They weren't going far. There was a clinic in the nearby town of Dendermonde. The doctors were already alerted and waiting for them to arrive. He continued his conversations with all the people who need-ed to be updated, watching the young girl and marveling at the ease with which she engaged the two paramedics. They went through the required medical procedures while enjoying the moment of joy and lightness that seemed to encircle ev-erything about Grete. As far they could tell there was nothing at all wrong with her.

"How do you say 'thank you very much' in French?" she asked the paramedic who was asking her whether she had a cough.

"*Merci Beaucoup.*"

"And how do I say 'my friends?'"

"*Mes amis*"

"*Merci Beaucoup ... mes amis,*" she told the two paramedics who laughed out loud at hearing one of their two native tongues spoken with a Norwegian accent. Hansen couldn't help but smile with them.

"*Tres bien*, Grete, *tres bien,*" they responded.

Hansen was only half paying attention. He had never been so proud, thinking about the young girl and his own career leading to this point.

His phone rang. It was his boss's boss's boss, the Norwegian Minister of Justice calling.

"Mister Minister?"

"Yes, Inspector. I understand that little Grete has been found safe and sound. Let me be the first to say Congratulations!"

"Yes, Mister Minister. I am with her right now in the back of the ambulance headed to a nearby hospital outside of Brussels. The paramedics say that she is in good health. She is keeping them entertained right now."

"Wonderful. And I cannot thank you enough for what you did. We are all proud ... very proud, of how you were able to find her and now bring her home. I just spoke with her parents. It was a nice touch to call the mother. Well done. But now, you know, Inspector, that our work is never so easy." He paused. Hansen knew it was not the time to say anything. "Now we have to deal with ... other matters taking center stage. Like, how did this happen, who was really behind this? What happened to the deputy who was in our country, the Mister Tosti? The list is long. You need to stay on this case. I have already spoken with your bosses. They will tell you the same thing."

"I understand, Minister."

"Very good, Fredrik. Again, on behalf of this department and our country, thank you Detective Superintendent Hansen. I look forward to hearing more on this after you make progress. Stay on it."

"I will, sir." The call ended.

⚓

On the N47, passing the village of Asse north of Brussels, Pascal was driving his Range Rover at just under the speed limit in order not to garner attention from traffic control. He was on the phone using his Bluetooth connection, getting an update from Vlad about the events to the north in the news media.

"What are they saying?" Pascal asked.

"That three bodies were taken away, no identification as yet. The police, someone named Betón, is supposed to be speaking shortly."

"Okay, what about the FBI involvement, what else have you learned?"

"I'm building a dossier on the principles starting with the guy named Rodriguez and also on his team."

"Why are they involved?"

There was a pause on the line. Vlad answered thinking it was obvious, "... because, they were asked to help ..."

"No! Listen to me, Vlad. That is not the reason. There has to be more, something else. The FBI doesn't just pop into European affairs, not at this level and not at this depth. Figure it out. We can take care of the Tosti affair. I hadn't told you this, but I had decided that Tosti had become too great a liability. He was going to be out of the picture anyway—but not this way. Whatever happened at the house, the concern is that it stays inside the box of a criminal abduction. That we can deal with."

"Wait, there's more in the news. A policeman is coming to the mic, he's speaking now. He says that they rescued a girl, a Norwegian girl that had gone missing. He is thanking his Norwegian counterpart, Hansen, who is with the girl, he says. Also, that there were two unidentified remains of ... but that there were three people, a woman and two men. They say that one of the men was Tosti ... that he was working for, ... what the hell? ... for the Belgian police to help find the girl. Can you believe this? They are saying that Tosti is a fucking hero!"

"Take it easy, Vlad. I told you I was taking care of the situation. Now you do your job and find out what is happening with this FBI involvement. Stay on Hansen's tail."

"Okay, I got it. But I need those mobile phones and laptops."

"Call me later when you have more."

"Yes, will do."

PART FOUR

"I've seen things you people wouldn't believe. Attack ships on fire off the shoulder of Orion. I watched c-beams glitter in the dark near the Tannhäuser Gate. All those moments will be lost in time, like tears in rain. Time to die."

Roy Batty, Blade Runner

CHAPTER 37

OSLO, NORWAY
FRIDAY, 6TH OF APRIL
LATE EVENING

Monika was in her apartment filling out papers for her new job. She had been tentatively accepted for the same malware analyst type of role that she had back in Moscow. The apartment was located on the north side of Oslo, near Holmenkollbakken, the old Olympic ski jump site. She was stuck looking at the same online documents for a while now, a new job working for a new firm but doing the same thing. Not very exciting, *but a job is a job*, she thought. Norseman Labs seemed to be a good place to work, as demanding as her old job, but back home in Oslo, where she belonged. Try as she did to concentrate on the task at hand, there was something else that kept coming back to the top of her mind.

She opened the Messages application on her Mac, the computer she used for everyday stuff. She checked her phone—again, for the umpteenth time. She had called Frank's number several times and left several messages, "call me ... please," "call me, pretty please," "Frank, you're pissing me off, call me!" And finally, "Frank, you're scaring me. Call me. Please!"

Still nothing. She opened her newsreader application and updated her Google subscription, again, for any breaking news coming out of *Belgium*, this time, not just Brussels. She was worried. "Something was wrong, he would have sent a text message by now," she thought. The text messaging application showed that the last entry from Frank had been sent earlier in the morning. It read, "arrived at the airport," then nothing.

Monika scanned the list of news stories. There were over a dozen from various media feeds. She was about to close the newsreader when a caption caught her eye ... *Young Norwegian Girl Rescued*. She had almost missed it. The link pointed to a France24 article. A lump of fear grew in her throat as she read about the "Belgian Police Chief Betón stating that "the Norwegian girl had been rescued ..." That there were "three bodies found, two men and a woman. One man, a Belgian and EU government executive called Silvio Tosti, is being hailed as a hero."

She continued reading the story, unwittingly holding her breath. "The other, a Norwegian adult male, died in the fire ... name withheld pending notification to the Norwegian authorities ..." Monika stopped reading gasping for air.

Her hands went instinctively to her belly.

A flood of uninvited tears came, her face a reflection of tormented grief, her world spinning out of control. And then it hit her again, a second wave, the emotion of overwhelming loss piled on top of the devastating disappointment of a future gone. It was so overwhelming. She wailed, "No, no ... no!" It was all she could say.

Monika tried to stand up but her legs wavered, she wanted to throw up, and then her legs crumbled under her as she fell to the floor curled up in the fetal position. She had waited twelve years for Frank, the man that she had loved all her adult life, lost, and re-found, now lost again—this time forever. Hope was gone, her hands stayed at her belly with the surprise that she was waiting to tell him—when he returned.

The apartment was actually a loft in a private home, belonging to a "sweet older lady, Mrs. Johannesen, like a grandmother, the daughter of a famous Olympic speed skater," she had told Frank. From the windows she had a view to the north, up to the hills where on clear days she could see the top section of the famed ski jump. That's what she had been doing before reading the news from Belgium, looking out the window, the sun setting over the mountains, her mind drifting far away to the east, to another apartment in the outskirts of Moscow where she had lived and from where she had worked not one but two jobs. Somehow, her Moscow-based employer had not figured it out, the fact that she worked for them and also for their opposition.

On the wooden floor covered by the red carpet, her cat Maggie licked at her face, drying her tears. Monika heard it again, the soft knocking on the door. It was soft but persistent. She dabbed at her eyes with the back of her hand, picked up Maggie and walked carefully to the door regaining her composure with each step. She heard it again, three knocks and then the sweet voice of Mrs. Johannesen, *Er alt bra, kjære?*—are you alright, dear?

Monika put Maggie back down on the floor, opened the door and walked into the open arms of the little old lady, Mrs. Johannesen. In her arms, Monika became the young girl that had cried once, a great many years back, before she could even remember, when her mother had left her, and it was only her and her father who had also died ... suddenly from some "accident," leaving her alone in the world.

That is all they, the police investigators, would tell her. It wasn't until she started working in Moscow that she figured it out for herself with the new skills she had developed working for her new bosses. The police had told her that her father had died under mysterious circumstances, but officially it was called an accident. Hacking into the police files she was able to connect the dots and why they had told the young girl privately that "... it was better for her if she not inquire further about the case, that the murder was unsolved and would most likely stay that way."

The dots she connected in those long nights breaking into the police case files pointed to the very same NoSaints that had taken ownership of Frank. She had also discovered why it was that the police told her to stop asking. There was an unconnected dot, like an open question, why a certain mid-level prosecutor in the Ministry of Justice had taken an unusual interest in the case. His influence had led to the end of the investigation, telling the KRIPOS Investigator, the woman named Brit Jahn, that there was "insufficient evidence to prosecute." That's what Chief Investigator Brit Jahn had bitterly put into her case notes.

That prosecutor had continued on to a successful career. Sitting there in her Moscow apartment and many years gone from Norway, she thought she had heard the name before, but wasn't sure why. It only took one search and it was clear enough. The man named Lars Mortensen was the now middle-aged but still handsome Minister of Justice of Norway.

She saw it clearly. The connection was the missing dot for how a certain government prosecutor gave cover to criminals and how her father had died with no chance at justice, not when justice was compromised by the very people in the government whose job it was to uphold the law. Her father had simply run afoul of the chemistry of power and ambition. The investigator woman named Brit Jahn had told her as tenderly as she could, speaking to a girl barely ten years old to "dry your tears, Monika, and grow up. The world is full of injustice. Your father was a good and honorable man trying to stand in the middle of old fashioned greed; that is all. Your father died of an 'accident,' that is all you need to know. Grow up, and put it in your past, little Monika."

The old woman, Else Johannesen, held Monika in her arms lending her the strength that she had inherited from her famous father. "Whatever it is, dear, we will find a way to solve it. There is nothing that my God cannot solve, my sweet dear girl."

CHAPTER 38

MOSCOW, RUSSIA
TWO YEARS PRIOR

"So, our Viking girl graces us with her presence."

"Stuff it, Viktor! I'm not in the mood." She paused by his cubicle, rested her arm over the partition, looked him in the eye and told him, "It was a long night. But a successful one."

She flashed her colleague, Viktor Orlov, a mischievous smile. Viktor leaned back in his chair. "The Viking is ... pretty," he thought, "... when she smiles."

Viktor was a year older than Monika, twenty-nine and not liking the idea that his success depended on the Viking girl. He had been waiting all morning for her to show up. He was stuck on a problem and needed to know what she thought.

His demeanor changed from peer to puppy dog waiting for the morsel of treats that Monika doled out. He knew that she knew—what everyone in the office knew—that Monika was the star. She knew and she knew how to keep them as allies not competitors. It was her way of keeping the boys in check. They all knew it, resented it too; but without Monika pointing the way, chances were that they would not be holding the high paying jobs they occupied as members of the elite Borovsky malware analysis team. Where they came from there were countless others spewing out of the emerging Russian tech industry who would work for less.

But she was also liberal with her treats, the morsels of credit for discovering new threats, the zero day exploits, how they worked, who was controlling what in the underworld of spam, botnets—the kind of fodder that kept Borovsky in the news, sometimes making the news about the ever-expanding awareness in the public domain that hacking had become big business. It was open season on business IT systems; and not just business, but government as well.

Monika had started her new life after leaving Oslo, to begin anew—after being disappointed by the *boy* Frank—as she had thought of him back then, angry with him for going to work for the "insipid, fat, stupid, Tom Whanamum," as she had named the businessman. That's what she had told Frank, but he hadn't listened. In time she started to realize that it was not disappointment, it was sheer naked heartbreak, the kind that makes it hard to breathe, every thought hostage to the one-and-all consuming thought of a love unreturned.

To compensate, Monika sunk her heart and soul into the new line of work, the work that Frank was in, but with a real purpose of legitimate business. She began working as one of the first employees of a startup company led by the brilliant Eugene Borovsky, named after a famous Russian Chess Master seeking to get into the nascent game, as it were, of hacking and security defenses. During the day Monika was a highly-regarded security analyst at Borovsky, dissecting malware code for Borovsky labs. She became their resident expert on rootkits and botnets and on the players of the underground game. Like all professionals in the game of cyber sleuthing, Monika had to taken on a new personality.

So it started that Monika, the Borovsky Viking girl during the day, became her alias, M0k1, in the chat rooms that operated in the wee hours. She didn't have a social life, not like normal girls anyway. Her social life was the double life of Monika during the day and M0k1 at night fitted into one person. It was Dr. Jekyll and Mr. Hyde. What she learned at night she used during the day. She never took the lead in any of the chat rooms, but she absorbed all and with time she made some additional discoveries about herself.

When the Computer Emergency Response Team in the U.S. released notice of the vulnerability in the Internet addressing software called BIND back in 1998, she was one of the first to realize its potential impacts. What it meant to the growing installations of Linux servers around the world was nothing less than a huge gaping hole in the operating system—the kind that let hackers gain unauthorized access at the administrators level, also called root access. Linux servers in 1998 were mainly in use by the big boys, not the kind of technology that the garden-variety companies would mess with. Getting root access to one of these servers meant that you had gained access into something big, like the US Defense Department.

What she learned about herself was the realization that she was as good or better than any of the best. And she had the advantage, or rather that she lacked the disadvantage of the boy hackers who were all about showing off the size of their dicks. Monika was quite content following them, befriending them, and learning from them, what they did that was brilliant and where they failed. In a small way, Monika was getting even with Frank, by being better than him.

Borovsky Labs prospered with her and she with them. They called her Borovsky's little Dark Viking. She learned how to write her own rootkits, testing them, erasing her trail, and she rarely took credit. She didn't compete in dick size competitions so she became ... *trusted*. In the underworld of cyber sleuthing, reputation is everything. She was the chick hacker that everyone respected because she didn't try and compete with the boys—the ones who were getting the press and sometimes getting caught.

But things changed in her head. She started to see beyond the Goth mystique, a maturing view of the world that became more sophisticated, more aware and more to the notion that there needed to be a point to it all. Nihilism was not much of a point. Along the way she joined Internet Relay Chat (IRC) channels consisting of supergeeks and wannabees. Anonymity simply meant connecting from a public "shell" service and choosing a bland nickname. Joining the popular Undernet IRC network, her chosen M0ki nickname slowly became known and trusted by those online denizens who worked at night like nocturnal mystic creatures called vampires. Over time, she was trusted with channel operator status, then invited to hidden private channels where those who decided that digital freedom required anonymity, active protest, cyber-disobedience, and the like.

It fit her sense of self perfectly, becoming a contributor to a new group maturing away from the world of hacking for greed to hacking as a form of social justice. The group evolved into the infamous *Anonymous* and she, M0k1, expressed *mohkee one*, was one of the most influential of the Anons. M0k1 became queen of the Anons until the day that she disappeared.

Borovsky brought security technologies to the legions of enterprises connecting to the Internet and needing virus protections. That was her day job as Monika NLN. That is what she told Borovsky who she was, Monika with No Last Name and they could take it or leave it. At night M0k1 learned how to attack those enterprises—with impunity, to bring them down to size and to disclose their hypocrisy. Borovsky never knew.

She had found the double life exhilarating until the discovery of an adversary working for some of the most greedy of them all—organized crime, and now also the super rich oligarchs that had re-emerged by entering the world of cyberspace mixing old school breaking heads with the new school of breaking into IT systems.

They stuck to breaking heads—what they knew how to do, but employed a small squad of hacker *bitches* that served their need to break into the IT systems of the rich *phat* prize. One of those, the best of them, was using the alias TWhnum. When she saw the name, she first thought, "no it couldn't be." But it was. Frank was that very *bitch* adversary.

Monika had grown up, and with the years she began to realize that there was no good side and no bad side to the conflicts of the world—there were only shades of gray. It was like the old rock-n-roll song said, welcome to the revolution, where the new bosses are the same as the old bosses—maybe even worse.

So the Dark Viking Borovsky girl had a choice to make, and she chose ... selfish love. It had been her dream, even as a young girl, to raise her own children with a husband, with the only man she had ever loved, Frank Becken.

CHAPTER 39

THE HOUSE
NORTH OF BRUSSELS, BELGIUM
FRIDAY, 6TH OF APRIL
LATE EVENING

By the time Pascal arrived, the evening had advanced, and the sun's last rays allowed him to see the aftermath of the devastation that had once been the Seraphim farmhouse. He parked his car and looked around, making himself the curious passerby.

The place had that unique smell of burned wood turned charcoal black and charred brick doused with water from the fire trucks. Police crime scene tape encircled the compound with vestiges of what had been a large police and public safety force now wrapping things up.

Pascal looked left and right to the east and west of Paradjis Street. The site of the devastation that had attracted so many people earlier in the day was now getting empty. He walked at the periphery. When the last of the response teams left he ducked under the tape walking inside the burned out compound.

If the laptops and phones are still here somehow buried in the debris, then they are nothing more than melted blobs of plastic, silicon, and aluminum, he thought to himself. *Or, these blobs are in the hands of the police*, he thought further. In either case he knew how to deal with the situation. The first problem had been taken care of with the call to the Director General, Tosti's boss, who was connected in the chain of command ultimately to Inspector Betón. A frenzy of favors had been called in, and by the time Betón got in front of the microphone to talk to the press, the situation was under control. Tosti would no longer be a link to Seraphim. He was now only a memory as the heroic, but out of his element public servant, who had discovered the abduction of the Norwegian girl, and had given his life to save her.

He finished the inspection of the grounds but did not find the laptops or smartphones. Pascal got back in his Range Rover and called Vlad. "Any news?"

"Yes. I've been working on what happened inside the house. Four people went in and three died. What happened to the fourth? That's the question."

"Right. We have to assume that the fourth walked out. It wasn't Berta and it wasn't Tosti. That leaves either Rigo or that Norwegian, the one they talked about in the news."

"I'm thinking it was Rigo. It would have been easy, kill the others and start a new life. There was plenty of money ..."

"Don't assume. Find out for sure. Rigo is the smaller of the problems. The Norwegian ..."

"I understand. What about the laptops?"

"It's a burned out debris field here. If they're still here then they are burned beyond use. I've walked around a bit—didn't find anything. The police will be back here in the morning, I'm sure."

"I'll keep working trying to figure out number four."

"Good. I'm headed back now. Call me in the morning."

CHAPTER 40
CLINIC IN THE TOWN OF DENDERMONDE, BELGIUM
FRIDAY, 6TH OF APRIL
LATE EVENING

D SI Hansen had finished all his update-the-bosses calls. He caught a glimpse of his counterpart, Inspector Louis Betón, speaking to a group of reporters on the television news channel about the fire and the rescue of the young Norwegian girl. The doctor came out of the examination room.

He was signing the forms clearing Grete to return home. He spoke passable English. "The young girl, Grete Enberg, is good, in good ... health, no physical problems except for smoke from the fire, but there is no damage to her lungs." He looked up from his paperwork. "What she needs is to see a psychiatrist to deal with the psychological ..."

"Yes, doctor. Her parents are arriving shortly from Norway. I will inform them. Is she cleared to leave now?"

"Yes, of course, but we did get a phone call from the Police Chief, Monsieur Betón, saying he wanted to meet with you and the young girl before you left the hospital. He said he is on his way."

"Bon, merci, doctor."

He went back into the examination room to find Grete sitting up tying her shoelaces. "Your parents are on their way, Grete. We will meet them at the hotel."

"I want to see them. When will they get here?"

"They are due in later this evening. It will be best if we wait for them in the hotel where you will get some rest. Okay?" She nodded her head and blew her nose in a tissue that she had in her hand.

"Are you okay to speak with me, Grete—to answer some questions?" She nodded again. "How did you get out of the house? Did someone help you?"

"Rigo. It was Rigo who helped me. He kept me safe. Rigo kept his promise. And then it was Rodrigo. Why do they have these funny names?" she asked. She didn't expect an answer.

"Who is ... Ro ...?"

"Rodrigo. He was the man that Rigo asked to help me. He is Norwegian, like you and me." She let go a laugh and yawned, her arms stretched out.

"Are you tired?" She nodded. "Can I ask you just a few more questions? And then you can sleep a little?" She nodded again.

"Rodrigo spoke Norwegian?"

She nodded. "Yes, I don't think his real name was Rodrigo," she said as a matter of fact. Hansen smiled. This little girl was nobody's fool.

"And where did the Norwegian-speaking Rodrigo go?" he asked.

She shrugged. "He helped me escape the house through the window. We crashed into the hedges, then he told me to find you. That was all. No! Wait. I also gave him Le Petit Prince."

"Le Petit ..."

"Yes, the rag doll. It has the secrets. I gave it to him. Can I sleep now?" She said with some exasperation.

Hansen pulled the blanket up to her chin. She was fully dressed. Grete fell asleep in an instant. He turned around and went out of the room to find his friend Louis Betón there waiting for him. Two other police officers were with him.

"We need to talk, Fredrik."

"Okay."

"No, not here." He turned around and spoke to the two police officers. He motioned for Hansen to follow him. "They will watch her," he said, motioning to the two officers with him. Hansen followed him out the door of the clinic. Betón pulled out a cigarette and offered one to Hansen. It had started to rain, a light rain to cleanse the world.

Betón lit the cigarette as Hansen cupped his hands around the match. He pulled the smoke deep into his lungs.

"Funny, they won't let me smoke in my office anymore."

"Me too, what's the world coming to?"

"Fuck if I know." Betón lit his own cigarette and did like Hansen, sucking in a lungful of the smoke, letting it out in one long stream.

"Did you see the TV interview?"

"No, I was asking Grete about what happened. She's quite the little girl. More there than first meets the eye—a lot more. Brave, very brave little girl."

Betón looked over at his friend. "You're not going to like what I'm going to tell you."

Hansen looked back and said, "Whatever you tell me can't dampen what I'm feeling right now ... this little girl ... it's why I joined the police."

Betón nodded, "Me too."

"So tell me what you must Louis. I know it's a fucked-up world. But it would be more fucked, if it weren't for us."

"You sure about that?"

Hansen smiled, "Well, maybe not. Okay, it's fucked, all we can do is keep it from getting completely fucked."

Betón took another pull of the cigarette. "That call I got from my boss ... it was a call to tell me what I was going to say. He got a call from his boss, who got a call from who the fuck knows how many calls it took to get this message to me." The guy Tosti, who you were looking for ..." he paused.

"Yeah?"

"I was told that Tosti was to be the hero in this thing."

Hansen dropped his cigarette and put it out with his foot. "I'm listening."

"It's politics, Fredrik, they don't want to be embarrassed. Someone is covering his ass, what the fuck, it could be all of them covering their asses. All of them and ... me. I had a choice. They know my sins, Fredrik. I was threatened. I could be the Police Chief that handled it their way, or the one who got to take the fall, my fuckups from way back exposed, and my incompetence discussed in the public, my resignation accepted, my pension under review."

Hansen listened, his face a poker-player's mask. "Anything else?"

"Yes. We found your boy."

"No you didn't."

It was Betón's turn to be surprised, but he too kept the poker face. "And ..."

"And what I am going to tell you is that it's not over. You got another smoke?" Betón pulled out his pack and offered Hansen a second smoke, lit it for him.

"I'm all ears, Fredrik."

Hansen pulled on his cigarette. "You ever hear the expression it's not over 'till the fat lady sings?'"

"No, I can't say that I have. You going to keep me in suspense talking in riddles?"

"The Americans are a funny people. When you think you have them figured out ... well, let's just say that they have some funny ways of saying things. It means that you don't quit the game until it's really over ... when the fat lady sings ..."

"I have the image in my head, Fredrik ... can you tell me later about the fat lady?"

"It wasn't Frank in the house burned like overdone bacon. Frank is alive, probably on the road, maybe in one of your hospitals.

He looked his friend in the eye. "This is not over Louis, it's not over 'till the fat lady sings.' The question is ... are you going to work with me to figure this out ... or are you going to let the politicos fuck us?"

"Fuck the politicians."

Hansen burst out a laugh. "Fuck the politicians. I like that."

"Now about that fat lady singing ... I can't get that horrible image out of my head, Fredrik ... save me." The two old veterans let out a good laugh.

"Did you find any computers?"

"Yes, the place was wired like a digital fortress." Betón put out his cigarette stubbing it out with the heel of his shoe. "The computers were in backpacks in the RV and in the Audi. They are a bit crispy on the outside, but the internals survived intact. That blast from the gas tanks basically put the fire out for us ... before everything burned down."

"I need them. I need them, and I need you to put it in your report that they were completely burned, unusable, no forensics possible. These laptops and the phones may give us the clues we need to find out what was really happening in this house."

Inspector Louis Betón extended his hand to his friend. "Fuck the politicians!" The two grasped hands, eyeing each other with the bond of conspirators on a cause.

"One more thing, Louis. Frank was one of the good guys. It was he who saved the girl. Without him ... we had nothing.

This guy found out about these assholes, he came here, and he got the girl. Now he's in danger. They find him, he's a dead man. Can you keep it that he died in the fire ... that he was working for me?"

"Yes, I can do that. The autopsy will reveal that he was Frank the hacker that you told me about."

"Good. Thank you."

"Fredrik?"

"Yes?"

"If I can't get that image out of my head tonight when I go to bed ... I'm calling you up—to wake your ass up."

CHAPTER 41

SAINT-LUC UNIVERSITY HOSPITAL
BRUSSELS, BELGIUM
SATURDAY, 7ᵀᴴ OF APRIL

Two IV bags hung from a long metal contraption by the side of the hospital bed. The band around his wrist said that Mr. Rodrigo Kajctan, age 30, Hungarian citizen, was admitted the evening before. The first IV was for hydration, the second for the medicine including the sedative that kept him in dreamland and minimized the pain of a busted eardrum, gunshot wound, the head wound, and multiple punctures from shards of wood.

The doctors had no personal history, only that he had been admitted as a casualty of the fire north of Brussels near the town of Dendermonde. The police would show up eventually.

He wasn't going anywhere ... not for a couple of days at least. Outside the hospital the world continued to spin, but for Frank there was only one thing in his head. He dreamed of a little blond girl full of curls in a jacket with two kittens and a ball of yarn. The little girl was running away from him with a rag doll tucked under her arm and her words that she said over and over again, "The secret is in his heart."

CHAPTER 42

OSLO, NORWAY
SATURDAY, 7ᵀᴴ OF APRIL
EARLY MORNING

Monika woke up with the sun peeking through the curtains. She had a splitting headache. Mrs. Johannesen had made her a large pot of chamomile tea that she drank with a sedative to help her sleep. The two women had talked until Monika couldn't keep her eyes open any longer. Alongside the bed was a small note in Mrs. Johannesen's handwriting inviting her to come for breakfast when she woke.

Monika sat up in the bed and looked out the window, the tears welling up again. She fought them down. She would not be crying anymore. The words of the inspector lady still resonated in her head, "Dry your tears, Monika, and grow up. The world is full of injustice."

"Yes, the world is full of injustice, but the wicked will be punished." She had resolved it in her head. It would start with the NoSaints. Monika NLN was going to be the punisher.

She got up and went to find Mrs. Johannesen.

CHAPTER 43

CORPORATE OFFICE, WONG SHIPPING AND ENTERPRISES, INC.
SINGAPORE
TUESDAY, 10TH OF APRIL

Jim Wong answered the last of the five questions: *Do you like French fries with your hamburger?* The software detected the keystrokes. Mr. Wong would never willingly eat a hamburger or French fries for that matter.

The question was presented on the screen for precisely five seconds and he had ten seconds to complete his answer. He was seated in front of a table in a secure room using a virtual keyboard on a touch-sensitive display embedded into the table. His irritation at answering the silly question came across in the manner in which he typed. It was expected—matching his personality profile.

A second display on the wall showed the status of the twelve participants joining the call from various parts of the world. They were in the process of making their credentials known and getting validated for access. They came up one by one. There were four women. Jim Wong was the last that remained to complete his initiation. It should have been completed by now, another reason for his irritation.

The famous White House Situation Room at 1600 Pennsylvania Avenue did not have near the electronic sophistication of this room. A Faraday Cage embedded in the concrete prevented any inbound or outbound leakage of electronic signals—cell phones didn't work in this room, not that they were permitted—the sensors continuously scanned for the presence of any unauthorized electronics. Mahogany wood walls gave the illusion of an old style executive suite, pleasing to the eye but electronically dead.

The illusion was part of the plan. Behind these walls, and embedded in the eighteen-inch steel-reinforced slab-to-slab concrete floor, ceiling, and wall construction lived an array of electronics to make a spook green with envy. In the world of government this type room was called a Sensitive Compartmented Information Facility, better known as a SCIF. Everything ran on batteries fed by a protected and filtered power source. Mr. Wong's voice was being recorded and pattern matched. Facial recognition software also matched him to the pattern in the database. This was the one and only Jim Wong, CEO of Wong Shipping and Enterprises, Inc., based out of Singapore.

Across the world a similar process was taking place in eleven different locations. The Asian contingent included an Aussie in Sydney, a Chinese from Shanghai, a Japanese in Tokyo and a Korean in Seoul, all Chief Executives in their own corporations and each representing a different sector of industry. There were four Americans, out of Bogota in the South, Mexico City in Central, Washington DC in the US, and Montreal, Canada to the north. Europe had two, in addition to Pascal, a Frenchman out of Marseille and a German out of Berlin. An Israeli and an Indian out of Mumbai completed the twelve.

The authentication system in the SCIF sampled what Wong knew, the answers to the questions, and how he typed the answers. It also required that he present a token with an encryption key, one that he wore as a necklace with an embedded a tiny passive Radio Frequency Identification device known as an RFID chip. That was just for starters. The system also sampled the biology of Jim Wong, how he talked. Even his mannerisms were part of the pattern-matching profile. This was indeed Jim Wong and there was no one else in the room. Body temperature was also measured. The presence of another person would be known. Nothing was left to chance.

Wong thought that all he needed to do to be granted access was answer five silly questions correctly. Little did he know.

The room had been designed and installed by HII, otherwise known as Haywood Industries, Inc. HII was one of the many so-called Beltway Bandits that dotted the landscape around Washington DC. They had once built these

SCIFs for the Intelligence Community, the select member agencies that had, like all things in Washington, been converted into an acronym—in this case the IC. HII served the IC and many other government clients. Like its peer competitors, HII had become a global brand growing so large that it was counted in the Fortune 100 of the largest firms in the world.

But of late they had struggled. Washington had changed the rules of acquisition, and the ever growing partisan stagnation had made it all the harder to win the deals. So HII diversified at the insistence of its third in the generation of Chief Executives at the helm of HII—

One of the twelve joining the call, Mr. Alexander Haywood, III, was CEO and Chairman of the Board of HII. Its information technology systems integration division served many of the agencies in the IC with its SCIF technologies—an expertise that had once been reserved for the member countries known as the Five-Eyes. It was a throwback to World War II, a members-only club that included the United States, the United Kingdom, Canada, Australia and New Zealand. Its Research and Development offices in Kista, Sweden, and Herzlia, Israel made it all the more flexible to take their particular skill from the service of government and into the service of the so-called private sector of commercial companies. HII won the contract to install the sophisticated SCIFs for a private not-for-profit organization known as Seraphim.

Up on the screen, in the SCIF located on the same floor as the office of the CEO of Wong Shipping and Enterprises, was a digital avatar; not the cartoonish version, but a digital-animated replica of the shipping magnate. When Wong spoke, his voice was changed into the digital voice of the avatar with only the slightest delay; his expressions looked uncannily like its real biological source. At the bottom of the screen was the Seraphim logo of a six-winged dark angel holding a broken chain in its two hands and the caption, *Until the day when we transcend.*

"Welcome everyone." The avatar called Pascal Du Relo spoke to initiate the session and the other twelve responded with a "hello Pascal," in English.

"Let's begin. As a reminder, this is a recorded session. We are making history, ladies and gentlemen. The date of transcendency approaches; now only seven years, four months, and eight days remain. Everything is proceeding according to plan. Your vitals were all processed; everyone was well within the parameters. We had hoped to complete the initiation by this date, but unforeseen circumstances caused us to postpone the date with Mr. Wong. It is being rescheduled. A new date has not been determined but certainly we expect to have the initiation completed by the time of our next scheduled meeting in the next quarter. I know you have questions so I will pause and take the first one. As always, please indicate so on your screen."

Almost immediately there were four questions, one from the Avatar of the man who led the largest chemical industries conglomerate in the world, and the same for nuclear energy, military hardware, and agriculture. The Count Du Relo was nonplussed. He had expected questions. He raised an eyebrow. Wong was not one of the ones asking a question. He suspected that there was a proxy, someone asking for Wong. Which one was it, he wondered. He guessed Nuclear. "Your question, Henri?" was directed at the Frenchman and CEO of the French nuclear energy giant.

CHAPTER 44

OFFICE OF CHIEF INSPECTOR LOUIS BETÓN
BRUSSELS, BELGIUM
TUESDAY, 10ᵀᴴ OF APRIL

"There are three possibilities that match your request, Inspector. Starting with the top one, at the ING Uz, the Saint-Luc University Hospital here in Brussels. The name you gave me matches a male registered as Rodrigo Kajetan from Hungary. The hospital said that the police had been there as required when a patient is admitted with gunshot wounds. The police, they said, had made it clear that they would return when he was conscious. What would you like to do?"

The young woman Laura stood there in front of his desk waiting for his instruction. Betón was thinking it over—again.

He had a suspicion that whatever he decided would have consequences—later.

"Nothing at the moment. Get me the information for all three."

"I have it printed." She pulled the report from her folder and passed it to him.

"There is one more thing, Laura. Get me the phone number of my counterpart in Hungary. I am going to make this his problem."

The Inspector's Assistant, Laura Souci, left Betón's office and headed back to her cubicle She wondered what was troubling her boss. He was normally more decisive on these matters and he was loath to get involved with trivial things—like this one. She let it drop. It didn't appear like the Inspector was going to do anything with it anyway.

Betón thought he could kill for a cigarette right about now. He walked out of his office past Laura's desk. "Laura, I'll be outside." She knew this was code. The inspector would be taking his office work to his car where he smoked his cigarettes and made calls on his mobile.

Once inside the BMW X5 police vehicle, the Inspector's Vehicle, Betón lit up, took a long drag and made a few preliminary calls, then dialed Hansen. DSI Hansen picked up on the second ring. "Fredrik?"

"Louis. You have news?"

"Yes. Your boy. We located him. I have to act ... unless he disappears ... soon. You understand what I'm saying?"

"How much time?"

"Twenty-four hours max, not more than that."

"Okay. Twenty-four is enough. How is he?"

"Still sedated. Just spoke to the doctor. He says they can wake him anytime. The critical period is over, and they don't want to keep him sedated any longer than necessary. I told him that someone would be there to visit him. To wait until he arrived. He agreed, but he said that he would not wait longer than the twenty-four."

"Thank you Louis, twenty four should be enough ..."

Betón interrupted, "... he needs to disappear. It took my assistant less than a day to locate him. For all we know, whoever is behind this has already figured out that your boy is the missing fourth person, may even have someone already on the way to the hospital. We had an advantage—we had his first name and we knew approximately when he would have been admitted. These are not insignificant ..."

"I know, I know. Twenty-four hours max, and sooner if possible. I would go there myself, but that would create the very trail we are trying to avoid."

"Me too. Everything I do becomes a matter of record ... and I cannot afford to have this one come back and bite me ... I am on thin ice as it is, the politicos have me by the balls. What about the American you told me about?"

"That's what I was thinking. He has a vital interest in keeping Frank alive ... and access to resources. I will call him as soon as we hang up. Can you arrange it with the hospital?"

"Yes. Tell me when you have it worked out with the American—assuming he agrees."

"Will do. Again, thank you."

"Don't thank me yet. We're still in the swamp on this one. Sooner the boy is out of that hospital the sooner I will breathe easier."

"I'll text you confirmation and details of his arrival."

"Very good. One last thing."

"Yes?"

"When they have a vise positioned around your balls, they don't have to squeeze very much to get your attention. You understand? I want this vise gone ... but until it is gone ..."

"You don't have to explain, I get the picture."

"I hope you do. *Au revoir* ..."

CHAPTER 45

NORTH OF NEW YORK CITY
TUESDAY, 10ᵀᴴ OF APRIL

Jaime was on Interstate 684 headed north. North on I-684 was where the rich people lived; people like Bill and Hillary Clinton, who made their home in Westchester County when they weren't out traveling in the business of politics. He was in the Bu car, pronounced Beu and short for Bureau as in Federal Bureau of Investigations. The radio under the dash crackled every so often with the voice of the dispatcher. Many of the FBI field offices remained stuck on an old convention of reporting the comings and goings of its agents over a radio network with a frequency band set aside for the FBI. The network was a throwback to the Hoover era. Some traditions changed very little. It was background noise—nothing that Jaime paid any attention to any longer.

ENIKITA

The Bronx was to the south, less than twenty miles as the crow flies. The contrast was like night and day. The Bronx was a forest of concrete, steel, stone, bricks, and black-tar roads. Jaime was on the highway running from the south northbound where the scenery changed to the lush springtime forests of magnificent oaks, elms, and evergreens of every variety. He felt like he was driving in a foreign land. He missed the noise and bustle of the city and the particular neighborhood they called The Bronx.

The Bronx had been home back in the day, the days of youth and innocence. That is where he and Caro had grown up. Now they lived north of the city—in the township of Armonk in Westchester County.

It was all thanks to Caro's income. He had caved in on her insistence that she wanted her children growing up in a safer place. He had argued, chafed, and finally gave in. Caro usually got what Caro wanted. It was also her money that paid for the house in Armonk. Bureau pay did not match up to the idea of living in Hillary's neighborhood.

It had been a good day, the kind of rare day when he thought about breaking away early and seeing the kids ... and Caro. He had called her earlier, asked her out on a date.

It was Friday. "I deserve it," he thought, the hint of a smile creeping across his face with the thought of "chilling out with Caro, a bottle of wine, a nice Italian dinner out in Fairfield, Connecticut, maybe catch a concert, walk the shore of the

Connecticut beaches on Long Island Sound." The phone rang and broke his reverie. His smile disappeared. It displayed an area code for somewhere in Arizona, but he knew better. It was Norway calling. This could not be good.

"Inspector!" Jaime liked calling him by his title. It conveyed a sense of respect for his senior friend.

"Hello Jaime. Can you talk?"

"Yes, no problem. I'm in the car, almost home. How's Grete?"

"Doing well, back with her parents, a bit of a celebrity, if you know what I mean, but the parents are keeping the press at bay, and it seems that the media are behaving themselves. We owe a great debt of gratitude to you and the FBI. It won't be forgotten." There was a sense of melancholy in his voice. Jaime knew something else was coming, but a few moments of idle chatter wouldn't do any harm.

"I will tell you one thing, Inspector, this was the most personally rewarding case that I have ever worked on ... the entire team feels the same. They wanted to make sure that I told you so. We thank *you*—happy we could do our part." He decided to give DSI Hansen his cue. "But I guess that's not why you're calling."

⋏

Finishing the call, it took Jaime a moment to shake off the home persona and to go *operational*. Then it was all business. In ten minutes he was at the house, the old colonial style home that Caro had fallen in love with. He went straight to his ready room, picking up his go-bag, on the phone the whole time; first with Caro, who was inbound; his Section Chief to get the travel approvals; Special Agent Jillian Rose, who was second in charge of the squad; and to the travel office to get the tickets lined up. Analyst Atkins had his firearms travel forms filled out for him, and sent it to him on his mobile phone. All he needed was to wait for Caro. The flight out of JFK would not wait and he needed to be on that flight.

Her Mercedes Benz finally pulled into the driveway. She opened the door and ran to his arms. Jaime embraced the skinny Nuyorican girl of his youth who was now the lusciously attractive and smart as the dickens head banker of the Boston Federal Reserve. He could feel the operational persona slipping, his loins starting to hurt and his need to go begin to crumble. "You're gonna owe me one," she said, as she nipped at his ear in secret. The kids, Caro and Jaime, respectively six and five years old, were standing there sullen at not getting to Mom first. He looked briefly at his mother-in-law standing there by the front door. She had a big smile on her Puerto Rican face. Jaime knew from where it was that Caro had inherited her looks.

Caro pulled away ... she knew it was time—time for him to go and time for her Special Agent husband to get his game face on. "And you'd better not come home without lots of Belgian chocolates."

"Chocolate!" The kids screamed. They all did a group hug. Supervisory Special Agent Jaime Rodriguez buckled up and pulled out of the driveway with a screech of the wheels.

CHAPTER 46

OSLO, NORWAY
TUESDAY, 10ᵀᴴ OF APRIL

"**W**ho the fuck do you ..."

"Frank is dead."

It took a moment for The Voice to process what he had just heard. It had taken him by surprise—the call from this number and then the woman's voice. He thought it was Frank calling him.

She kept him on the hook, "... and if you're asking who the fuck I am, the answer is Frank's replacement, a better version."

She canceled the call and put the phone down on the desk, chewing on her fingernails—an old habit she had not lost despite the years.

"This is going to work ... or not," she thought. She started thinking "not" when the phone rang. It had been a full ten seconds, but seemed like an eternity. "Now to keep playing the game," she thought, "Don't Panic" was her motto, like from the Hitchhiker book. She didn't answer. Four rings and still she didn't pick up. On the seventh ring, she accepted the call and started speaking.

"Seems I was right, ... you need a new Frank ..."

"And who the fuck ..."

She hung up on him again. This time he called back in seconds. Monika let it go to the seventh ring—again. Then she answered.

"You need a new Frank. Except this girl plays by different rules. That shit you pulled on Frank ... try that on me, and ... let's just say I've got bad friends, like in good friends who are bad people ... the kind that speak Russian and who wouldn't give a flying fuck who you are or how much money you have."

The phone was silent for what seemed like an eternity to her. "Don't Panic, this is going to work, or ..." She heard him laughing.

She could tell it sounded ... forced, like a bad actor. "You gotta pair of balls," pause, "I'll give you that," pause, "figuratively speaking of course," longer pause, "... talk, what happened?"

Monika told him—first the short version. She filled in the details with his questions—as much as she knew.

"And what makes you better than Frank?"

"Well for one, I'm not a pussy like he was. Figuratively speaking, of course." This time The Voice laughed out loud for real. No acting this time.

He regained his composure and got almost—chatty. "But that doesn't tell me a thing about you, where you're from, how I ..."

She interrupted. "No it doesn't. But then, if I told you, it would be like ... like if I were talking to you in Mandarin. You wouldn't understand a word I was speaking. Only way you're going to know is to give me a mark ... then you'll see."

Silence—again.

"Just so happens ..."

"No, first we meet. You get to see me. I get to see you. Send a flunky and game over. We meet in person, give me the details of the mark, and then you'll see. And so you know now, I'm not taking your phone calls in the middle of the night. I'll show you how to send me information—privately. How do you think I found your number? That's how good I am ..." she suppressed a giggle, "never figured you for a fat business executive." She giggled.

"You don't know shit…"

"Like hell I don't."

Silence. Longer this time.

"We will meet ..." pause, "have any suggestions—Monika?"

"Actually, I do. In a public place, you see me, I see you, we go to a coffee house, I leave a newspaper on the coffee table, you pick it up, no one sees us together ... then you know who I am, and you'll know how to reach me, secure, private, no electronic trace."

"The parliament building, there's a kiosk a block away, in the park, sells ..."

"Sells newspapers. I know it. I'll be there ... at nine thirty on Wednesday, tomorrow?"

"Nine thirty, Wednesday it is."

"How do I recognize you?"

"Black hair, purple reflective sunglasses, white skin, purple scarf, five-ten, wearing a black leather jacket. I'll be the only chick at that kiosk wearing purple that morning."

"And you?"

"You know what I look like."

"Yes, I do."

"All right then." Monika hung up the phone.

She then promptly got back on her computer and watched. It was a hunch, nothing more. Monika had pushed his ego buttons, the kind she suspected made The Voice tick. No way he was going to lose control—not to a girl.

It didn't take long. She had previously taken control, or "owned," access to The Voice's computer well before she had called him. She had turned on log captures; the data got sent to another server that she owned, rather that she borrowed from a university to store data, like the stream of log data getting generated from The Voice's computer. At night, Monika didn't read novels or watch movies. With a glass of red wine, under the cover of her bed or listening to Mrs. Johannesen talk about her past, Monika combed through logs looking for clues. The previous nights had revealed all she needed, everything about the organization called NoSaints, and about the group's money manager and handler of Frank. He had not been the only one, she realized.

In the middle of the most arcane computer data she found everything she was looking for, all the many needles in the haystacks of machine data that told the story of websites visited, orders placed, monies wired. And she found out about the double life of one Hans Pettersen, also known as The Voice, businessman and executive for a charitable organization helping immigrant families in Norway.

She watched in real-time on her screen. He logged into what he thought was a protected web portal for a flower delivery company. The keylogger software captured the ID and password that he typed in. The website was designed for the most eccentric of online buyers, the clients that ordered specialty flowers. One could order anything—including black roses at various price ranges. It was open to the public—and to a select set of clients like Pettersen with a specialized access code.

That's what Mr. Hans Pettersen did.

With a few clicks of the mouse Hans Pettersen ordered a dozen black roses to be delivered on the specified date to *a black haired, pale-skinned woman, five feet, ten inches tall, purple-colored reflective sunglasses, a purple scarf and wearing a black leather jacket—to be delivered at the kiosk just outside the main entrance to the Norwegian Parliament building on the corner of Rosenkranz and Karl Johans. A dozen black roses, no less, at nine thirty in the morning. Will send confirmation text message when spotted in front of Kiosk.*

Payment for the dozen black roses was set at five hundred Norwegian Krones, depicted as 500 NOK, roughly $100— what one might expect for the away *from the mainstream flowers* as the website said. Only the actual price sent in the transaction to the bank for the select clients like Pettersen added two zeros at the end. Payment was processed.

Monika smiled. "It was priced to include the short notice," she thought.

She saw him log off the website. The confirmation would be sent to him on his smartphone—like any legitimate business online transaction—and copied to her. As soon as he logged out, Monika gained access to the web site and made a few of changes.

It was now set to deliver the same flowers, same date and location, but the description changed to *sometime between nine and nine thirty in the morning for a male, six feet tall, middle aged, in a business suit, arriving in a gray Mercedes Benz C-Class. Will text confirmation with any additional description when he arrives to receive the bouquet.*

In the notes section she made an additional comment, *a reward bonus of 250 NOK for delivery as planned.* She smiled again. It wasn't her money she was spending. The NoSaints could afford it, now that she had access to their bank accounts.

Hell hath no fury like a woman ... who needs revenge ... and can hack the fuck out of anything, she thought. *For Frank*, she thought, again, ... and for my little one growing in my belly.

"Now to own the NoSaints. First them. Then the bastards who killed Frank."

She sipped on her red wine. That was her next task, and she had a lot of work to do.

CHAPTER 47

BANGKOK, THAILAND
JANUARY 1997

"When God is Dead, that's what Nietzsche said." Pascal was drinking his Vodka cocktail, a cube of ice was still floating and twisting in the clear drink—like an iceberg floating into tropical seas. He watched it, thinking about what he was going to say next, "... and so is government ... as we've known it."

He looked around the scenery of the outdoor bar in the fancy hotel, the sun beating down, glistening off the crystalline blue water of the hotel pool.

He looked at Silvio. "... when will that day arrive? I cannot wait." He said it not as a question and not as anticipation, but as frustration.

"These old anachronisms of the past, they are like the suits of armor from the time of Medieval Knights. Maybe useful in its day, but today ... of no use whatsoever, except for making movies for the romantics ... thinking of chivalry and codes of honor." He snorted a short laugh.

Silvio stared back at him through the sunglasses. Pascal had been moodier of late, not as carefree. The vacation was winding down. Maybe that was it.

"There's a better way, Silvio. These people, here in Thailand, the poverty is everywhere; in Europe they are the bourgeoisie, wherever you go it's the same, ... they are like sheep, bleating stupid sheep, blah, blah, blah sheep that need to be led. But they are also people, honest people who want nothing more than to live in peace, to have their basic necessities met. And the governments of this world are failing them, they always have. War and more war, the earth's resources all taken up, pollution everywhere, gods of all kinds polluting the mind, religious gods, capitalist gods ... is there no end to the stink of it all?"

Pascal took a sip of his cocktail, took his glasses off and wiped his brow with the wet paper napkin. "I think we can—you, me, others—shake off the old ways and govern—really govern ... intelligently, forcefully, efficiently; take down all the barriers of stupid country borders, help kill off religion like Nietzsche said, only help it along. That's what I think," he said, putting his sunglasses down and diving into the pool.

Silvio didn't know what to make of the latest outburst. Pascal didn't ask him his opinion. And he had one. The fact was that nothing stirred his soul like it did when Pascal reminisced about what the future could be, a place where a new aristocracy would arise, not one of blood, but of capability.

CHAPTER 48

BRUSSELS, BELGIUM
WEDNESDAY, 11ᵀᴴ OF APRIL
07:30 CET

Special Agent Jaime Rodriguez exited through passport control with all the other passengers. It was seven thirty in the morning. He was starved. The Bureau did not pay for business class travel and what passed for breakfast on the economy class was something he decided he would rather pass. With no checked-in luggage he was able to register the paperwork for his firearm and exit out to find Legat, Special Agent Robert Levin, out of the Brussels Office there waiting for him. The two men had worked in the same Field Office in a past assignment. Levin was a large black man who had made his way into the FBI by way of the U.S. Marine Corps. They shook hands and headed for Levin's car.

"We've got you staying at the hotel near the office. I've got your reservation printed in this folder. I'm guessing you want to head straight to the hospital?"

"Yes, but can we find a place for coffee and a bagel or something?"

"Can do—once we get started. Best we get a head start before the traffic starts picking up. This has been the most unusual arrangement getting you clearance to operate in this country. Normally, we have mountains of bureaucracy to go through, but I got the call from none other than the Chief Inspector. Said that the sooner this guy named Frank is our problem and out of the hospital, the happier he will be ... and they want to be hands off. This is a new one. By the way, remember Inspector Lieuvin, from the Europol Office?"

"Yes, I remember, the one who helped get the Belgiques to stand down the police from combing the area. Turned out to be the right call."

"Yes it was. Anyway, Lieuvin is going to meet us at the hospital. She wants in on what is happening. You good with that?"

"I am. She helped us. She done good."

Levin started up the Ford Taurus and headed to the exit looking for the E19 around the city of Brussels that would take them east on the northern curve of the beltway and to the hospital. Once in the car, SA Rodriguez called Inspector Hansen and brought him up to date.

CHAPTER 49

OSLO, NORWAY
WEDNESDAY, 11ᵀᴴ OF APRIL
06:30 CET

Monika didn't sleep much that night. By half past six she was showered, dressed, and had her first Red Bull of the day. She was biting her fingernails—furiously. Waiting made her stir crazy. It wouldn't do to leave too early. So she waited. By seven she could wait no longer. She headed out the door and to her car. Mrs. Johannesen watched her go peering out the window from her kitchen and said a little prayer for the girl that she had taken in, her "little orphan girl," as she thought of her. She had heard the pacing in the room upstairs. Something was going to happen today. Mrs. Johannesen wondered if she would see her

Monika again. She said another prayer. "It was now in God's hands," she thought.

Monika got in her black Mini Cooper, started the engine and headed downhill towards the city. It was going to be a brilliantly clear day; the air was crisp, colder than it had been for days—her kind of weather. She was about to enter the highway when her phone beeped to tell her that she had a new message. She thought about taking a peek then decided best to wait when she was parked, "it's probably a tweet," she thought, from her Twitter account feeding her the morsels of information and gossip posted of the people she followed—people in her field.

She continued on, her mind focused on the one thing she needed to accomplish today, to clean the slate of Frank's past, and her past, so she could face the future with her new child. She so wanted it "to be a boy, so I can give him Frank's name. I will love him more than any child has ever been loved," she thought.

A horn woke her from her thoughts. She drove the Mini Cooper past the stop light, dabbed at her eyes and chewed on her fingernails, refocused on the necessary delivery of the bouquet of black roses to the one called The Voice.

When she had done her research, Monika had not wanted to know more, not about the family that Pettersen had; the wife and two children, a boy and a girl, teenagers, probably completely unaware that dad, Mr. Hans Pettersen, well-regarded humanist in the country that celebrated humanists, was also the operational head of the NoSaints.

The Grand Hotel was just ahead. She maneuvered the Mini Cooper into the underground parking lot, not more than a block away from the hotel. She locked the car and walked up the stairs exiting out onto the bright sunshine of the morning. The street was busy full of delivery trucks and service vehicles stocking the chic shops of Oslo's city center. Reaching the corner she also saw the street cafes setting up the tables and chairs. The city's service workforce had been up early to get everything ready for the day's routine.

A parade of office workers were already out, just like her, walking up the slight incline past the shops getting ready to open. The sidewalk was busier by the moment.

She was wearing a cream-colored blouse, with a string of small pearls to accent her neck and to accent to her otherwise pale skin. Monika had dressed as conventional as any of the others walking to work.

Frank would not have recognized her, the nicely coiffed brunette wearing a black skirt, dark pantyhose and black rounded-front pumps, with her morning coffee in a paper cup getting ready for the day. Two small pearls, one for each ear lobe, accentuated the entire look. She looked ... attractive, not head-twisting attractive, just pretty with a small twist of lime put in the drink to give it that sense of the exotic. No one gave her a second look at this time of day, but after work would be a different thing. The pedestrians were in their robotic routine, headed to work, many of them already at risk of being late.

CHAPTER 50

ING, Uz Clinic
Outskirts of Brussels, Belgium
Wednesday, 11ᵗʰ of April
07:31 CET

Frank opened his eyes. It was like waking from a long and deep sleep, the mind trying to bridge the gap from when it had its last conscious thought. He heard a voice. It was the doctor talking to him.

"I am Dr. Solis. Can you hear, Monsieur Kajetan?" He said it in English.

"Water," he croaked. Dr. Solis passed him a bottle of water with a straw. It felt good. Frank could feel the coolness of the water slide down his esophagus.

"You are feeling better, yes?"

Frank nodded in assent. "Where am I?"

"In hospital, near Brussels. You are very sick, Monsieur Kajetan, your lungs and your ear. But you are young. You will get better."

Frank grabbed the doctor's arm. He had an intense look on his face, his eyes watering. There was a patch on his abdomen. He remembered. "My pack? My backpack, where is it, Doctor?"

Dr. Solis went to the closet and brought him his backpack. "I leave you now, come back in two hours, will check on you then. Much better."

The elder gentleman in the white frock headed out to make his early morning rounds, as was his custom. The night before he and the hospital administrator had a professional argument about keeping to the requests of the police chief.

"I have no intention of keeping the patient sedated any longer. There could be lasting harm," he told the administrator. They compromised. Dr. Solis could stop the sedation first thing in the morning.

Frank opened his backpack and found his phone. His mind was reconnecting memories and urgent tasks—foremost that he had to maintain his new identity and to keep a low profile. He had many questions; the kind of questions best answered by his phone, like what day is it, and the most important task, to talk to Monika.

The phone would not activate, he could see that the battery had died. With the help of a nurse, he connected the charger and watched as the phone came back to life. He had to be patient.

The charge would take some minutes before he could place a call. The text-messaging app came up first. "Best to text her, we can talk when she's up," he thought. He checked the date. It was Wednesday, 9th of April. "Five days," he thought, "five days of not knowing, and Monika with no news." He used her handle, so she would know it was really him. "M0k1. New phone. Note number. Am ok—in hospital in Brussels. Will catch flight to Oslo tomorrow morning. Must see you!!! Call me. F."

He next picked up the rag dog, Le Petit Prince, and stared at it, turning it every which way, trying to piece together what it was that Grete had told him. He remembered, "This is for you, Mister Rodrigo," she had said, "The secret is in his heart." He looked again. There it was, in the seam under the chin, where the head was attached to the body, a small strip of Velcro that he pulled open.

The pocket was a few inches deep leading down to where the heart would be. Frank was able to fit two fingers in and pulled out little folded up strips of paper with Spanish writing ... in pencil, and there were a few others, written in German. There was also Grete's contribution, written in her native Norwegian. His heart beat fast. Frank did not want to read what was in these small scraps of paper. Yet he did. He started with Grete's, and learned how she had discovered the secret compartment and about her fears. His heart calmed.

Opening the next note Frank mouthed the words trying to make sense of the message written in Spanish. The handwriting was in miniaturized script—written in tiny print like the work of a young teenager writing the formulas for a school math test. He struggled to remember the little Spanish that he knew, restarted from the beginning reading a word using Google Translator to aid him. It came slowly. And then, like bringing a microscope into focus, the message in the small bit of paper finally became crystal clear. It was worse than even he had feared.

Tears of horror streamed down his face. He shook his head, his hands covering his face like he could hide from the message in Julia's notes. Frank's heart began to race. The machine that kept track of his vital signs starting to squeal. He let loose a watery gruel of vomit on the bed sheets. "Toilet," he thought, "... got to get to the toilet when he fell in a tangle of the metal stand and the IV tubing that had ripped out of his arm.

The nurse from the front desk came in hurriedly through the door running to find him in a seizure. Three other nurses arrived shortly after to give her a hand.

One of the nurses called Dr. Solis, but he was tied up with another patient in an urgent matter. Another doctor was luckily there having just arrived.

Dr. Mila Josefino took charge, and together with the nurse, they placed the patient, Mr. Rodrigo Kajetan, back on the bed, his knees tucked in under his chin, still crying but calming down, whimpering. The nurses reattached the IV and Dr. Josefino told the nurses that he had it under control. He came out a few minutes later, filled in his report on the clipboard and told the nurse that he had given the patient a mild sedative to calm him down; the rest he would leave to Dr. Solis. She thanked him profusely and went in to check on her patient. Frank was sleeping peacefully.

CHAPTER 51

ARRIVING AT THE ING, UZ CLINIC
OUTSKIRTS OF BRUSSELS, BELGIUM
WEDNESDAY, 11TH OF APRIL
08:30 CET

Inspector Patricia Lieuvin saw the two FBI Agents in the parking lot. *They're cute*, she thought, *very cute, in a very American sort of way.* She allowed herself a momentary smile. She exited her car and met the two Agents. The three of them walked towards the entrance, the thirty-something blonde- haired woman walked between the two men. Her pictures did not do her justice. She had the athletic build of a swimmer, which she was. Lieuvin was in her business attire wearing a navy blue jacket and skirt, hose, and black leather pumps. Inspector Lieuvin was flanked by the two big men, carbon copies of each other, well dressed in their blue American-style suits, thickly- soled shoes, white button-down shirts.

The three entered the lobby of the non-descript white ING, Uz hospital with its two multi-story wings. Lieuvin registered their visit as official law enforcement business. The escort took them down the hallway and up to the second floor, where they were handed off to a middle-aged nurse in the white uniform and nurse's cap. They were expected. The nurse was "happy that the government had sent in a doctor, he had been so helpful."

Rodriguez and Levin looked at Lieuvin, who made the cross-cultural shrugging of the shoulders. Before Inspector Lieuvin could ask, the nurse offered that "Dr. Solis is the attending physician and he should be available in a moment. He is with Monsieur Kajetan at this time."

An audible alarm went off, persistent but low key, just enough to get attention. The nurse had a momentary look of concern, looking up the hall and then to the panel behind the counter. It was blinking red ... from Monsieur Kajetan's room according to the label on the monitor.

"Will you excuse me, please," she said hurriedly, "... and please stay here, I will be back as quick as I can."

The nurse turned the corner around the L-shaped nurse's station and hurried, without running, down the hallway to the fifth room on the left side. Rodriguez sidled up to the nurse's station and took a discrete look over the partition wall. Room number 205 was blinking red, what appeared like precisely where the nurse had entered. Another nurse came from the opposite side of the hallway and also entered the same room.

Rodriguez turned around to look at his companions and also shrugged his shoulders. There was nothing to indicate that the alarm was initiated in Becken's room, but his misgiving fueled a growing apprehension. *Are we too late?* he thought.

The three law enforcement officers were about to sit down when they all spotted the nurse returning, the look on her face confirmed to Rodriguez that the erstwhile hacker, Frank Becken, was indeed not the luckiest guy around. And he knew, that without Frank, his part of the investigation was in trouble. It had not been all about cross-Atlantic cooperation that had convinced the FBI leadership to put their best and brightest on the case.

The nurse went straight to Inspector Lieuvin. She was visibly upset, her cheeks glowing red from the exertion.

"The doctor will be out as quickly as he can," she said. "He knows that you are here." She kept averting her eyes.

Rodriguez had enough years in his career listening to people evade and lie when being questioned. It was clear that the nurse would rather not speak further. *It must be Becken*, he thought. He also thought again about what Frank had asked him to do before he went in to find Grete, the message he had been asked to deliver to Monika in Oslo. He hoped not to have to deliver that message. The nurse asked them to take a seat in the waiting area and they obliged. There was nothing for them to do at the moment.

It was nearly half an hour later. Lieuvin had gone twice to the nurse and inquired about the status of Monsieur Kajetan and each time got the same evasive answer, that the doctor would be out shortly to speak with them. And then he did.

The elderly doctor had been practicing medicine for over thirty years. He had learned how to be tender with the families of his patients. With the police, he had also learned, it was best to get to the point. But it was never any easier.

He introduced himself and beckoned the trio to join him in the consulting room. The four of them walked into the small nondescript room adjacent to the nurse's station. It was not a place where people lingered for very long. He spoke in English. "Monsieur Kajetan is in a coma," he said, "... and recovery...is, how do you say, ah yes, uncertain. We will make further tests ... to see the brain. He may have brain damage, it is uncertain. That is the situation, as much as we know."

Lieuvin took the lead to ask the obvious questions where they learned the truth about what had happened. The doctor avoided speculation and did not convey any false hope, only that "Monsieur Kajetan is young, and with youth there is always the potential of recovery. Rodriguez wanted her to get to the most pressing question, and eventually she did. He could see that she was being careful. To build trust, one had to convey concern first—empathy. She handled it well, so he stayed patient.

"And how did this happen, Doctor? He came in with smoke ..."

Doctor Solis interrupted her. He knew this question was coming, and he knew that this is where he and the hospital could be in for some legal jeopardy. He proceeded nonetheless, angry at what had just happened. He wanted the police to understand, to help them find who did this.

"We don't know why, or who he really is, but a doctor Josefino was here when Monsieur Kajetans was having ... an emotional breakdown. I had just left him, my patient. He was awake, we spoke, he was doing ... well, could be released maybe tomorrow." He paused for a second. All three investigators saw the change in the doctor's facial expression, the visible anger.

"This Doctor Josefino, gave my patient a sedative, a lethal dose ..." he hesitated, "... that would kill him ... in minutes." The elderly doctor was visibly distressed, unable to fathom how anyone, especially a doctor, could do such a thing to a healthy young man. "I looked in the registry. There is no Doctor Josefino, not in Belgium." And then he broke his own rule by offering a conjecture. "This, this doctor is no doctor. That is my opinion. Find her, Inspectors—please, find this woman."

Special Agent Rodriguez broke his silence. "Can we go in to see him, sir? There may be valuable evidence that can lead us to understand who and how this happened. And one more thing, doctor. We will need to move him…to a safer place. I don't mean any disrespect ..."

"None taken, Monsieur ...?"

"Rodriguez, sir"

"Yes, Monsieur Rodriguez. I agree. He would be safer elsewhere. With an ambulance, he can be moved, yes. I will allow it."

Outside the clinic by their cars, the trio of Leiuvin, Levin, and Rodriguez huddled together. "How about K-Town, Landstuhl?" Levin had been a military brat when his father had been stationed with the U.S. Army's First Armored Division and he knew about Landstuhl, the U.S. military medical facility in Kaiserslautern, Germany where he had made frequent visits to see his father recovering from battle wounds. "Landstuhl is not far and he would be under military protection there."

It was agreed.

They were about to get into their cars when they saw the nurse, the same one that they had just left, come running out of the door. She spotted them.

"Please," she said, "Inspector Lieuvin, can you come back, please?" The trio of law enforcement investigators walked back to the entrance of the building.

The nurse for some reason went directly to Rodriguez. She had something in her hand. She was shaking, in anger, her hands were trembling. Nurse Madeline Vervloet, herself not a small woman, took the right hand of the tall Special Agent Rodriguez and deposited several small scraps of paper. She closed his fingers around the papers and shook his hand vigorously.

She looked at Inspector Lieuvin and said in French, "They were in his hands, clutched in his hands. We had to pry his fingers open and that is when we discovered this. Find them inspector, find the bastards who did this."

Supervisory Special Agent Jaime Rodriguez and then Legat Special Agent Levin and Europol Inspector Lieuvin each read the notes in succession like passing family photographs. The notes from Grete, a young German girl named Angelina, and finally the diary of Julia Michaela Santander made each of them angry. It was resolved in their minds. If it was the last thing they did in their lives, it would be to find these "bastards" as Nurse Vervloet had called them. Julia had given them some clues, more pieces to the puzzle. Special Agent Rodriguez could think of a different choice of words right now.

In the car, headed to find the hotel and a place for the two men to catch a late morning breakfast, Rodriguez called DSI Hansen. He gave him the update and told him about the text message that Frank sent out to Monika and about the two phone calls that Frank had received unanswered, and finally that he would be flying in to Oslo's Gardermoen International Airport on the first available flight.

The two men agreed that Jaime's visit to Oslo would also serve as the opportunity for Jaime to take possession of the laptops and smartphones they had found in the partially burned out RV.

"Inspector, one more thing. Can you meet me at the airport? I will send you specifics of the flight when I've made the arrangements. I suspect that Monika may be there in the morning, waiting to see if Frank arrives. Would make sense, given his last text message."

CHAPTER 52

DOWNTOWN OSLO, NORWAY
WEDNESDAY, 11ᵀᴴ OF APRIL
08:30 CET

Monika reached the front doors of the Grand Café and walked into a setting made to convey the idea that culture was of prime importance here: elegance, courtesy, and of course, money. She looked around and found the spot she was looking for, by the corner, next to the door looking eastward where the target kiosk was perfectly visible. The waitress came by.

Monika asked her, "Do you have Red Bulls ... and could you take this coffee cup away?" The paper cup was empty, all for show.

Settling down in the chair, she glanced at her phone, keeping an eye out the window. There was one text message from an unrecognized phone number, not anyone she had listed in her contacts. "Later," she thought. Now she needed to keep an eye on that Kiosk. Looking right on Karl Johans Street, Monika could see motorcycles and scooters of all kinds parked along the sidewalk. A line of European, Japanese and the Swedish brand cars passed in both directions. Each one that passed obstructed the view of the Kiosk. It was unavoidable, "a risk," she thought. Not one she could solve, not without possibly getting spotted.

The waitress brought the Red Bull and offered to pour it in the glass. Monika would have said no on any other occasion, but dressed like she was, drinking the Red Bull from the can would have seemed unusual. "Unusual" meant that she might be remembered by the waitress, when the investigators came by later, as surely they would. She let the waitress pour it in the glass and took a long gulp, savoring the sweet, almost synthetic taste of the drink. It quenched her thirst and gave her the energy she was craving. She looked at her phone. Its digital clock read 08:55. "Soon," she thought, "patience."

Her impatience and her curiosity took over. She opened the text message and gasped. Monika put her hand to her mouth, letting out an involuntary tiny squeal like a young girl might make. Her face flushed. *This can't be ...*, she thought. Her brain, the part that formed the calculating, disciplined part of her makeup, fought to regain control. It won the moment. And none too soon to see a tall man in his fifties pass by the kiosk wearing sunglasses with a walking cane. He had on a black knee length overcoat, enough cover to keep the morning chill at bay, and he carried a newspaper tucked in under his arm. He walked, stooped over some, slowly—like an old man would, but not exactly. "Something doesn't fit," she thought, but then she lost sight of him with a passing truck that obstructed the view. Monika was up out of her chair, straining to see past the cars that blocked her view, but the man was nowhere to be seen. She looked left and right down Karl Johan Street but saw nothing. *Maybe that wasn't him*, she thought ..., "but she could have sworn ..."

Monika fought to keep the other half of her brain from pushing itself to the front. A tear formed and dropped down her cheek. She ignored it; kept looking for the old man. A Range Rover passed, and then she saw him, again, now standing in front of the kiosk, looking left and right. She was sure—almost. It took a second more, but then she knew. It was arrogance. That's what The Voice had, oodles of it, the kind that couldn't be kept hidden, not with sunglasses and a walking cane. That's why she had been so sure—that he would be here to see it for himself. She smiled; she had played him like a violin. People could not escape their nature, which was the whole point of social engineering. Next, he would go to some point of observation, just like she had, to see the whole thing play out. *He might even come to this very spot*, she thought. She frantically typed a text message to the number for the flower delivery service, "in front of kiosk now—using a cane—black knee- length jacket," and hit the send button.

The deed was set in motion. Nothing more to do but wait. Monika looked back at the message on her phone. Her training told her to keep her focus on the task at hand ... and not to believe. This was surely some cruel, demented joke ... from that *"helvetes forbanna gjengen av pedofile"*—motherfucking group of pedophiles, her mind screamed. A second teardrop fell, this time onto the phone. She didn't care anymore.

Monika wiped her face with her hands and looked back out at the street. That's when she saw the two slim Asian men dressed all in black, including their sunglasses. They calmly walked in front of Hans, The Voice, and spoke to him briefly. Pettersen started to look at his watch, then realized.

But it was too late. He dropped his walking cane and froze. Monika was mesmerized. She heard the staccato volley of the weapons as they emptied into the fifty-year-old distinguished-looking gentleman, who was doing a sort of backward dance into the front of the kiosk and then fell back into the spread of newspapers and magazines, his arms splayed wide, his mouth drooling a spittle of blood. One of the two assassins pulled out a handgun and did a double tap on Pettersen's forehead, just to make sure.

Monika ran out the door stopping at the edge of the sidewalk and caught a short glimpse of what she needed to see. Pettersen's black overcoat masked the red blood; nothing showed in the front. The sunglasses had fallen off his face. The newspapers splattered with his blood had fallen off the racks, a few pages flapping in the wind. Pettersen would be the lead story in these same papers—tomorrow...

The two Asian men looked up and down the street as a darkly tinted BMW pulled in front of the kiosk and they stepped in like they had just hailed a taxi.

The BMW made an immediate left turn, right past the corner of the café where Monika watched with a cold satisfaction. It drove down Rosenkrantz street and disappeared at the next corner.

While everyone panicked around her, Monika went back into the café and paid for her Red Bull with a green fifty Krone bill on the table. A melee of screams now registered, people fleeing the spot of Pettersen's demise like a foul smell was spreading viciously outbound to every corner from ground zero and everyone wanted to get as far away as possible. She looked over her shoulder and saw again what she needed to see. The deed was a done thing.

"The Voice," she thought, "is ... history."

Walking down the street, it didn't take long before Monika heard the sirens of police cars headed to the scene of the dead man lying like he lay when completing his death dance falling into the newspapers of the day. When they got there, they found him. The man named Hans Pettersen was riddled with bullet holes in a pool of his own crimson blood. A dozen black roses rested on his chest.

Monika walked down the stairs to the underground garage. She found her car and started the Mini Cooper. The sound of the engine revving up was magnified in the close quarters of the garage. She came out onto the street headed back to her place, to think over the message on her phone.

Monika wasn't sure whether she should call. At the next intersection, waiting for the stoplight to turn green, she did. The phone rang and rang, but no one picked up. She tried again, but again nothing. Not even a voicemail message prompt.

"Out the front door and down Rosenkrantz Gate. She was a brunette girl, dressed for business. She paid and left, nothing more." That's what the waitress later told the police investigators looking for witnesses and possible accomplices. "And, oh yes, she ordered a Red Bull. I thought that was a bit odd ... that early in the morning." That's what they wrote down on their notepads. It wouldn't amount to anything, but they had to write down every detail.

CHAPTER 53

HOME OFFICE OF DR. PASCAL DU RELO
IN THE OUTSKIRTS OF ANTWERP, BELGIUM
WEDNESDAY, 11ᵀᴴ OF APRIL
07:01 CET

"They were never found. We have to assume the worse." The renowned Doctor of Advanced Biotechnology Research, the Count Pascal Du Relo, had his feet propped up on the desk in his home office, on the first floor of his country estate located just outside of Antwerp in the Flemish countryside. The estate dated back to the sixteenth century, from where the count derived his lineage. He had always found the aristocracy something to be derided, not that he was "so stupid as to ignore its advantages," which was the way he often said it to Tosti when they were alone and drinking.

Vlad had his own feet propped up on his desk in his home in Reykjavik. "What about the laptops?" asked Pascal. The two men were at ease. The immediate danger had subsided. But they also knew not to be complacent. He continued saying what they both knew, "Without knowing the disposition of those laptops and the phones, there is still much to be worried about."

"I've got scripts running on various computers, the Police Inspector's in Oslo and on Betón's computer, actually his secretary's computer. I can read their email and am also watching for any new case information going into the databases. There's no mention so far."

"That Agent Rodriguez was there in the hospital. He didn't travel all this way just to meet up with a two-bit hacker. Hansen and Betón are the tripwires. They start meeting together, it can only mean one thing."

"Then you have to get them ... find out what Tosti was doing behind our back."

Vlad just couldn't pass up the chance to take a swipe at Tosti, even a dead Tosti. Pascal was getting irritated with the call. Talking with his insolent bastard son was always a challenge for him, not the same as talking to Tosti. He already missed Tosti.

Vlad wouldn't let up making the point. "I can't hack something that doesn't connect and I think there's more that we don't know about what Tosti was doing."

"Yes, speaking of Tosti; we have to set up a new Nikita. Wong still has to initiate. I'm thinking of just doing it in Bangkok. Easier there."

Vlad knew that Pascal was changing the subject. And he was not asking him his advice. He was just thinking out loud. He let it pass. Vlad saw an opening to bring up a related topic.

"How about all the other stuff that Tosti did for you? He was an arrogant ass, but he had his uses."

Looking out the window of his country estate, the gardens outside on this calm sunny day, Pascal couldn't stop thinking about Tosti, his best friend in life, the only one he had ever really confided in. And the one who had betrayed that trust, he reminded himself.

Vlad was right, he thought. *We, no, I need a new Tosti.*

"I'll think of something. We do need a new Tosti." Pascal was thinking that this was the first time that he had actually heard Vlad say something about Tosti that was the semblance of a compliment. Vlad's next statement surprised him.

"I could do it."

Pascal put his feet down and got up from the chair, walking to the window. It caught him by surprise, but there was some merit to the idea. It would solve a lot of problems. Only Vlad was not Tosti. He would have to give it some thought.

"I'll think on it. Tosti had access, a position…"

"Yes, but we don't really need that as much anymore. Once Wong is initiated …"

"Yes, yes, I get it. I *will* think on it. We'll talk later."

"Before you hang up, think on one more thing, Father. If the FBI really does have the laptops, you've said it yourself: we have to assume the worst. That means they can break the encryption, or worse, Tosti had unprotected information, like the limo receipt. So what then?"

Pascal took note of the "Father" appended to the statement. He chalked it up to insolence, again.

"I have been thinking on that very point, night and day. It may be that we have to apply some pressure. Real pressure. Anyway, leave it alone for now. We'll talk on this next time. Goodbye."

"Goodbye ..."

The two hung up, but each stayed on the topic in their own ways, working out the meaning of their most recent conversation and what it meant to their evolving relationship. Pascal was happy to keep it as it had always been.

Vlad wanted a new one. He had always dreamed of a father, one that was proud of his son. Pascal had never given him that. He had given him everything else—but not the idea that Vlad was his acknowledged son. That was all that Vlad had ever wanted—a father. And his own status. He mouthed the words of his favorite line from his favorite movie—Scarface. *"First you gotta get the money. Then, when you get the money, you get the power. Then, when you get the power, you get the women. That's why you gotta make your own moves."*

CHAPTER 54

OSLO AIRPORT, NORWAY
WEDNESDAY, 11TH OF APRIL
MID MORNING

Monika went home and the cold outer shell of control she had been maintaining fell apart. Hacking had always been the distant, impersonal activity, far removed from what actually happened on the pointy end of things. Not this time. She saw firsthand, what the pointy end actually did.

Monika knocked on Mrs. Johannesen's door and waited. She was fighting a rising tide. It only happened with her, the little old lady, she had only known for a couple of months. In Mrs. Johannesen's arms, Monika was able to let go of the practical, operational M0k1. With her she could be the little girl she never got to be when she was young ... Mrs. Johannesen opened the door and the two women embraced inside the entrance hallway. In the kitchen with a cup of chamomile tea, Monika told her everything.

"I'm a bad girl, Mrs. Johannesen, if you want me to, I will leave." I killed somebody, someone who needed dying. She explained the rest, about her father, about the prosecutor who had dropped the case and about the NoSaints including the one called The Voice also known as Hans Pettersen.

Monika saw the expression in Mrs. Johannesen's face change as the words registered into meaning. "I am so sorry. I," a sob escaped her lips, "... I will start packing."

It came as a shock to her. Mrs. Johannesen had never actually known anyone who could kill, much less someone who had actually done the deed. But in a few seconds of time, the shock of hearing Monika's story wore off and she started to understand. Mrs. Johannesen was also old enough to remember the stories of an older Norway when she was a young child, the events still fresh in the psyche of the nation when Norway had fallen into the hands of the Nazis and of the ones who had collaborated. But she also knew that there had been others, the ones who had fought back and had reclaimed their land. This was the Norway she was proud of, the one she herself had helped rebuild. She knew. Evil must be fought. And sometimes it takes blood. She made up her mind, the mind of resolve and a steely determination.

"Stop," she said, as sternly and as warmly as she could. She smiled, the smile of love. Mrs. Johannesen took Monika's face in her two hands and looked at her. Their faces were only inches apart.

"*You* are like my daughter now. I never had a daughter. And I always wanted one. I had a son once, but he was sickly, only survived a few days. But what I really wanted was a daughter."

Monika wiped away her tears. A new emotion found its way into her heart, an emotion that had never been tapped. It was the emotion of love for a mother. Another sob escaped, this time smaller, only a gasp. She smiled for a moment and then the face contorted into unabated tears of joy.

"Okay, go ahead and cry, my little girl. Go ahead and let it out. We can talk later." It took a while, but the tears subsided.

Then the two women spent the day together, making chit-chat, cooking, and baking. It was the happiest day of her life. Monika had never known that a person could be so happy. They also talked about Frank and the text message. Monika was convinced that it was some demented hoax being played on her. Mrs. Johannesen was not so sure and convinced her to make the trip to the airport, like she had done, in disguise. She had to "face reality, head first," she told her. "That is how you live your life."

CHAPTER 55

OSLO AIRPORT, NORWAY
THURSDAY, 12ᵀᴴ OF APRIL
07:05 CET

The airport was an hour or so drive in early morning traffic. The earliest flights from Belgium would start arriving at 08:00 in the morning. She was there by seven, waiting and wondering what would happen. She was dressed like a businesswoman, a pretty young brunette, with makeup done in the style of a professional office worker with a stylish purse. Around her neck Monika wore a silvery scarf that Mrs. Johannesen gave her, "for good luck," she said as she had wrapped it around her neck.

Monika had never actually felt "pretty," but that is the only word she could conjure up about how the scarf made her feel ... she actually felt, "pretty, like a woman should," is what

Mrs. Johannesen had said to her. It lifted her spirits. And she now hoped against every possible experience that she had ever had that the sun would shine today, outside and in her life. Mrs. Johannesen had already brought her a love she thought was long gone, but now she needed to hope that she could have the other kind of love, the love for the partner in her life, the love for the father of her unborn child. *Frank,* she thought. *"Please, God, let it be him.*

Waiting in the reception area where the automatic doors opened and closed as passengers exited was like a knife tearing at her insides. Most people exited and walked on to find their transportation, but a few found their mates, children waiting with a handful of flowers, lovers. The smile on their faces reminded her what it was that could be ... or not.

The third wave of people finally dispersed. Only a few of them remained, lingering to check schedules or find their keys. If she could have found a quiet place, she would have gone there to scream and let go of the emotion of anticipation unfulfilled. But she stayed and stared at the door. She saw on the periphery of her vision that there were a couple of men talking; the younger one had come out with the latest group of people. Then her phone rang.

For a moment, Monika was unsure what it meant. She looked down at the phone and saw that it was the same phone number, the one that had registered with the text message she had received the day before presumably from Frank. She was about to answer it, but it only rang twice and then it stopped. That's when she noticed that the two men she had seen before were now staring at her. The younger one had a phone in his hand. She looked at him.

He said, "Monika?"

It took a moment to realize that he was speaking to her and to make the connection that he had been the one who had just dialed her phone. She turned to him.

The two men approached her. Her first instinct was to run. But it was something about their faces. There was something there that she didn't understand ... and then she did. It was sympathy. Monika raised her hand to her mouth, like doing so could hold back what was building up inside and could not be stopped. Once again, the tears came. She shook her head and said "no," and said it again and again and again ... until the world above her started to spin and her legs turned to rubber and her knees buckled.

Special Agent Jaime Rodriguez rushed forward and caught the attractive young woman before she hit the floor. With Hansen's help, the two of them took her outside for some fresh air and sat with her on a bench as Monika recovered.

She could see his lips moving. He was saying something in a weird language. The other man, the older one, was also speaking. She understood him. "Frank is alive, Monika, just sick, very sick, in a coma." He kept saying it ... until she understood. The clouds above in the morning sky had blocked the sun, but she saw a ray of sunshine peeking through.

She had only one question now. "Can I see him?"

CHAPTER 56

Staten Island Ferry leaving Manhattan
New York City, USA
Tuesday, 17th of April
08:05 PM EST

A gentle evening breeze blew across Manhattan harbor. FBI Analyst
Nick Williams buttoned his overcoat tighter around the
neckline. It was still cool in April. He had made this commute
on the Staten Island Ferry so many times that his mind wan-
dered off hardly conscious of the rocking, the boat making its
way full of the passengers on their commute home. Nick always
made it a point to sit in the back where he could see the beauty
that was the famous New York City skyline. It always looked
better at night; *all cities look better at night*, he thought. He was

seated in the back, shoulder to shoulder with other commuters like him.

A Spanish woman sat to his left clutching her plastic bag full of the things she took to work every day, food and a pair of work shoes. A man in a business suit and long black overcoat was seated to his left reading the New York Times. He recognized them but they never spoke. He could see the growing towers that now reached higher than all the others. That's why he always sat in the back, to see the new tower, the Freedom Tower rising from what had been the ashes of the old Twin Towers when they had fallen.

Nick thought again of his old mentor, Supervisory Special Agent John O'Neil, who had gone down with the towers. It was for him that he had first applied and it was still for him, the dashing maverick Special Agent O'Neil who lived his work on the edge. Williams wanted above all things to be like his hero O'Neil.

He pulled out the application that he had printed to review when he got home. It was his third try. *Like baseball*, he thought. He had applied right after 9-11 to the FBI academy at Quantico, Virginia that was situated alongside the famous Marine Base. That had been a mistake. The FBI had been swamped with so many applications. His had likely gotten lost in the crowd of so many that had volunteered. Strike one. Strike two had been the one, everything ready, all the prerequisites taken care of, except for the one thing he could not control, a less than enthusiastic letter of recommendation from his squad supervisor. Strike two.

This was his third try. Strike three, and he would be done, his hopes dashed. Williams wore his hair long, gelled and pulled back like O'Neil used to wear it in the dashing man-about-town style—made for Manhattan's nightlife.

A long sigh left his lips. The letter of recommendation remained the one problem. He was not sure about the new boss, SSA Rodriguez. Atkins told him not to worry, but he did anyway.

He felt the bump that meant the ferry was docking. His mind reconnected to the present. It was time to catch the train next, for a fifteen-minute ride that would eventually get him home in the heart of Staten Island. The herd of people like cattle edged together pressing forward to the exit, everyone lost in their own thoughts.

CHAPTER 57

LANDSTUHL HOSPITAL
NEAR KAISERSLAUTERN, GERMANY
WEDNESDAY, 18TH OF APRIL

Monika knew what she would see, but when she did the tears came anyway. Frank was wired up like an astronaut in a space capsule. She had cried enough, she said to herself. It was time to be the other Monika, the operational one, M0ki, the one who always knew what to do.

She bent over and kissed him on his forehead, the person that was Frank. He lay there on white sheets on a hospital bed, the head of the bed raised a couple of degrees, his long hair framing his long face, his body as placid as a replica from Madame Tussaud's wax museum. Still, the life was there. That's what the American doctors had said. There was no discernible brain damage.

He could recover, not would, but could. There was a difference. But they couldn't say when. It was all up to Frank. So she sat next to his bed and told him about how she had missed him so terribly much when she was in Moscow and now more than ever.

And she also told him about the baby growing in her womb, and how she had already picked out the names, Else if a girl, and Frank if he was a boy.

Excerpt from the Case File from DSI Hansen

16 April

Nikita Case resolved successfully. No prosecutions. At direction of MoJ, new case opened, Seraphim Case.

Purpose to uncover the organization behind the Nikita Case and determine what threat it poses to Norwegian safety. Will be working in collaboration with Europol and FBI. Laptops, smartphones and a separate external hard drive found by Betón at crime scene from Nikita Case transferred to FBI for forensics. This may serve to generate the first leads.

CHAPTER 58

Highway 95
Somewhere in Massachusetts approaching
Boston, USA
Monday, 11ᵀᴴ of June
08:32 AM EST

Carolina Maria DelBarco-Rodriguez answered her Bluetooth-connected car phone. She was already a few minutes behind schedule, working her way north on the interstate. A steady rain fell onto the pavement showering the cars and trucks on the highway. The clock on the dashboard was digital. It read 08:32:22—precision. The traffic was reaching its peak at this time of the morning, ferrying a bustle of people in their cars each weaving through the congestion to be at some place and start the day's agenda.

Her first appointment was a meeting with her peers from the other *banks* as they called them. These were no ordinary *banks*. Caro was already deep in thought about her own schedule, the Mercedes Benz S-Coupe making it an island of calm in the turbulent environment of the interstate.

The phone rang. Caro pressed the green button on her steering wheel to answer the incoming call. She had been expecting a call.

"Hello. This is Mrs. Rodriguez." she said.

"Carolina Maria DelBarco-Rodriguez. That is a long name for such a beautiful woman ..."

"Who is this," she asked? The voice continued—uninterrupted. She was startled. Caro yelled the same question a second time, but the voice did not respond—like it was a recorded call, incognizant of her question.

She wanted to hang up, but something kept her from clicking the end-call button, "... in such a beautiful car, on such a dreary gray day." There was a sigh.

"You don't know me, but you will, Mrs. Carolina Maria DelBarco-Rodriguez. Such a long name, can I call you Caro?"

The voice conveyed an exaggerated frustration with the length of her name. It continued, "Jaime, your very own FBI Supervisory Special Agent does. Why can't I? What's it like to have your very own, your very, very own Special Agent? I wonder."

It's not a voice she recognized. It sounded like something that was recorded, *something mechanical about it*, she thought, *but the phone number says it's a call originating from my own home and it knows I'm in my car. And something else*, she thought, *I've heard this before—just can't remember when or where.* For a moment she thought it might be one of Jaime's computer toys making the call.

The voice on the call continued, "What's it like Caro, to be you, to be so young and beautiful—already the head of the Federal Reserve in Boston, and to have the handsome FBI Special Agent as your husband? So many *ands* ... What a lucky woman you are, Caro, a husband and those two ... very beautiful ... children." The line went dead.

Her heart raced. Caro's first and only thought was "the children." She choked down the urge to panic. It felt like someone had punched her in the gut. She turned across two lanes to get to the right side as quickly as she could. The blare of honking horns voiced displeasure over the erratic and dangerous move. She took the nearest exit and stopped the car at the nearest gas station.

Caro was in a full-blown controlled panic—the kind that usually gave her energy – but not this time.

"Call home," she said. The car obeyed her command and within two rings the call was answered. It was her mother who lived with them at their home in Armonk, part of Westchester County, New York.

"*Los niños están bién, mija.*" Señora DelBarco told her daughter. They are doing their reading lessons, she told her. They were fine.

The panic subsided. But the pit of bile had worked itself into her gut. She got out of the car oblivious to the rain that had picked up and threw a jet of half-digested breakfast onto the black tar paving. She wiped her mouth with her sleeve and soaking wet made her way back into the car.

She gave the car a new command, "Call Jaime."

At about the same time in that virtual place of electronic signals flowing across endless connection points called the Internet an email went out. It was addressed from a Doctor Mila Josefino. The addressees were a blind-copied list of email accounts. It was all heavily encrypted. It had a short message:

A friendly reminder from your doctor to take your new dosage of pills. And don't forget to send in your blood samples.

It was signed Doctor Josefino. Under the name was the symbol of a black angel with a broken chain around its shoulders. It had a caption underneath it that read.

"Until the day when we transcend through Tannhauser Gate."

We hope you enjoyed eNikita and appreciate your review in your favorite online bookstore, www.goodreads.com and any social media.

Join the Seraphim community on Google+ and Facebook to meet the authors, get access to research notes and pictures, participate in related discussions, and, of course, find the latest updates on the follow-up to eNikita. Will Frank wake up from the coma? Is Jamie's family threatened by the Seraphim? What will Monika do next?

Google +	Facebook

http://bit.ly/18d5mNJ	http://on.fb.me/MzFHHp

Author's Note

"I'm not sure how to write on this topic, not sure that I even want to." That was the first reaction to the idea we were kicking around about the plot for this crime thriller where it begins with the darkest of subjects—the subject of pedophilia. That was the start of the conversation. It took some amount of thought and conversation that eventually led to the conclusion that we would try. The approach we decided to take was to deal with it like one might describe a sealed box describing its surface but not what goes on inside. But even at a surface level, the topic of pedophilia that starts our crime thriller called *eNikita* is abhorrent. That reaction we don't shy away from, because that is what it is—abhorrent.

So we walked a fine line to achieve an honest (if gut-felt) reaction but not so that we ventured inside this dark box. Julia's diary was placed in the story to convey the very real thing that it is, not an abstract condition that *happens* to some people. This book starts there, but leaves the topic behind to focus in on another topic that one may argue is even a broader, more sinister danger.

As fans of technology we are constantly reminded that for every good that technology brings to the life of humankind there is also its ugly side. It was the trust one places in these new applications like Facebook that was used to first dupe Julia and then Grete's grandparents. We are left with the fact that the bad comes with the good. It should be a law of physics if only one could put it into a mathematical formula. Maybe it is a formula; one found in the sequencing of code that we call deoxyribonucleic acid, otherwise known as DNA. We are left with what we have always had, free choice, for good or evil. In cyberspace we know it only too well. The Internet is living proof, but just one example among many.

Technical advancement is transformative, this we know. But to date, we can still walk away from it; make a choice. Abstinence from technology is *still* a choice. The transformation that is enabled with technology is incremental, to enhance the human experience, good or bad. It has not been the case, however, that the transformation cannot be reversed, that abstinence is no longer a choice. Try and get any government service, or buy anything and you will find out.

What if the day arrives when that frontier gets breached and the human transformation comes with no ability to "undo it." What happens when the transformed reach not an incremental step, but a leap forward so vast that it creates a new species of human, altogether different when biology and computing mesh at the cellular level? What happens to the divide between those who transform and those that don't, the ones left behind. What do we call this moment in time? Is it only theoretical?

What is this transformation? It has a name. It is the new frontier called *The Singularity ... When Humans Transcend Biology* that Ray Kurzweil writes about. Do we know what we are doing? Is this a good thing? Or is it like all other technology—packaging the *bad* with the good where a certain détente settles into place? And how *bad* is the "bad?" Shouldn't we at least ask the question with an open mind that maybe it, the *transformation*, is not what was meant for us—that we should step back from that precipice where we cannot undo the damage? There is a well-known saying, "The road to hell is paved with good intentions," after all. Hell is not a place we can undo.

The sad reality is that for all the many motivating reasons that include, greed, power, the thrill of exploration, no one has a clue what we are getting into. The argument for ... is that we won't know unless we try. We have to dive into the abyss and then we will know the answer. That may be true. But once we do, like Pandora's box, our own drive of curiosity may indeed be our undoing. Do we gamble with our souls?

This novel is fiction, but the topic is not. Not the topic of Pedophilia and not the topic of Transcendency. In the next book we dive deeper into the *transcendent* topic in fictional form. For those readers who want to understand more about what law enforcement is doing about the other topic, we send you to the following website: www.missingkids.com

CARLOS C. SOLARI

@ccsolari

Carlos was born in Colombia, South America, raised and educated in the US, a graduate of Washington and Lee University and the Naval Postgraduate School. He served 13 plus years as an officer in the US Army, 6 plus years as an executive in the FBI, and 2 plus years as CIO of the White House from 2002 to 2005. In the private sector Carlos worked for Bell Labs of Alcatel-Lucent, CSC and others. He is an Adjunct Professor at George Mason University teaching on the topic of Information Security. Carlos lives with his wife Sabine in the Shenandoah Valley of Virginia. eNikita is his third book.

JOHN-PATRICK SKAAR

@jpskaar

JP was born in Norway, educated in Germany and in Norway with 18 plus years in the IT sector emphasizing information security. He is an expert in bringing together business concerns, cultural differences and IT to solve real world problems. JP is also a prolific world traveler, guest lecturer at the Norwegian Police University College on cyber security, prolific blogger and social media contributor. JP lives in southern Norway. eNikita is his first book.

Excerpt from

EL CAPITÁN

A NOVEL
BY
CARLOS C. SOLARI

CHAPTER 1

A scissors-kick is a rare thing when done right. But *this* ball was coming in way too high, not where he could make the kick in the normal fashion. It cut across the field, bending on a long curving arc and angling slightly away from the goal line.

He could not align horizontally and still reach the ball, so he reached higher, swinging his body the way a pendulum sweeps through its arc to reach a zenith. He did not think – he just jumped to reach the ball.

It came towards him spinning on a trajectory ten feet in the air.

It was still coming too high; so he extended his leg even further to reach it. He only saw the ball; everything else was dim background. Up was down, down was up. It didn't matter. He could see it coming at him like a scene from a movie; the bullet captured in slow motion as it exits the barrel – spinning and pushing the air around it in bow-wave fashion.

It was instinct borne of training. The eye caught the flight, the brain calculated spin and distance, the curvature of its path, speed of travel.

He met it at the top of its flight – the leg cantilevered by the weight of his body.

"There is no time to think the play, Rio; you must let your body respond to the situation, to where the ball will be." He could hear the calm voice of the wise old maestro, Sebastian. *"Nothing else matters but the eyes focused on the ball. Don't worry about the body, the training will take care of this – the body knows what to do."*

With his right foot he found the *futbol* dead center. Up was down, down was up. It didn't matter. He was in a near vertical line, the arms stretched laterally for balance, his head and neck twisting around, following the path of the ball as he smacked it at the pinnacle of his jump.

Like the crack of the bullwhip, the curve of his foot hit its target hard, leather-to-leather. He nailed it right where the cuboid bone is thick and strong.

Like the report of a rifle, he heard it hit. Energy transferred, a lightning bolt that coursed through his body, out his foot and beyond, like an explosion. He was sweating profusely.

The ball immediately obeyed, rocketing off in a new direction.

In that instant, Rio locked eyes with the keeper. He saw him fly to meet the ball, his arms stretched to their limit; his legs slung back trailing like a comet's tail. Rio tumbled from the sky, trying desperately to land without breaking his neck. He hit the ground hard, lost sight of the ball. Someone grabbed him screaming. Up was down, down was up. He looked frantically. Where did it go? Someone grabbed him again. *Where did it go?* His heartbeat raced. He screamed out loud, "Where did it go?"

"It went nowhere, you asswipe. Go back to sleep!"

Rio gasped for air as he bolted upright in his lower bunk, the words still formed in his mouth. He looked across the room and saw his older brother Rodrigo glaring at him from his bed. Rodrigo flipped over and rolled the pillow around his head. They were in their Queens apartment. Rio heard the siren of a police car as it raced down his street and off into the start of the morning. Miguelito, Rio's five-year-old brother, popped his head down from his perch on the top bunk.

"You had the dream again." Miguelito whispered, his hair dangling as he hung there upside down.

For a moment this picture reminded Rio of his upside-down eye lock with the goalkeeper of his dream, and he rubbed his eyes. Miguelito was talking at him again; he could see the lips moving, but his brain was still in the dream. Soon the words came through, as if the volume had been turned up. "You had the dream again," Miguelito repeated.

"I heard you, squirt," Rio said back. He grabbed Miguelito by the arms and pulled him off the top bunk, starting a mock battle with him on the bed. Miguelito squealed in pure delight. Fighting with his older brothers was his favorite thing.

Rodrigo, now sixteen, had no patience left for young Miguelito. It was different for Rio; at thirteen he was light years closer to Miguelito in terms of boyhood innocence. Rodrigo used to be like that, but not anymore.

"Yuck, you're wet," said Miguelito as he freed himself and jumped down to the floor.

Rio sat up on the edge of the bunk bed, careful not to hit his head on the upper beam of the bunk. He was soaked in his own sweat, as if a fever had broken, his body expelling the poison in the night.

Rodrigo's muffled voice came out through the pillow covering his head, "Wake me up with that stupid soccer dream again and you'll regret it."

Rio ignored him. He yawned and stretched his arms wide and stood. Their small bedroom was lit up with the morning sun that revealed the debris of three boys living in the same room: sneakers, dirty socks on the floor, the walls plastered with posters of the soccer greats. Rio knew that his mother would complain about the smell of the room, so he walked to the window's edge and opened it to let some fresh air in. It was Saturday, so he would spend his day playing soccer with his maestros. The day promised to be perfect for spending it outside.

Miguelito stared at him in that stupor of being half asleep, his brain teetering between sweet slumber and consciousness, his stomach telling him to find breakfast. Rodrigo was under the covers, the pillow still over his head. He wouldn't get up until later, much later.

The evaporating sweat felt cold on his back as Rio lumbered off down the hallway and to the bathroom. He saw the door to his parent's room still closed. It was early. They were probably still asleep he thought. The door to the bathroom creaked as he walked in. He stood in front of the mirror. The dream had come again. It had been a month since the last time. Where *did* it go—did the ball go into the net or did it fly out of bounds? That was the question that he could not answer, for the dream always ended with this question in his lips. But there was also another question: What did it all mean? He stripped off his clothes and got in the shower.

Get your copy of **El Capitán** on Amazon.com today!

ALSO BY CARLOS SOLARI

Security in a Web 2.0+ World   http://amzn.to/HRVVJ5

El Capitan   http://amzn.to/1aJRdnt

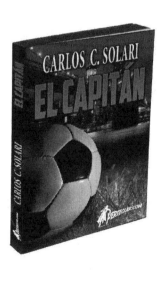

Made in the USA
Middletown, DE
16 March 2021